A Dangerous Lady

The count's hand landps
followed and she stru pe
was the last thing she he
erotic sensations and ed
he was stripping her. The lacing on her bodice snapped
and he pulled the garment from her body. He untied her
skirt and pulled that off, too, roughly. By the time she
was down to her stockings and shoes, she was gasping
with exertion and delight. He turned her over, pulled
her on to her knees and knelt in front of her, his
excitement obvious.

'Now let's play a different game,' he said. 'But first, let
me see how much you want me.' And with that, the
count parted her legs.

A Dangerous Lady

LUCINDA CARRINGTON

BLACK
lace

Black Lace novels are sexual fantasies.
In real life, make sure you practise safe sex.

First published in 1998 by
Black Lace
332 Ladbroke Grove
London W10 5AH

Typeset by SetSystems Ltd, Saffron Walden, Essex
Printed and bound by Mackays of Chatham PLC

ISBN 0 352 33236 0

Chapter One

'Submit?' When he was excited Jack Telfer's soft Cornish accent always grew more pronounced. And Lady Katherine Gainsworth could certainly see that he was excited now.

'You cheated!' She lay naked on the bed, her shoulders pinned down by Jack's strong brown hands. His knees gripped her waist.

'Cheated?' He laughed, still holding her. 'I'm the superior wrestler. Admit it.'

'Never,' she said.

'I'll keep you here forever,' he threatened. 'Or until you repeat after me: Jack Telfer, you are my superior in every way.'

She smiled sweetly. 'Very well.' Her hand sneaked forward. 'Jack Telfer, you are my superior in every way.' Suddenly, she grasped his balls. 'Except when I'm holding you like this.'

'Katherine,' he gasped, 'you she-devil! You're hurting me.'

'I'm not,' she said. 'Much.' She tightened her fingers. 'But I will. Unless you admit that I have won.'

'You don't fight fair,' he objected.

1

She massaged him, more gently now. 'And who taught me to use every weapon at my disposal? Fair means or foul?'

'I taught you there were rules,' he said unsteadily. 'And even a man without a title to his name can have a sense of honour.'

'All's fair in love and war,' she said. She moved her fingers more strongly, and then reached forward with her other hand to grasp his semi-erect cock. He was hard now, and throbbing in her hand. 'So soon?' she teased. 'Sir, you are insatiable.'

'Only when I'm with you.' His voice was hoarse. He reached between her legs and she parted them for him. His fingers quickly sought for proof of her arousal and found it. 'If I'm insatiable, how about you? You're warm and wet and you want me.'

She felt him entering her and relaxed, allowing him this final pleasure. As he began to thrust, she began to respond. And then, much too quickly, it was over. He came with a groan of satisfaction, his body shuddering, lay on top of her for a moment then rolled off on to his back. 'How will I survive when you're gone?' he muttered.

She laughed. 'You'll find someone else.' Teasing him, she added, 'You've probably got someone in mind already.'

He turned towards her, angry now. 'I have not. Ever since I first saw you, there's been no one else. You know that.'

She ruffled his hair. 'I believe you.'

She did believe him. He would have kept his marriage vows to the letter. He would be faithful ... and boring. Even if she had been given a choice, Jack Telfer was not the man she would have elected to spend the rest of her life with. It had nothing to do with the fact that he was a groom, and she was the daughter of Sir Henry Upfield Gainsworth. Jack was well mannered, and knowledgeable about horses and the countryside. A champion, back in his native Cornwall, in his own strange style of wrestling. He had broad shoulders, a broad chest and narrow hips. He was hard with muscle and tanned by the sun. Any woman would have been delighted to see him stripped, and then enjoy him perform.

When she thought of him in those terms, he sounded like the perfect man. But their lovemaking always left her with a sense of frustration. He became erect quickly and took her quickly, with the minimum of foreplay. He told her he loved her body, but he rarely explored it. He only ever kissed her briefly and, she had to admit, rather clumsily, and she had never felt his lips anywhere else other than on hers. He had never given her the extremes of pleasure that she could give herself, in the privacy of her bed.

He seemed oblivious to her needs, and unteachable. When she tried to move his hands to different parts of her body and encourage him to linger there, he moved them back. He did not mind her handling his cock and balls, but he seemed totally unaware of the pleasure his own fingers, or his mouth, could give her. She would have liked to feel his tongue exploring her, and she would have liked to have pleasured him in the same way. She had only once made a tentative move downwards, hoping that this would encourage him to respond, but he had pulled her up, and asked her what she was doing. She remembered that it was one of the few times she had actually felt embarrassed while she was with him.

She had expected him to be her erotic tutor. She would have enjoyed learning to please him. She had to admit that she had been disappointed when his imagination did not seem to match her own, although she had never told him so. Perhaps, she thought, it was a good thing that fate had provided her with an excuse to end this affair without hurting Jack too much. Jack understood about duty, even if he did not approve of it.

'If fate had been kind to us, we would have spent our life together.' He briefly stroked her tumbled hair. 'I could have given you children. Lots of children. A house full of children. Would you have liked that?'

'Of course,' she said.

But she knew it was a lie. She remembered the local women she had seen, old before their time from the drudgery of yearly births. She imagined Jack Telfer in ten years' time, his body thickening, his skin weather-beaten, still making love to her in the same way, whispering the same endearments, thrusting into her fast, too fast, then rolling off and quickly snoring.

'But instead you are to marry a man you hardly know,' Jack said. 'Doesn't the prospect frighten you?'

'We can't all have the luxury of marrying for love,' she said. 'I'm sure I shall become very fond of Ruprecht.' She added kindly, 'This kind of thing happens all the time.' Although I never believed it would happen to me, she thought.

Jack moved suddenly, rolling over and pulling her towards him. 'Run away with me,' he said passionately. 'We'll go tonight.'

She laughed gently. 'That's a very sweet thing to say, Jack, but you know it's impossible. I have made a promise, to my father and to my future husband, and I intend to keep my word.'

The wind on Albion Hill always blew strongly. Katherine sat astride her favourite mare and stared at William Shannon. 'I shall miss these meetings,' she said.

'So shall I,' he said.

He was slimmer and taller than Jack Telfer, but she guessed that he was equally strong. She had gazed at his lean thighs, hard from constant riding, and wondered what it would feel like to have them imprison her on a

4

bed. When his hand patted the neck of his horse she imagined his fingers fondling her, opening buttons, finding her nipples, coaxing them into hard buds, taking them in his mouth. She suppressed a sigh. William Shannon had always been scrupulously polite, impeccably respectful. It had taken nearly a year before she had persuaded him to use her name without her title.

'I hope you will be able to continue with your riding,' he added.

'I'm sure I will,' she said. 'But not dressed like this.'

She saw his eyes travel over her body, lingering on her thighs in their tight breeches. 'There's nothing wrong with the way you're dressed,' he said.

'A woman in breeches, riding astride?' She smiled. 'I'm sure it would shock my new family. When I'm married I daresay I'll have to wear skirts and ride side-saddle. I'll have to behave like a lady.' She paused. 'I hope I won't be bored.'

There was a brief silence. 'Do you really want this, Katherine?' he asked softly.

'Yes,' she said. He stared at her intently. 'Well, no,' she admitted. 'But I'm resigned to it.'

He edged his horse forward until his knee was level with hers. 'So this really is our last ride together?'

'Yes,' she said.

'By next week you'll be in the Duchy of Heldenburg. I'll probably never see you, or speak to you, again.'

She tried to smile. 'Don't sound so mournful, Will. You'll hear news of me. And no doubt I shall visit my father from time to time.'

'With your husband at your side? What use is that to me?'

She stared at him, surprised at the sudden bitterness in his voice.

'Don't you understand?' He turned to her. 'Knowing that I would meet you each week has kept me sane.'

'Will,' she said in surprise, 'what exactly are you saying?'

'I'm saying I'm in love with you!' He made it sound like an accusation. 'I think I've been in love with you from the first time we met, although I've tried to deny it. From the first time we met and we argued. Do you remember? You were on horseback and I was driving Sir George's trap. You wouldn't move out of my way.'

'And you pushed forward, and my horse shied,' she continued. 'And I was nearly unseated, and you felt *very* guilty.'

'And you said how you hated riding side-saddle. And I told you a woman's legs weren't strong enough to ride astride.'

'So I challenged you,' she finished. 'Challenged you to teach me to ride like a man. I think you were somewhat surprised when I turned up dressed as a boy.'

'I was even more surprised when I found out who you were,' he said.

'But you still agreed to go on meeting me.'

He paused. 'By then I needed you. Like some men need brandy or gambling. I lived for the evenings when I could see you, and talk to you.'

She could hardly believe it. 'And you've only just found the courage to tell me?'

'Courage has nothing to do with it,' he said, stiffly. 'I live in a tied cottage on Sir George's estate. You're the daughter of Sir Henry Upfield Gainsworth.'

She gazed up at him. 'Do you really think our social positions would have mattered to me?'

'Maybe not to you,' he said. 'But they would have mattered to just about everyone else. Including your father.'

She moved her horse closer to him. Their knees touched briefly. She gazed up at him. 'Did you think about me often, Will?'

He stared above her head. 'All the time,' he said.

'During the day?'

'Yes.'

'And at night?'

He still refused to look at her, but she noticed that he had not moved away. She edged forward and their knees bumped again. 'Yes,' he said, his voice less steady now. 'Especially at night.'

'What did you think about – at night?'

He pulled his horse round until he was facing her. 'Can't you guess?' he said, harshly.

'Then do it,' she said. She saw his expression change. 'Do it now!' She realised that he was actually backing away from her. She urged her own horse forward. 'I want you to, Will. You'll never get another chance.' He stopped. She was level with him again. 'In a week's time I'll be preparing for marriage to a man I don't love. Give me one last lesson, William Shannon. A memory to take with me to Heldenburg.'

She could sense his indecision and felt like shaking him. What was the matter with him? He wanted her, didn't he? He'd just admitted it. Why didn't he dismount, and drag her off her horse? Drag her into the trees, fling her on the ground, and make love to her? Open her shirt, unbutton her breeches, let her feel his hands on her flesh, his mouth on her lips and her breasts? And maybe elsewhere. She had always believed he would be more exciting than Jack Telfer. He had an air of authority about him. She had imagined he would take charge. She certainly hadn't expected to have to virtually order him to perform!

'Do you want another man to have me first?' she demanded. 'A foreigner?'

He looked at her in amazement. 'Here?' he faltered. 'You want to do it out here?'

'Where else?' She was getting angry now. 'Back at your cottage?' She swung her horse round. 'All right, Will. We'll do it back at your cottage. In your bed.'

'No, no,' he said hastily. 'Too many people would see us arrive.'

'Does that bother you?'

'I'm thinking of you,' he said, sharply. 'Of your reputation.'

She swung her leg over the saddle and slid to the ground. When she dropped the reins, her horse immediately began to graze. 'I don't care about my reputation,' she said. 'It won't follow me to Heldenburg, anyway.'

He dismounted. His horse joined hers. He reached for her hands. 'You really want this, Katherine?'

She suppressed a sigh of frustration. 'Yes,' she said.

'Over there then,' he said. 'In the trees.' They walked over to the trees together. Once there he grasped her suddenly and turned her so that her back rested against an oak. His lips touched hers, lightly. 'So I'll be the first,' he said. 'I'll be the one to make you into a woman. I like the thought of that.'

'I thought you would,' she said innocently, wondering why men seemed to find virginity attractive. Why didn't they value experience?

Her jacket was already open. He began to unbutton the man's waistcoat she wore underneath. She leant back against the tree and closed her eyes. She could smell the scent of his skin. She waited to feel his hands under her shirt. She wanted his fingers on her breasts, arousing them, and then his lips, sucking her nipples gently. She wanted him to play for a while, exploring. She would enjoy it selfishly, doing nothing in return. She had imagined it often enough, longed for it, tossed and turned in her bed, bringing herself to a climax while she moaned his name.

But she knew she would not be able to keep her hands off him for long. That lithe body had excited her visually for months. She wanted to touch him, smooth her palms along his thighs, unfasten his breeches and feel him swelling, large and hard. She was sure he would be as impressive as she had always imagined. She wanted to lie beneath him and let him strip her, to watch his face when he saw her naked, see his eyes enjoy her, then feel his hands again, and his mouth roving over her skin, seeking out the hollows of her arms and behind her knees, teasing her as he travelled towards more exciting places. She wanted to see his expression when he reached between her legs and discovered how aroused she was, and then decided to let his tongue explore there too. She wanted him to force her to lose control.

The shirt parted as he pulled the buttons open. She felt the cool night air on her skin. His fingers closed over her breasts. She knew her nipples were hard with desire. Then he stopped. 'Katherine,' he said hesitantly, 'are you sure you want this?'

She gave an audible sigh of frustration. 'Yes,' she said, more sharply than she intended.

'If it wasn't your first time . . .' he muttered.

She took his hand and pressed it against her breast, regretting that she had lied to him about her past experience. 'Will, I want it to be you. You want me, too, don't you? You said so.'

'Yes,' he said. 'But I don't want to hurt you.'

'It won't hurt,' she said.

'It always does, for a woman,' he insisted. 'If we were married, it would be different. There would be time for you to grow to like it. But this way, when you remember me, you'll think of the pain.'

'It won't hurt,' she repeated. 'It doesn't have to hurt. I've been riding astride for over a year, anyway. It isn't going to hurt me at all.'

'Perhaps it's wrong of me,' he mumbled, as much to himself as to her. 'I shouldn't have told you how I felt.'

'But it was the truth, wasn't it?' she demanded.

'Yes,' he said, startled by her tone.

'Then fuck me!' she said furiously. 'Damn you, Will, you've half-stripped me. Now finish it.'

9

She could see the amazement on his face. He reached out for her and this time she responded. She caught him round the waist and slid her hands over to his buttocks, pulling him towards her. She felt his erection bulging against his breeches, moved her hands and deftly unbuttoned him. She heard him gasp as her fingers closed round his cock.

'Well, now,' she murmured, close to his ear. 'It seems you really do want me, after all.'

'Of course I do,' he muttered hoarsely. 'But . . .'

She squeezed him harder, unfastening her own breeches with her free hand, fondling him with the other. She wondered if she should kneel and take him in her mouth, a service she had often imagined performing for him. Maybe then he would do the same to her. She briefly imagined his warm tongue on her, probing and circling, exciting her in ways that Jack Telfer had never even thought about. They would lie together on the ground, exploring each other, discovering new pathways to pleasure.

'Teach me, Will,' she requested. 'I'll be a willing pupil.'

Suddenly he seemed to lose control. His hands grabbed at her clothing, pulled at her breeches. His nails scratched her skin. She tried to slow him down, but his sexual need, suppressed for so long, made him thoughtless and clumsy. He pushed her back against the tree, entered her roughly and then thrust wildly, a groan accompanying each movement. She found it impossible to match his uneven rhythm. She heard his laboured breathing, and her own name muttered over and over again, and then he came with a shuddering cry. His arms tightened round her as the orgasmic tremors shook his body, and he held her close while they subsided. She felt nothing but disappointment. The sudden assault had doused her rising excitement.

He kissed her then, calm again, his mouth warm on

her cheek. 'I'm sorry,' he said. 'I should have been more considerate.' He kissed her again. 'Did it hurt much?'

'Not much,' she said, truthfully.

But her lack of an orgasm made her feel frustrated and irritable. She had dreamed of him for over a year. Even when she made love to Jack, she often thought of William Shannon. She had imagined him in a series of fantasies where he always performed as an authoritive, experienced lover. The fantasies had been so real to her that she had forgotten they were not based on fact.

His lips were on her neck. 'But I've made a woman of you, Katherine. I'm glad of that. I'm glad you let me be the first.' He stood back and smiled at her, and for a fleeting moment she felt a pang of regret. He really was an attractive man. To look at, anyway. But then so was Jack Telfer. What a pity neither of them could match up to her imagination when it came to making love. Would anyone? she wondered. Or were all men only really interested in their own satisfaction?

'Do you think you've packed enough clothes?' Sir Henry looked at the two brass-bound trunks and the smaller leather-covered box. 'Your mother, God rest her soul, used to take far more than this when we travelled to London.'

'I've packed all I have,' Katherine said.

'You still have some beautiful dresses, I hope?' Her father was stooped now, but once he had been over six feet tall. He had lost the good looks that she knew had captivated her mother. The looks that had persuaded her to continue to give him all of her inheritance, although she certainly knew it would be lost at the gaming tables. 'I don't want my only daughter looking like a pauper's child,' he said.

'I shall look respectable enough,' Katherine promised. 'And if I don't, I'm sure my new family will provide for me.'

11

Her father said suddenly, 'What have you packed in that box?'

'Just a few personal things,' Katherine said sweetly.

He shook his head. 'I won't even ask what that means, but do try and remember that your new life will be very different from the one you've grown accustomed to here.'

'I'll have to behave like a well-brought-up young lady, you mean?' She smiled. 'I think I can manage that.'

'They're a stiff-necked lot in Heldenburg, so I've been told,' her father said. 'That's the German influence, I suppose. You'll have to conform to their rules.'

'Of course, Father,' she agreed, demurely. She curtsied deeply. 'You see? I know all the social graces.'

Her father did not look convinced. 'I should not have let you run wild,' he said. 'I've allowed you to grow up more like a son than a daughter. You've mixed with all the wrong people. Gamekeepers and servants, and the penniless reprobates who still visit me here.'

'And gamblers?' she interrupted, smiling. 'Don't forget them.'

He returned her smile then. 'And gamblers.' He nodded. 'I class them with the reprobates. But I should have arranged for some women to ... talk to you.' He looked suddenly embarrassed. 'There are things your mother would have told you. You are to be married, after all. And we know almost nothing about this Ruprecht von Krohnenstein. I would not have you upset.'

'Don't worry, Father,' she said, gently. 'I shall not be upset at all. I have discussed certain things with Cook, who is a married woman, as you know, and very sensible too.' It wasn't true, but she was pleased to see that her father looked relieved. She added, 'I shall not be upset by anything that happens to me in Heldenburg.'

Least of all by innocent little Ruprecht, she thought. She remembered her two brief meetings with her husband-to-be. She did not believe that Ruprecht had ever kissed a girl, let alone done anything else. Far from shocking her with his husbandly demands, she thought it far more likely that the poor boy would bore her to death.

But jolting through the darkness in the coach, with Mr Barkstowe's voice droning in her ears, Katherine began to wonder if she would expire from boredom before she ever reached her destination. Until they reached the port of Harwich, Katherine's travelling companions had been a taciturn elderly man, and an older woman who read a small Bible. Katherine had deliberately introduced herself as plain 'Miss Gainsworth', in order to forestall anyone from trying to force themselves on her because they were impressed by her title.

She met Mr Barkstowe on the boat, and realised with resigned horror that, as he was travelling to Italy 'for his health', she would have to endure his company until she reached the borders of Heldenburg. Mr Barkstowe almost immediately expressed disapproval at the idea of a young woman travelling alone, and took it on himself to protect her from future contact with foreigners. Katherine could have tolerated protection, irritating though it was to be treated like an idiot incapable of ordering a bed or a meal in France, but Mr Barkstowe also talked non-stop, and it was his interminable life story, in all its tedious detail, that frequently made her wish she could grab him in one of the wrestling holds Jack Telfer had taught her and pitch him head-first out of the carriage window.

Yvonne Tressilian boarded the coach at the Westphalian town of Stolz, a cloak pulled over her low-cut dress and rustling satin skirts. Katherine judged her to be older than she was trying to appear, but she had a strong face, with good bone structure, that would age well. Having first obliged Mr Barkstowe to move his valise so that she could sit next to Katherine, Yvonne proceeded to outtalk him, and cap every story he started with a better one of her own. She not only told the stories brilliantly, but played all the parts, with appropriate accents and gestures. It came as no surprise to learn that Yvonne was an actress, going to Bavaria to join a troupe. Her arrival proved to be such a welcome relief that Katherine made a more obvious overture of friendship towards her than she might have done if she had met Yvonne in a different social situation. Mr Barkstowe sniffed his disapproval. Yvonne Tressilian chattered on, ignoring him.

When the coach finally halted at a small border hostelry, Mr Barkstowe managed to corner Katherine. 'If I may give you a little advice, my dear child?' He pushed his face close to hers. 'Do not encourage that Tressilian woman. She will take advantage of your generosity.'

Katherine treated him to an innocent look. 'But she's the most amusing company. And it's difficult to avoid someone when you're travelling with them.'

'She calls herself an actress,' Mr Barkstowe warned. 'But to a man of the world, such as myself, it's quite obvious that she is, in plain words, a whore.'

'It isn't obvious to me,' Katherine said.

'You have only to look at her painted face and her immodest dress.' Mr Barkstowe glanced round furtively. 'And I have to tell you, she has already propositioned me.'

'When did she do that?' Katherine asked sweetly. 'You have never yet been alone with her.'

'She has given me certain looks,' Mr Barkstowe said. 'You would not have noticed, but a man understands these things.'

Yvonne choose that moment to come storming out of the hostelry in a temper. 'Idiots! They claim they have no rooms reserved for us.'

'Nonsense,' Katherine said. 'They knew the coach was arriving.'

'All that sausage-eating oaf in there could say was "*nein*" and "no room"!' Yvonne fumed. 'He practically

14

pushed me out! I wish I could speak German. I'd teach him some manners!'

'Well, I can speak German,' Katherine said. 'And if he knows what's good for him, he'll start saying "*ja*" and "welcome".'

'It's hardly appropriate for a young lady to argue with these people.' Mr Barkstowe stepped forward pompously. 'I believe I should intercede on your behalf.'

Yvonne rounded on him angrily. 'Do you speak German?' When he shook his head, she gave an irritated snort. 'Then keep quiet – for once!'

Leaving Mr Barkstowe outside, Katherine followed Yvonne into the hostelry. The air smelled faintly, and not unpleasantly, of herbs and beer. A heavy-set, angry-looking man in an apron glared at Yvonne. '*Nein, nein*! No room.'

'Surely rooms have been kept for us?' Katherine interrupted, in fluent German. 'You knew the coach was arriving, and the von Krohnenstein family told me you would be expecting me. I am to wait here for transport to take me over the border to Heldenburg.'

The effect on the inn-keeper was immediate. 'You are the Lady Gainsworth from England?' Katherine nodded. The man was practically bowing now. He glanced quickly at Yvonne and then back to Katherine again. 'You will forgive me, gracious lady? If this woman had told me she was your servant –'

'She isn't my servant,' Katherine interrupted. 'She's a travelling companion.'

'Naturally we have rooms for *you*, gracious lady.' The inn-keeper was grovelling now.

'And for Miss Tressilian?' Katherine insisted.

The inn-keeper smiled, showing surprisingly even teeth. 'Surely you won't want that sort of woman to stay with you, gracious lady?'

'*What* sort of woman?' Katherine asked, with dangerous calm.

The man obviously noted her tone of voice, and decided not to make his intended remark. 'Whatever you wish, gracious lady,' he conceded. 'I believe we may have a room to spare for Miss Tressilian, and one for the gentleman.'

'Just Miss Tressilian,' Katherine said. 'The gentleman can find another hostelry.'

'What's going on?' Yvonne asked. 'I don't care for the way that oaf keeps looking at me.'

'Don't worry.' Katherine smiled. 'We've both got a room for the night, and we won't have to suffer Mr Barkstowe's company, either.'

'How did you manage it?' Yvonne asked admiringly.

'Influence,' Katherine said.

After a simple but filling meal, the two women sat together at a small table and chatted. For an inn that claimed to have no rooms free, there seemed to be very few guests around. Several glasses of a local wine had made Yvonne Tressilian even more voluble than before. She leant across the table and took Katherine's hand. 'You're a mystery, you know that, *Miss* Katherine Gainsworth. You confronted that fat sausage-eater like a woman who is well used to dealing with servants. I'd guess that you have servants at home. Am I correct?'

'A few,' Katherine admitted. The ones who were loyal enough to stay on without pay, she thought wryly.

'That Prussian pig didn't want me here, either, did he?' Yvonne persisted. 'But you gave the orders, and he was all but kissing your feet. You're a real lady, aren't you? Maybe you even have a title?'

'Maybe,' Katherine teased.

'You're not going to tell me?'

The wine had loosened Katherine's inhibitions. 'I might. If you tell me something truthfully, too?'

'I'll try,' Yvonne said.

'Are you really a whore?'

That silenced Yvonne for a moment. 'What makes you ask that?' Her voice was cold.

Katherine wondered briefly if she had gone too far. 'Mr Barkstowe said you propositioned him.'

Then Yvonne began to laugh. 'Did he, now? Well, it's true I was a whore, and I don't really care who knows it. But I've given it up. I always wanted to be an actress, and pretty soon I will be.' She gulped another mouthful of wine. 'Propositioned him, indeed. The slug! I wouldn't service him if I was starving. I've had men like him before. They lecture you on the error of your ways, fuck you, and then haggle when you ask for your fee. Or want a refund because they can't get it up. As if their floppy cocks are a whore's problem. I always used to tell them, "I'm ready to perform. Is it my fault if you're not?"'

'I thought there were certain tricks you could use?' Katherine hinted.

'Sometimes,' Yvonne said. 'It depends on why they can't get stiff. If it's drink, you can forget the fun and games. They'll snore.' She smiled at Katherine. 'And why are you so interested? A well-bred, single women like you?'

'I'm going to Heldenburg to be married,' Katherine said.

'And you think you'll have problems on your wedding night?' Yvonne laughed. 'With a face and figure like yours? Your problem will be getting some sleep.'

'He's very young,' Katherine said.

'Lucky for you,' Yvonne said. 'You'll be his first teacher. You can train him!' She leant forward conspiratorially. 'You're not a virgin, are you?'

'No,' Katherine said. 'But he thinks I am.'

'Does that worry you? You think he'll guess – and be upset?'

'Not really,' Katherine admitted. 'I doubt if he'll know the difference.'

'Are you madly in love?'

17

Katherine laughed. 'Good heavens, no!'

'But you're a titled lady, aren't you?' When Katherine hesitated she added, 'Tell the truth, now. I did.'

'Well, yes,' Katherine said. 'But –'

'You're marrying out of duty?'

'Yes.'

'What's his name?'

Katherine hesitated. She did not really want to divulge too many details about her private life. Maybe she had said too much already? She tried to think of a way to change the subject without making it sound too obvious, or too unfriendly.

The door of the hostelry banged open suddenly, causing a welcome diversion. The man who walked in was over six feet tall. He wore an ankle-length, high-collared military cloak, and a distinctively shaped kepi-style cap with a dull metal badge and a bright-red cockade. The stiff peak shaded his face. When he swung the cape off his shoulders Katherine saw that his uniform was dark blue. A short fitted jacket with silver braid emphasised his wide shoulders and narrow waist. His tight dark trousers with a wide red stripe fitted smoothly into knee-high boots. He was armed with a cavalry sabre.

'Herr Leutnant Bruckner.' The inn-keeper was all smiles. 'How nice to see you again. You will want your usual room? A drink? A meal?'

The young officer removed his cap and rubbed his hand over his face. His hair was cut plainly, and gleamed gold in the lantern light. His clean-shaven face had strong, straight features.

'All of those things,' he said. He spoke in fluent German, but with an accent Katherine did not recognise. 'Give me the drink first, though. Night patrols always make me thirsty.'

The inn-keeper obliged. Yvonne watched with undisguised interest. 'Now that,' she breathed, in admiration, 'is what I call a man.'

'Is anything interesting happening on the border?' the inn-keeper asked.

Katherine watched as the young officer sat down by the fire and stretched his legs towards the flames. He swallowed a mouthful of beer and surveyed the room. His eyes reached her, and stopped. She felt them linger on her face, then descend to what was visible of her body, chastely covered by her fitted travelling jacket. His glance stayed just a little longer than necessary on the tiny buttons that drew a line from her neck to her waist, swelling over the curve of her full breasts, and his mouth quirked slightly. His gaze moved to Yvonne and gave her a similar assessment. Yvonne smiled, and moved so that the low scoop of her neckline was more obvious. The officer smiled back. Then he turned to the inn-keeper.

'Nothing much is happening outside,' he said. 'But things are looking promising in here. Ask the two ladies if they would allow me to buy them a drink.'

'They're foreigners,' the inn-keeper said. There was a warning note in his voice. 'English. They're travelling in the same coach.'

'Even English ladies drink wine, I believe?' The officer lowered his voice. 'Those two certainly do, judging from the glasses on their table. Ask them. If they refuse, there's an end to the matter.'

'Is he talking about us?' Yvonne asked.

'I believe so,' Katherine said.

The inn-keeper had come over to their table. He said, in German, 'Herr Leutnant Bruckner would like you both to accept a glass of wine.' Katherine realised in surprise that he sounded distinctly nervous. She wondered why. Surely there was no harm in relaying a sociable offer?

'What's he saying?' Yvonne asked.

Katherine translated, and Yvonne smiled. 'Shall we accept? It could mean that our gorgeous soldier will take it as an invitation to join us.'

Katherine looked at the young Leutnant again. 'Maybe he'll be amusing company.' She glanced up at the inn-keeper. 'Thank the officer for his generosity. We accept.'

The inn-keeper shuffled his feet. 'He does not know who you are, gracious lady.'

'Then don't tell him,' Katherine said. 'I would not wish to embarrass him.'

The wine arrived almost immediately. The Leutnant raised his tankard to toast them, and smiled. Yvonne lifted her glass in return. 'In a minute he's going to come over to us,' she predicted. 'Do you like the look of him?'

'He's very – interesting,' Katherine said.

'Would you bed him?'

'Heavens!' Katherine hoped she sounded suitably shocked. 'What an immoral question!'

'You mean you haven't considered it?' Yvonne laughed softly. 'Well, I have. And so has he. I recognise the look on his face. He'd like a little fun this evening. With us.'

Katherine stared across at the officer. He gazed back, a slight smile touching his mouth. She remembered the way his eyes had assessed her. It had given her the distinct impression that he would not have needed much encouragement to undo her jacket buttons, and all the other hooks, laces and fastenings he found underneath. And the thought of letting him do it had definitely aroused her. As she watched, he stood up, unhurriedly. He drained his tankard and put it down, and walked towards their table.

'If he asks us,' Yvonne persisted, 'will you agree? Your last adventure, before you get married? Perhaps you owe it to yourself?'

Perhaps I do, Katherine thought. Once I'm settled in boring Heldenburg I'll be expected to play the dull and dutiful wife. I probably won't get a chance to stray, even if I want to. If this attractive young man is after a little fun, why shouldn't I oblige? I'm not married to Ruprecht von Krohnenstein yet.

The officer had reached their table. He towered above them, in his dark uniform, and bowed. 'May I introduce myself?' he said formally, in excellent English. 'I am Leutnant Markus Bruckner, currently inspecting the border patrols. I hope you were not offended by my forwardness in offering you wine?'

Yvonne lifted her glass. 'Why should we be offended? It's excellent.'

Bruckner smiled. 'Are you, perhaps, travelling for pleasure? Or maybe you plan to visit a spa for your health?'

'Neither,' Yvonne said. 'I'm a working girl.'

'An independent woman?' Bruckner held her gaze. 'I like that. What work do you do?'

'I'm an actress,' Yvonne said.

'An interesting profession,' he said. 'Do you play a variety of roles?'

'Whatever I'm asked,' Yvonne said. She paused. 'I'm very versatile.'

He stared at her for a moment. 'I'm sure you are.' His eyes moved to Katherine. 'I'm sure you both are. Maybe one day I shall see you perform.'

'Maybe you will,' Yvonne agreed. She stood up. 'But now, if you'll excuse us, we're both quite tired. I think we'll retire to bed.'

Leutnant Markus Bruckner stepped back immediately, and bowed again. 'Of course. It was inconsiderate of me to take up your time.'

When they reached the upper corridor, Yvonne said, 'I think the inn-keeper will give Herr Bruckner my room number, not yours. You're a lady, remember!'

'And you think he'll ask for the number?' Katherine said.

'He's probably asking now,' Yvonne laughed. She opened the door. The lamp was already lit, giving out a warm golden glow. 'Maybe I'll see you perform, indeed!' She ran her fingers round the neckline of her dress, loosening it, and then began to unfasten the hooks at the back. She slipped out of the dress and draped it over one of the carved upright chairs. She slackened the laces of her corsets and fluffed out her hair. 'Herr Bruckner can remove the petticoats,' she said. 'And everything else, if he wishes!'

Katherine took off her travelling jacket. Her fingers hesitated over the buttons of her blouse, but she did not undo them.

Yvonne watched her. 'Are you sure you're happy about all this? You wouldn't prefer to leave?' She smiled suddenly. 'I have to tell you that, if you do, poor Herr Bruckner will be *very* disappointed.'

'I doubt that he'd even notice,' Katherine said. 'I believe it's you he's interested in.'

'You're wrong,' Yvonne said. 'I can read the signs. Given a choice, he'd choose you.' There was a tap on the door. 'Guess who that is?' Yvonne murmured. She invited, 'Come in, Herr Bruckner.'

Markus Bruckner had removed his uniform jacket and was wearing a round-necked white undershirt, half open. His tight trousers hugged his hips and thighs and made it quite obvious that he was already excited about the entertainment he was expecting.

'What delayed you?' Yvonne asked sweetly. 'We thought you'd changed your mind.'

Bruckner smiled. His deferential manner had disappeared. 'I wanted to give you a chance to undress,' he said. 'You did say you were going to bed, didn't you?' His eyes moved from Yvonne to Katherine. 'Together?'

'Certainly not,' Yvonne said. 'We're respectable women.'

'I hope not.' Bruckner sat down on the bed, and leant back, resting on his elbows, stretching out his long legs.

His smile shifted from Yvonne to Katherine. 'You are both actresses?'

'I'm not,' Katherine said.

'She's getting married,' Yvonne said. 'Poor girl. To some virgin boy she hardly knows.'

Bruckner looked surprised and intrigued. He turned to Katherine. 'But why would you do that?'

'Necessity,' Katherine said, wishing Yvonne had not brought the subject up.

'I don't believe you,' Bruckner said. 'A beautiful woman does not have to marry anyone out of necessity.' He patted the bed. 'Come and sit here. Let me educate you.'

After a moment's hesitation Katherine obeyed. She found his closeness pleasantly disturbing. She wanted him to touch her. The knowledge that he was a complete stranger, and she would probably never see him again after the night was over, was surprisingly exciting. She was no longer Lady Katherine Gainsworth, promised in marriage to Ruprecht Wilhelm von Krohnenstein, marrying out of duty. She was as free as Markus Bruckner. Her body was her own. She could be as uninhibited as she liked. She could enjoy him or refuse him. The choice was hers.

His fingers touched the tiny buttons that fastened her blouse. He played with them for a moment, and then very slowly began to undo them. The edge of her corset lifted her breasts upwards and outwards. She could feel his fingers moving lightly, backwards and forwards. 'A beautiful woman,' he said softly, 'can always find a way to pay her bills.'

Her eyes held his. 'That sounds like a very immoral suggestion,' she murmured.

'A very sensible suggestion.' He pushed her blouse back over her shoulders, and began to loosen the front lacing of her corset, opening it and freeing her breasts. 'You should find yourself a protector.' She felt his hands

23

cup her breasts. 'If I had the money I would offer my services.' He began to caress her slowly, smiling as he felt her nipples harden under his teasing fingers. 'But all I have is my army pay.'

Yvonne sat on the bed behind them. 'Don't even consider falling for a soldier,' she warned. 'You never know what they're doing from one day to the next – or who they're doing it with.' She rested her hands on Bruckner's shoulders, and began to massage them. 'Don't listen to this seducer. Your little virgin boy is the best option. At least he'll be married to you, fair and square.'

Is that thought supposed to make me feel happy? Katherine wondered. Bruckner's lips touched her neck and then moved quickly downwards. His hands pushed her breasts up, guiding her nipples to his mouth. He kissed first one, and then the other. His tongue circled and caressed. She felt a shudder of pleasure course through her. Jack Telfer had never handled her like this. She had always hoped William Shannon would do so, but that was a lost dream now. Would Ruprecht von Krohnenstein be as accomplished? She doubted it.

Bruckner's hands travelled downwards to the waist of her skirt. He loosened it, removed it, and then began to work on her petticoats, all the time exciting her with his lips and tongue. It kept her mind off what he was doing, and soon the rest of her undergarments had followed her skirt.

His movements were smooth with experience. How many other women has he stripped? she wondered. How many others have felt their bodies respond, as his hands worked their expert magic? Not that she felt any jealousy. She was not asking him for fidelity. What she wanted was to be aroused by someone who was willing to take the trouble to please her, as well as satisfy himself. The thought of all the things he might do to her was making her damp with expectation. The idea of watching him make love to Yvonne excited her too. And, she realised in surprise, performing with him while Yvonne watched was an equally stimulating proposition.

She felt Bruckner's palm slide up to the bare flesh of her thigh, above her stocking, while his mouth still sucked her gently. Because it was all so unhurried, and he seemed to feel no need to prove his virility by quickly displaying his erection and entering her, she felt both relaxed and eager. She wanted to feel his hand search between her legs. She wanted his mouth to follow, to pleasure her slowly, until she was finally desperate for relief.

This is how it should be, she thought contentedly. A long, slow build-up. Not a quick fumble, almost immediately followed by penetration, leaving her with a sense of disappointment. Jack Telfer had often left her unsatisfied, although she had never told him so. Sometimes, she thought, their wrestling matches on the bed had been more erotic than their lovemaking – especially when Jack held her down, and she felt deliciously helpless.

She was vaguely aware that Yvonne's arms were circling Bruckner's waist and her fingers were pulling at the buttons of his tight uniform trousers. She heard Yvonne's voice scolding playfully, 'Come on now, Herr Bruckner, I need some help. Whoever designed these trousers didn't intend them to come off easily.'

Bruckner lifted his head and grinned. 'Don't be so impatient, my dear girl. We have plenty of time. I will satisfy both of you.'

'This – ' Yvonne rubbed the impressive bulge of his erection ' – will only manage to satisfy one of us.'

'Both of you,' he promised. 'The honour of my regiment is at stake. The honour of my country.' He smiled at Yvonne. 'If you think I'm not up to the challenge, you've never met an officer from the Heldenburg Fifth before.'

'Heldenburg?' Yvonne said, surprised. 'I thought you were a Prussian. Don't they patrol their own borders?'

'They share the duty with us,' Bruckner said. He shook his head in mock reproof. 'Didn't you recognise my uniform?'

'No,' Yvonne said. 'But Katherine probably did. Her little virgin boy comes from Heldenburg.'

Katherine felt a slight stab of apprehension, but dismissed it. Ruprecht was hardly likely to know this young officer. She doubted if he knew anything about the army. Or cared. He was the most unmilitary person she had ever met.

'I've never been here before,' she said. 'I wouldn't recognise anyone's uniform.'

Bruckner's hand slipped between Katherine's thighs. 'So your future husband is a fellow countryman of mine, and I'm going to have you before he does?' He shifted his position slowly, caressing her all the time, and ended up astride her. She felt his knee between her legs, keeping them apart. 'That's amusing.' His fingers explored. One hand found her swollen clitoris and stroked it, gently but firmly, arousing it even more. The other reached up and touched her nipples. 'Hard as little brown berries,' he said, softly. 'Will your new husband please you as much? Perhaps you should introduce me? I can give him some advice, tell him the things you like. Maybe I even know him. What's his name?'

Katherine ignored the question. She did not want to think about Ruprecht. Ruprecht was part of a future she was beginning to wish she did not have to face.

'You're not likely to know her husband, Leutnant,' Yvonne laughed. 'He's nobility.'

Bruckner smiled. 'Really?' It was clear that he thought Yvonne was joking. 'And I suppose you'll be telling me next that this little wanton girl, who is wriggling about with such delight because I think I've managed to find out just the right way to play with her, is a duchess?' He smiled at Katherine. 'Is it true?'

'No, no,' Katherine said. She hoped Yvonne would take the hint and keep quiet. 'Of course not.'

But Yvonne persisted. 'She's just being modest. She's a lady. A real one, I mean.'

'I'm sure she is,' Bruckner agreed, condescendingly. 'But to me, all women are ladies, until I persuade them to be otherwise. And I have a feeling that I will persuade both of you tonight.'

'When I said a lady, I meant a *lady*!' Yvonne was obviously getting annoyed at not being taken seriously. And, Katherine thought, maybe a little frustrated because Bruckner was not paying her any physical attention. She wished Yvonne would change the subject. 'A lady as in Lady Katherine,' Yvonne insisted.

'I believe you,' Bruckner murmured, his attention focused on Katherine.

'And she's marrying someone called von Krohnenstein,' Yvonne finished triumphantly.

Bruckner sat up with such a jolt that he made Katherine jump. 'That,' he said, coldly, 'is not a funny joke!'

'It isn't a joke,' Yvonne smirked, clearly pleased to have caused a reaction at last.

Bruckner turned to Katherine. He stopped stroking her, and she felt a surge of irritation at the abrupt cessation of pleasure. 'Tell me this is nonsense,' he said.

'What does it matter?' she asked, more sharply than she intended.

How did Yvonne know of her intended connection with the von Krohnenstein family? She had never mentioned the name. Or had she? Yes, she thought, once. During her conversation with the inn-keeper. Yvonne's acute ear had obviously caught the name, remembered it and jumped to the correct conclusion. But why should it matter to Bruckner? She caught his hand and tried to encourage it back between her legs.

'Don't stop,' she said. 'I'm not married yet. And right now, I want you.'

27

He pulled away from her with brutal abruptness, and stood up. 'What you want is unimportant. Tell me the truth. Are you are promised in marriage to Ruprecht von Krohnenstein, the son of Count Werner von Krohnenstein?'

'Yes,' she said. And added lightly, 'Unless I change my mind.'

He began to button his trousers, fumbling in his haste. 'You obviously know nothing about your future husband. And you certainly know nothing about the von Krohnenstein family, or you would not be travelling with this whore.'

'Just who are you a calling a whore?' Yvonne interrupted, angrily. 'You were calling us both ladies a few minutes ago.'

Bruckner had finished buttoning up. Katherine suddenly realised what she must look like, sprawled half-naked on the bed, her legs apart. But Bruckner was no longer gazing at her with lust in his eyes. She realised in surprise that he looked afraid.

'I did nothing.' He backed towards the door. 'Nothing, you understand?' He stared at Katherine, his face hostile. 'I don't know you. We have never met.'

Katherine sat up on the bed, and pulled her dishevelled clothes around her. She was no longer angry, just curious. What was it about the von Krohnenstein name that could cause such a reaction?

'And as for you – ' Bruckner turned to Yvonne ' – you would be well advised to forget this incident too.'

'Just like that?' Yvonne taunted. 'Since it seems to mean so much to you, and since I'm a whore, you wouldn't like to pay me to keep my mouth shut, would you?'

Bruckner's face turned ugly. 'If you value the looks you still have,' he said, 'you will be sensible, and heed my warning.'

'Threats, now?' Yvonne laughed harshly. 'You do

change your tune quickly, Herr Leutnant Markus Bruckner of the Heldenburg Fifth.'

'Yvonne is my friend,' Katherine said. Her voice was quiet, but it held an underlying note of warning. 'Please remember that, Leutnant Bruckner.'

'You would do well to choose your friends with better caution in the future,' Bruckner said.

'At all times, it seems!' she snapped back.

He turned to the door, and then hesitated. 'Listen,' he said rapidly. 'I'm telling you this for your own good. Go home. Marry a nice, dull Englishman and have his babies. If you become involved with the von Krohnenstein family, you'll regret it.' The door clicked shut behind him.

Yvonne looked at Katherine. 'So what was that all about?'

Katherine shrugged. 'He's frightened. I wonder why.'

'Because you're going to marry a von Krohnenstein,' Yvonne said.

'That was a good guess of yours,' Katherine said, smiling.

'Wasn't it?' Yvonne agreed, smiling back. 'And it's correct, isn't it? Why didn't you tell me you were involved with such an important family?'

Katherine shrugged. 'I didn't know they were important.' She paused. 'Do you really think I should go back to England?'

Yvonne snorted. 'Of course not! Just because the mention of your husband's father reduced the size of that bulge in Herr Bruckner's trousers?' She put her hands on Katherine's shoulders. 'The von Krohnensteins are obviously powerful. Marry this virgin boy of yours, and you'll become powerful, too.'

But is that really what will happen? Katherine wondered later that night, as she tried to sleep. Is that my future? The wife of an influential aristocrat? Another thought nagged her. Why did Ruprecht's family want him to marry a girl from an English family? If they were that important, surely they could have had their choice of suitable wives from Heldenburg's eligible aristocrats?

Is there something about Ruprecht that I should know, but haven't been told? she wondered. Or something about the count? She knew Ruprecht's mother had died in childbirth, but he had hardly ever mentioned his father, and when she had pressed him for details he had always tried to change the subject. Katherine had assumed there was no love lost between the two of them, and that Ruprecht had been obeying his father's orders when he had proposed to her.

She realised that she really had no idea what the count was like. She imagined someone middle-aged, with old-fashioned ideas. Probably a man who thought pleasure was synonymous with evil. A man who ruled his son with an iron hand, and whose influence obviously extended outside the family circle. Far enough outside to make army officers like Leutnant Bruckner very nervous, anyway.

Just who is this Count Werner von Krohnenstein? she wondered, as sleep overtook her at last. And just what kind of a family am I marrying into?

Chapter Two

'*I*f you want to back out – ' Yvonne Tressilian held Katherine's hands in hers ' – there's still time. But do it now. Before you go across the border.'

Katherine smiled. 'I don't want to back out.' She had breakfasted with Yvonne and had voiced some doubts about her prospective father-in-law. Yvonne had obviously taken her remarks very seriously. 'I'm not marrying the count,' she added lightly.

'But he could influence your life,' Yvonne warned. The coachman was looking across at her expectantly. A glum-looking Mr Barkstowe was already aboard. 'Come with me.' Yvonne tugged Katherine forward gently. 'It won't take a moment to get your luggage. Come with me and be an actress.'

'Will I make a lot of money?' Katherine teased.

'No, but we'll both have a lot of fun,' Yvonne promised.

'Fun doesn't pay debts,' Katherine said. The coach horses were shifting about impatiently now. 'You have to go.' She gave Yvonne a friendly push forward. 'If you ever come to Heldenburg, make sure you send me a note, and we'll meet.'

31

'I wouldn't do that,' Yvonne said. 'I'm a disreputable actress. I'm sure your father-in-law wouldn't approve of me.'

'Who says I'm going to tell him?' Katherine asked.

'You might have to,' Yvonne said.

'You make it sound as if I'm going to be a prisoner,' Katherine said.

'With Count von Krohnenstein as your gaoler,' Yvonne agreed. 'Don't joke about it. I have this unpleasant feeling that your new life is not going to be as free as the one you've probably been used to.'

'Nonsense.' Katherine forced more enthusiasm into her voice than she actually felt. 'The count will probably turn out to be a nice old boy, and I'll get on splendidly with him.'

She knew Yvonne did not believe this cheerful prediction. And as she watched the coach pulling away, and saw Yvonne's hand waving at the window, Katherine wondered if she really believed it herself. Maybe the brash but likeable actress was right. She knew nothing about the kind of life she could expect as the wife of Ruprecht von Krohnenstein. It had been easy to dismiss the future as an adventure, back in England. The memory of Markus Bruckner's reaction to her future father-in-law's name had surprised and disturbed her. Maybe it would be fun to join a theatrical troupe. To have no responsibilities. To be free to live her own life, free to choose her own man.

A man like Markus Bruckner? She had to admit that she had found him attractive. What was so special about him? she wondered idly. He was certainly a splendid physical specimen, but Jack Telfer had the body of an athlete too, and William Shannon had been lithe and elegant. She decided it was not only Bruckner's appearance that excited her, it was the impression he gave of being in control. He was confident of pleasing her. She felt certain he would know just how far to push his erotic dominance. He would have enjoyed her, but made sure that she enjoyed him, too. He would not have lost control and taken her swiftly, and then apologised afterwards.

But she had believed that Jack Telfer and William Shannon would be equally accomplished, and they had both disappointed her. Would Markus Bruckner have disappointed her, too? She remembered his unhurried caresses, the sensation of his hands as they aroused her, his fingers expertly applying just the right amount of pressure as they played with her nipples and then moved down between her legs. She was certain he had been planning to explore her with his tongue. What would that have felt like? Would he have aroused her to the point where she would have been desperate for him to enter her, both of them giving and taking pleasure until they were exhausted?

It had never been like that with Jack Telfer. He had satisfied himself and had always assumed she had been equally contented. She had accepted it because she had not wanted to hurt his feelings. She had allowed the situation to continue because she never had an opportunity to alter it. Jack had never asked her opinion. They had discussed wrestling in great detail, she remembered wryly, but not sex.

How would Ruprecht treat her, if he ever managed to pluck up enough courage to make love to her? Would he approach her as if she were made of expensive porcelain and liable to break? Would he want the lamps out so that he could perform the dreaded act in the dark, probably with the quick speed of an animal? She assumed that she would be expected to produce an heir, but she hoped Ruprecht would delay the duty for as long as possible. What would happen if she did not conceive? No doubt she would be blamed, although Ruprecht did not look capable of impregnating anyone. Perhaps if I don't get pregnant, my father-in-law will

33

bribe me into a separation, she thought suddenly, and I'll be allowed to go home. It was an attractive idea.

Without Yvonne's company, time dragged. Katherine stayed in her room, amusing herself with a pack of cards, waiting for her transport to arrive. Despite her foreboding about the future, it was a relief when she heard the clatter of wheels in the yard outside. She went to the window and looked down. The coach was large, plain and dark. Rather like a funeral carriage, she thought. Four black horses reinforced this impression. There was a coat of arms painted on the door, and two men sat high on the driver's seat. As she watched, one of them swung down and strode towards the hostelry. He was tall and thin and wore an ankle-length black cape and a wide-brimmed hat.

Katherine's main luggage was already in the yard. When the inn-keeper came for her she only had to pick up her small personal bag. The man in the black cloak was waiting at the foot of the stairs. He had removed his hat. His face was bony and ageless, and his iron-grey hair smoothed back flat against his skull.

'Gracious lady.' He made a very slight bow. Just enough to be polite, Katherine felt, but not enough to imply real respect. 'I am Hecht. I have been sent to escort you to my master, the Count von Krohnenstein.'

Katherine inclined her head towards him with equally frosty disdain. 'Do you have any message for me from Ruprecht von Krohnenstein?'

The man allowed her to precede him through the door. 'I am my master's servant,' he said flatly. 'I do not carry messages for anyone else.'

He made his self-description sound like a title. And one that he was proud of, Katherine guessed. The faithful family retainer? Well, she could appreciate his feelings. Her father's gamekeeper still lived on their estate, fiercely protecting the river and the woods from poachers. She knew it was several years since he had received any money for his services. Dear Rothers. He had been a cheerful, talkative man, and a good friend. She felt a sudden pang of home-sickness. Hecht looked as if his thin lips had forgotten how to smile. She was very relieved when he made it clear he did not intend to travel in the coach with her. He made sure that she was safely inside and then climbed up to sit with the driver.

The coach was surprisingly well sprung. The seats were wide and upholstered with black leather. She slithered back on them and sighed. She knew this was going to be a long journey, and wished that her books were not packed away in her trunk. She was a little surprised that the von Krohnenstein family had not sent her a female travelling companion. At least it would have given her the chance of some conversation. And, she thought, a chance to ask questions. Then it occurred to her that perhaps this was exactly why no one had been sent to accompany her.

The rocking motion of the coach and the constant grumble of the wheels eventually lulled her into a doze. Before she closed her eyes, she glanced out of the window at the pine trees that lined the route. They were now a long way from any town. Do they have armed brigands in Heldenburg? she wondered idly. Was Hecht armed? Would he be capable of killing an attacker? She rather thought he was.

She let her thoughts wander. She imagined a mounted man appearing out of the trees. An old-fashioned high-wayman, a scarf covering the lower half of his face. He would be wearing a wide-brimmed hat, and a dark coat with a high collar. And he would be armed with a long-barrelled pistol. The coach would pick up speed, attempting to outrun him, but he would fire and wound Hecht, knocking him from his perch. The coachman would panic, leap down from his seat and run into the trees. The coach horses would bolt, but the highwayman would ride alongside and manage to guide them to a halt. Then he would edge his horse nearer to the window, to survey his prize. She imagined dark eyes assessing her above the scarf. A look that was an undisguised sexual appraisal. He would back away, his pistol levelled at the door, and order her out. Of course she would obey him. She had no choice.

She settled back more comfortably and prepared to enjoy picturing him more clearly. He would be tall, with William Shannon's long legs, and the kind of tight breeches and knee-high boots that Shannon used to wear, breeches that had emphasised his slim hips and the discreet bulge of his manhood. But this man would be less discreet. When he dismounted, leaving his horse free to crop grass, his long coat would swing open and it would be quite obvious that he was excited about the activity to come.

But she did not want him to look like Will Shannon, or like Jack Telfer, or Markus Bruckner either. Maybe he would have some of Bruckner's arrogant sexual confidence, but the similarity would end there. He would not back away from her at the mention of the von Krohnen-stein name. And she certainly did not want him to look like Ruprecht, with his smooth, almost pretty, face.

He would have a wildness about him, she decided. A hint of devilry that suggested his behaviour would be exciting both in and out of the bedroom. She imagined him removing his hat, his black hair blown into an attractively jagged fringe by the wind. And when he untied the silk scarf he would have a smile that could charm you into forgetting he was also pointing a pistol at your chest. He would offer a mocking apology for disrupting her journey, ask if she had any valuables, and laugh when she denied it. He would step closer, so she could smell the masculine scent of his skin.

'I cannot believe you have nothing to offer me.'

'I am not rich, sir,' she would reply, with the kind of meekness she would never adopt in real life.

'Are you sure you have no valuables hidden under that elegant jacket?'

'I have no jewels, and no money,' she would answer. 'You have wasted your time following me.'

She slipped deeper into her fantasy.

He pushed the long-barrelled pistol into his belt. 'I think not,' he said softly. He tugged at the buttons of her travelling jacket. She felt the jacket open and the cool night breeze touch the skin of her neck. Then his long fingers traced a line under her chin, moving gently to and fro, but the pressure increasing until her head was tipped backwards and her mouth was in the position he wanted. At the same time he had fully unbuttoned her coat and his hand was on the neck of her blouse.

She expected him to kiss her, and he did. One hand cupped the back of her head, holding her prisoner, as his mouth captured hers. Then his free hand ripped her blouse from neck to waist.

The vividness of the mental picture caused her to react physically, and she felt her nipples harden as the images formed in her mind. The thought of him completing the destruction in a few swift, strong movements excited her even more. She imagined her laced corset pushing her breasts upwards, invitingly, towards him.

He stepped back then, and looked at her. 'Remove your skirt,' he said softly.

'And if I will not?' she challenged.

'I'll do it for you,' he said. 'The choice is yours.'

She unbuttoned the skirt and let it fall to her feet.

'And the petticoats,' he instructed.

She realised then how exciting it could be to strip slowly in front of admiring male eyes. Jack Telfer had undressed her many times, but she had never felt that he had enjoyed it. It had usually been hasty, and his hands on her clothes and her body had felt as impersonal as a lady's maid. For Jack, it was necessary to be totally naked in order to make love, so he wanted her naked, and as quickly as possible. Sometimes she had undressed herself, but he had never indicated that he found it arousing to watch. Once she had left her stockings on, hoping that the contrast of white silk and bare flesh would encourage him to linger during his lovemaking. He had simply told her to remove the stockings 'in case they were damaged'. Once they were off (and he showed no interest in removing them himself, she remembered) he rolled on top of her and performed with his usual speed.

She was naked when he gave her his impromptu wrestling lessons too, but they always came after his sexual ardour had been satisfied. Sometimes their entangled bodies would writhe into positions where his mouth could have pleased her, or she could have taken his limp penis between her lips and probably stimulated it into action again. But she had never done so, and he had never taken advantage of his skill or strength to hold her down and enjoy her, either, although she would not have minded if he had.

It was as if he could shut his mind off from sex when he was thinking about wrestling, even if his pupil was a woman, and she knew he expected the same dedication from her. If she had tried to turn their bouts into a lovemaking session he would probably have stopped teaching her – and she had enjoyed the lessons. It was only during their last meeting that she had felt free to take advantage of the fact that his nakedness made him vulnerable, and that was because she knew their relationship, both as lovers and teacher and pupil, was over.

She had often imagined stripping for William Shannon. Disrobing slowly, teasing him. Then imagining him making love to her, with passionate dominance. Hearing his quiet voice telling her what he was going to do to her, and what he wanted her to do to him. The thought of it had always made her feel damp with excitement. Just as she felt now, she realised, as she imagined herself half-naked, wearing only her laced corset, her white silk

38

stockings tied at her thighs, and her shoes. But she no longer wanted to imagine William Shannon's face watching her. When she thought of Shannon now it brought back memories of that disappointing, too fast consummation. The dark and dangerous man that she had conjured up, with his jagged windswept hair, was far more enticing.

He would take his time looking her over. His eyes would admire her full breasts, her neat waist, and linger on the bush of her pubic hair. One hand on her shoulder would turn her round, slowly, and he would give her rear view the same appraisal. The same hand would reach up to unfasten the pins in her golden-brown hair, allowing it to fall in loose natural curls to her shoulders. When she faced him again he would be smiling. 'You see? A beautiful woman always has something to bargain with.'

Then he would step closer, move his hands from her hair to her shoulders, and lightly trace a line to the tips of her breasts. She would try to mask her own excitement by making an effort to fend him off. She thought that in real life she could probably throw an unsuspecting man by using one of the tricks Jack had taught her. But she had no intention of throwing this man, even in her imagination. Instead she enjoyed the thought of struggling with him, feeling the roughness of his coat against her bare flesh, and the strength of his grip. She enjoyed the thought of him grasping her wrists and forcing her back against the coach door. She would fight just hard enough to arouse him, and she would know how excited he was by the bulge of his erection behind the tight trousers, as his hips pressed against hers.

Holding her with one hand he would push her into the coach, following her in and slamming the door. She would still fight him. What would he do? She knew exactly the kind of reaction she wanted. He would hold both of her wrists and force her into position across his lap, while her silk-stockinged legs kicked ineffectively. She imagined the pressure of his thighs against her stomach. She imagined the smooth leather against her naked breasts, as she struggled to escape. And against her face, as his long fingers entwined in her hair and held her captive. She would smell the aroma of leather and hear the creak of the coach springs as he shifted himself into a comfortable position and, despite her struggles, arranged her just as he wanted her.

His fingers would massage her scalp briefly, tumbling her hair forward. 'First,' there would be a hint of humour in his voice, 'a lesson in good manners.'

She imagined the slap of his palm against her bare bottom, hard enough to sting, but not hard enough to cause real pain. The spanking would continue, despite her yells of protest, until her flesh was tingling and she was breathless. Then he would turn her over, and confirm that the erotic punishment she had received had aroused her as much as it had probably aroused him. And he would take advantage of her obvious need for him, positioning her astride his lap, facing outward. His hands would cup her breasts and his mouth would search under the tangle of her hair and caress the nape of her neck. He would search for her ear, find it and run his tongue round it gently. She would feel his erection, hard and eager, pushing against her bottom. She knew that, before long, he would tip her forward so that she was supported by his outstretched legs, her breasts pressing against the smooth black leather of his boots, and his hand would give her clitoris some of the relief it required. The kind of relief she had often given herself in the privacy of her bed. The kind of relief, she thought, wriggling uncomfortably, that she wanted right now.

There was a tiny window connecting the carriage to the driver's high perch. It was covered by a flap that could be opened from the outside. Katherine wished she was wearing her male riding clothes. It would be easy to unbutton the trousers and slip her hand inside. She could then close her eyes and imagine that she was with her black-haired and desirable fantasy man. If the driver, or Hecht, started to open the flap, she would hear them and be able to make herself respectable in seconds. With her heavy travelling skirt and petticoats it would be much more difficult to rearrange her clothing quickly.

But she felt so wet and uncomfortable that she was tempted to take the risk. Why should the two men want to talk to her, anyway? They had travelled all this time without needing to do so. And she wanted to feel a warm rush of sexual pleasure while the erotic memory of her fantasy was still fresh in her mind. She pulled her skirts up to her knees. Her fingers slid over the silky smoothness of her stockings, reached the bare flesh of her thighs, and then moved higher. She caressed herself gently at first, picturing the darkly attractive face, the lean strong body, the experienced hands and mouth. Her own hand moved faster, and she moaned softly, writhing on the padded seat.

The knowledge that she could be caught behaving in such a wanton fashion made it even more exciting. She glanced up at the shuttered window. If either of the two men outside opened it now, she knew she could not control herself. Then the orgasmic sensations overwhelmed her and she moaned again, louder this time, and fell back against the seat. For a moment she lay there, panting, her skirts round her waist. Look in at me now, Herr Hecht, she thought, and you can report *this* to your master! But the window stayed shut. After she had rearranged her clothes she felt a warm drowsiness overtake her. Settling back in her seat, she allowed the rhythm of the coach to lull her into a comfortable doze.

A violent jolt shook her awake. Instead of the rocking movement she had become accustomed to, the coach was now bouncing erratically. She slithered over to the window and looked out. The coach had left the road and was now closely hemmed in by trees. Anger banished apprehension. She struggled over to the little shuttered window that separated her from the driver's seat and banged on it. It took several attempts before she heard the catches opening. Hecht's face appeared, staring down at her.

'Where are we going?' she demanded.

Hecht paused, and for a moment she thought he was not going to answer her. 'I am taking you to the count,'

'You're taking me into the middle of a forest,' she objected tartly. 'Or are you going to tell me that this is a short cut?'

Hecht paused again, just long enough to make his response sound patronising. 'This is the only route to the count's hunting lodge at Grünholz. You have no reason to be afraid. I have promised my master I will deliver you safely.'

'I don't want to go to a hunting lodge,' Katherine objected. The coach lurched and bounced. 'I demand to be taken into the town. I demand to see my future husband, Ruprecht von Krohnenstein.'

She saw a glimmer of expression cross Hecht's thin face. It might have been the trace of a smile. 'I have my orders,' he said. 'I am taking you to my master, the count.'

The shutters banged together. Katherine stared up at them furiously. She felt like battering them, but knew that such an action would be futile. Instead she sat back and tried to make some sense out of her situation. Maybe it wasn't really surprising that the old count wanted to see her. They had never met. Perhaps he wanted to confirm that she really was the right bride for his son? Perhaps, she thought, he would decide she was not suitable and send her home. At that moment, as she jolted uncomfortably in the lurching coach, the thought was appealing. She remembered Markus Bruckner's words: *a beautiful woman does not have to marry anyone out of necessity*. She would find a way to keep her father out of debt. Maybe being a rich man's mistress was preferable to being a wife? If the man started to bore her, she could always look for someone else.

The coach driver's voice, as he soothed the horses to a standstill, was her first indication that they had arrived at their destination. She could see nothing but trees from the coach windows. Hecht opened the door and stood waiting to help her. She deliberately ignored him, and climbed down on her own. Then she saw the lodge. It was a long low building, with a pitched roof, and it seemed to be built entirely of logs. A massive pair of antlers had been fixed above the carved front door.

Hecht said, 'Follow me.'

He turned and walked towards the lodge. Silently fuming, Katherine followed him. Hecht pushed open the carved doors. The entrance hall was decorated with more antlers, and several boars' heads. One particularly vicious-looking beast snarled down at Katherine from above the huge fireplace. When the coach driver struggled in with the first of her cases she turned imperiously to Hecht. 'Why is that idiot bringing my luggage?'

Hecht stared at her. 'You will stay here,' he said simply. It had the ring of finality about it.

She stared at him. She had the unpleasant feeling that he was enjoying himself, although no trace of emotion showed on his face. 'Stay?' she repeated, no longer bothering to try to control her anger. 'For how long? And where is the count?'

'I do not know where my master is,' Hecht said. 'He will decide when he wishes to see you. You will stay until you are given permission to leave.'

'Permission?' Katherine could hardly believe that Hecht was serious. 'This is intolerable. I have come to your country to marry into one of your most respected families, and I find myself treated like a prisoner. Since

43

your *master* isn't here to explain, perhaps you'd like to tell me why I am not being taken straight to Grazheim?'

Hecht said simply, 'We have our traditions.'

Katherine glared at him. 'And do they include treating visitors like criminals?'

Again she had the feeling that Hecht was enjoying her reaction, although his sombre face was as expressionless as before. 'There are servants here. You are a guest. You will be well treated.'

'And that's supposed to make me feel better?' she demanded acidly. 'In my country, I am accustomed to personal freedom.'

This time she was sure Hecht's lips quirked into a brief smile. 'But we are not in your country,' he said. 'You will learn that here we do things differently.'

'Tomorrow,' Frau Grussell said, 'the count will visit us.' She clasped her hands together. 'I will prepare you. Aren't you excited?'

Katherine made a point of stifling a yawn. 'No, I'm not. But at least it means I'll be able to leave here soon.'

Frau Grussell looked worried. 'You have not been unhappy, gracious lady? We have all tried to make you happy.'

Katherine looked at the tubby elderly woman and smiled. 'It's not your fault, Frau Grussell. I know you're only obeying orders. But I hate not being allowed to go out. And I'm bored.'

'We have tried to provide entertainment, gracious lady.'

Yes, Katherine thought. But I have nothing in common with the chattering girls who are supposed to look after me, and who seem to think that I want to spend all morning getting bathed and dressed, all afternoon deciding which piece of jewellery to wear, and all evening playing silly board games or charades. When she had suggested that a ride in the forest would be more to her liking, her companions had reacted with horror. There were wild animals in the forest. Hadn't the gracious lady noticed the boars' heads that decorated the lodge? No one went into the forest without a man to protect them.

Katherine was willing to believe the stories, but in her experience animals left you alone if you treated them with similar respect. And tucked away in her small, leather-covered box she had the means to protect herself without a man's help, although she did not tell the other women that. It was clear that they had been given instructions not to let her go out, and they would have produced any excuse necessary to justify those orders.

But once I get this meeting with the old count over, Katherine thought, I'll be able to go into Grazheim. Then I'll be free. She knew the Duchy's capital was surrounded by good riding country. It also had good shops, good restaurants, and splendid parks. She felt certain she would be able to enjoy herself in Grazheim. But first, she thought, I have to go through with this meeting.

Once again she wished she knew more about the count. What kind of woman did he expect her to be? She had no idea. Even the gossipy servant girls became flustered and unhelpful when she questioned them about her future father-in-law. They seemed almost as nervous as Markus Bruckner.

Frau Grussell was no help, either. 'The count is from an old Heldenburg family. Very patriotic, a close confident of the Grand Duke.'

'But what's he *like*?' Katherine insisted. 'As a person?'

Frau Grussell looked genuinely surprised. 'He is my master,' she said, simply. 'He has treated me well.'

'Can't you tell me anything else?' Katherine said. 'I want to be sure I make a good impression when we meet.'

Frau Grussell smiled ingratiatingly. 'Please don't worry, gracious lady. The count will like you very much. He is very anxious for the marriage to take place.'

Once again, Katherine felt curious. Why did an obviously powerful and very rich member of the Heldenburg aristocracy want his son to marry her? She was hard-headed enough to accept that love had nothing to do with Ruprecht's marriage proposal, and it certainly had nothing to do with her acceptance. Certainly she came from an aristocratic family, but that was not unique. There were women with more distinguished pedigrees than hers. And with more money, too. Did the count know exactly how impoverished her father was? Would he agree to the marriage if he did? Maybe, she thought, after the meeting tomorrow, I'll find out exactly what Count Werner von Krohnenstein is really planning.

By the afternoon on the following day Katherine was longing for her evening meeting with the count to be over. Everyone at the lodge behaved as if they were going to receive a visit from royalty. The wooden floors were polished until they shone. Windows were cleaned. Old rugs were suddenly removed, and new ones appeared. Fresh candles were placed in all the lamps. The younger women spent a lot of time giggling, and discussing which dresses they intended to wear – which rather surprised Katherine, as her mental picture of the count did not include someone who would be interested in his servants' clothes. Given their preoccupation with appearances, Katherine was rather surprised that none of them had questioned her about her own choice.

By late afternoon she had made her decision. The wine-coloured velvet gown, she thought. Its smooth lines emphasised her narrow waist. Its scooped neckline showed just enough of her breasts to be decently provocative, and would allow her to display her only good piece of jewellery, a diamond necklace that had belonged to her mother. Her father had sold most of the family heirlooms, but had never been able to bring himself to part with that piece. She laid the clothes out on her bed, and was trying to decide whether to pin her hair up, or leave a cascade of curls at the back, when Frau Grussell came into the room.

'We have prepared your bath, gracious lady.'

Katherine pointed to the dress. 'What do you think, Frau Grussell? Will the Count find my choice appropriate.'

Frau Grussell looked surprised. 'Choice, gracious lady? What choice do you have to make?'

'The dress,' Katherine said. 'That's the one I've decided to wear.'

Frau Grussell stared at the dress, and then at Katherine. 'But you must wear our costume. Our national dress. It's all ready for you.'

'National dress?' Katherine repeated. She had never seen Heldenburg's national costume, but she guessed it would be similar to those of other European countries, and based on peasant clothing. 'I won't wear anything of the kind. I don't intend to meet the count looking like an imitation peasant girl.'

'But you must,' Frau Grussell said, with unexpected determination. 'It's our tradition.'

Katherine was suddenly reminded of Hecht, and his claim that things were 'different in Heldenburg'. Well, if this was one of the differences, she wanted no part of it.

'Are you telling me that every woman meets her prospective father-in-law wearing fancy dress?' she asked acidly.

Her sarcasm was lost on Frau Grussell. 'This is not fancy dress, gracious lady. It's our national costume.'

'Well, it's not *my* national costume!' Katherine snapped back.

Frau Grussell had obviously not expected a rejection, and was unsure how to handle the situation. 'But you will become one of us, gracious lady, when you marry into the von Krohnenstein family.' She smiled, entreatingly.

'And you will look very beautiful in the costume. Very beautiful indeed.'

Katherine realised that the old woman was probably worried. It's Frau Grussell's responsibility to see that I follow this ridiculous tradition, she thought. What will happen to her if I refuse? The count doesn't sound as if he's a very forgiving master. And does it really matter what I wear? Once this meeting is over I'll be able to go into Grazheim and start to live like a civilised person. She gazed at Frau Grussell's worried face, and relented. 'Very well,' she said. 'Just this once.'

But after she had bathed, wrapped herself in a huge towel, and followed Frau Grussell into a small room to see her outfit for the first time, Katherine began to have second thoughts. The clothes were everything she had feared they would be. A circular skirt over multiple petticoats, a full-sleeved white blouse and a tight-laced, black felt bodice. The only item she did not think looked authentic were the shoes. They were black, with tiny heels and neat buckles.

'You will look beautiful,' Frau Grussell promised. She went to a huge chest of drawers and took out a pair of black stockings. 'Put these on first, and then I will help you into the skirt.'

Katherine was surprised to discover that the stockings were silk. Surely peasant girls would have worn wool? But she had no complaints when she rolled them on. They felt smooth and cool against her skin. She knew she had good legs, and the dark sheen of the silk made them look even better. What a pity no one will see them, she thought. She slipped on the buckled shoes, and was surprised to find that they were a good fit. The white blouse was another surprise. It had full long sleeves but no buttons at the front. Katherine tried unsuccessfully to close the two edges together over her breasts.

Frau Grussell wagged a reproving finger. 'No, no, that

is not necessary. You have the bodice. That will cover you.'

The bodice was made of stiffened felt with a small peplum. Frau Grussell fussed round, pulling and adjusting the front lacing until she felt the garment was correctly positioned. As she gave the laces a final tug, Katherine felt that she was being fitted into a corset. The bodice was comfortable enough where the neat peplum emphasised her waist, but higher up it only just covered her nipples, and forced her breasts backwards and upwards, giving her the kind of full, rounded cleavage that she felt was more appropriate to a whore than a lady.

Frau Grussell lifted the first of the petticoats over her head. The white frilled underskirts were made of fine cotton. There were three of them, and they were surprisingly light. The dark overskirt, with its intricate embroidery, was also fashioned from expensive cloth. It confirmed Katherine's suspicions that these were not genuine peasant clothes. This outfit had been made for someone who wanted to play at being a rustic. Or a man who enjoyed seeing his women dressed in this way.

Frau Grussell spent a few minutes rearranging Katherine's hair, and for a moment Katherine had a suspicion that the older woman was going to suggest that she braid her natural curls into plaits. But all Frau Grussell actually did was make sure the holding pins were firmly in place, before guiding her towards the full-length mirror.

'There, you see?' she announced proudly. 'How nice you look. The count will be very pleased with you.'

Well, Katherine thought, I certainly look different. She was surprised how erotic the outfit was. Quite apart from the effect the bodice had on her breasts, the full skirt made her waist look attractively tiny, and the black stockings and neatly buckled shoes emphasised her small ankles. She felt different, too. The full petticoats lifted the skirt into a crinoline shape, and were so light that she almost felt as if she was naked from the waist down.

She had an unexpected mental picture of the fantasy man she had conjured up during her coach journey into Heldenburg. She imagined him pushing her back, on to a soft bed. She imagined the petticoats riding up in disarray. She imagined the contrast between the dark bush of her pubic hair, her white thighs and the black stocking-tops. She imagined his smile as he admired her.

Frau Grussell's voice broke into her dream. 'Come now. It's time to meet the count.'

'He's here already?' Katherine was genuinely surprised. 'I didn't hear a coach.'

'He has been here for some time,' Frau Grussell said. 'He rarely comes in the coach. He likes to ride.'

Katherine followed Frau Grussell down the corridor. Ruprecht did not like riding at all. He had refused an offer to take a morning canter with her. If the count would rather travel by horse than by coach, she thought, maybe we might have something in common after all. Frau Grussell stopped outside a door carved with vine leaves and birds.

'This leads to the count's private rooms,' she said. 'This is where he stays when he hunts at the lodge. You go down the corridor and through the door at the end.'

The corridor was long and windowless, lit only by a single lamp. Katherine's shoes clicked on the wooden floor. When she reached the door she stopped and, almost without thinking, smoothed her hair and checked her clothes. She tugged at the bodice in an unsuccessful attempt to pull it up a little higher. Oh well, she thought, resigned to the fact that her breasts would have to remain half-exposed, perhaps this will make the old man happy!

She opened the door and walked into a room that was much larger than she expected, and warmly lit by numerous flickering candles. They threw moving shadows on the walls, and over the many hunting trophies that hung there. Boars' heads and stags' heads, their glass eyes seemingly alive as they reflected the many candle flames. A huge pair of antlers hung over the open fireplace. In one corner of the room she noted a table, also decorated with candles. She could see bottles of wine, two glasses, and two chairs.

'Welcome, Lady Katherine.' The voice startled her. A man came out of the shadows of an alcove and walked towards her. 'I am Count Werner von Krohnenstein. I'm delighted to meet you at last.' He switched suddenly to fluent and hardly accented English. 'I hope you don't mind if we converse in English? I get very little chance to practise it on anyone here.'

Whatever she had been expecting, it was nothing like this. Tall and broad-shouldered, he moved with the easy grace of a panther. He had the presence to instantly dominate any room he walked into, and she felt certain he knew it. He wore semi-military riding clothes: tight breeches, knee-high boots, and a fitted jacket that accentuated his beautifully proportioned and muscular body. His thick mane of dark hair, only very slightly flecked with grey, was elegantly cut, and longer than any army rules would have allowed. He had a strong face, clean-shaven but with a dark shadow that suggested he would need to use a razor frequently. He was not traditionally handsome, she thought, but he had something far more desirable. A strong sexual magnetism, and the kind of self-assurance that allowed him to move his dark eyes from her face to her body and back again, in one swiftly admiring glance, and leave her feeling complimented by his frankly physical appraisal, rather than insulted. It was the type of slightly arrogant male confidence that she found attractive.

'I am delighted to meet you, too,' she said. She did not curtsey, but held out her hand to him instead. 'At last,' she added sweetly.

51

His grip was strong and warm. 'No doubt all this seems very strange to you.'

'Yes,' she said. 'It does. First I'm kept prisoner here. Then I'm told to dress as a peasant girl. Perhaps you'd like to explain why?'

He smiled. 'A prisoner? That's rather a strong description of what I hoped would be a pleasant interlude for you. And as for the clothes, it's traditional for a woman to wear our national dress when she first meets her new family. I am a great believer in tradition.' His eyes moved over her again, slowly. 'You look very charming. Don't you find our costume makes you feel attractive?'

She suddenly felt as if he was seeing the tight bodice unlaced, and the voluminous skirts lifted to reveal her semi-nakedness. Black stockings and white skin, the darkness of her pubic hair, all displayed for his enjoyment. The thought was so unexpectedly exciting that she blushed. This is the man whose name made Markus Bruckner so nervous that he walked out on two willing women, she thought. Was that reaction understandable now? There was certainly an air of hidden danger about Count von Krohnenstein. And an aura of power, too. He gave the impression that he was used to being obeyed, and would not take kindly to opposition.

But it was disturbing to find that he was so much younger than she had expected. She discounted the grey in his hair. She knew that people with very dark hair often tended to go grey early. She also remembered Ruprecht saying that his mother had been very young when she died tragically in childbirth. The count could easily be in his late thirties or early forties. At one time she would have considered this too old to be sexually attractive. How ridiculous of me, she thought. This man is absolutely gorgeous, but I had better be very careful not to let him know how I feel. He looks as if he would be very quick to take advantage of it.

'The costume is quite pretty,' she said casually. She

looked at him squarely. 'I've heard the word "tradition" quite often since coming to Heldenburg. Of course we have traditions in England too, but in my country no one is ever forced to obey them.'

'You've been forced?' He smiled. He was still holding her hand. 'Strong words, Lady Katherine. But you must realise that this is not England. We do things differently in Heldenburg.'

'That's what your manservant told me,' she said.

'You mean Hecht?' He raised one well-defined eyebrow in amusement. 'Hecht would die for me.' There was no pride in his voice. He sounded as if he expected such loyalty. 'No doubt he was only trying to prepare you for your future.'

'And how do you see my future?' she asked.

He had guided her over to the table. 'Sit down,' he said, ignoring her question. 'And stop being so cross.' He let go of her hand and poured her a glass of wine. 'Drink this. It's local, and very palatable.' She was trying to prevent her full skirts from displaying too much of her legs. He watched her for a moment, in amusement. 'If you wish to preserve your modesty, stop fidgeting.'

She managed to tuck her legs, and the skirts, under the table. 'This costume obviously isn't designed for sitting down in,' she said.

'It is,' he contradicted. He poured himself some wine, then picked up a small bell and rung it. 'If you sit on the floor you'll find that the skirt spreads out in a circle, and behaves itself quite well.'

'On the floor?' she repeated incredulously. 'Is that another Heldenburg tradition?'

'Yes,' he said. 'For women.' Another smile touched his mouth. 'But I will not insist on it with you.'

'I'm glad to hear it,' she said, acidly polite. 'I wouldn't agree to it, anyway.'

'Really?' His eyes were bright with amusement, and once again she found herself thinking how attractive he

53

was. 'If you wish to marry into my family, you might find you have to – bend a little.'

For some reason his words made her blush again. What's the matter with me? she thought angrily. This is my future father-in-law. Admittedly he doesn't have a wife, he's younger than I expected, and under different circumstances I could certainly encourage his interest. But it's Ruprecht I came out here to marry.

There was a knock on the door, and a girl came in, carrying a tray.

'I've ordered a meal.' The count tapped the table, and the girl began to arrange the plates and covered bowls. 'I'm sure you must be hungry.' His tone implied that he did not expect her to disagree.

The delicate aroma of herbs, and the fresh smell of newly baked bread rolls reminded Katherine that it was some time since she had eaten anything. The count explained the various dishes to her, and encouraged her to try the crisply baked vegetables smothered in a delicately flavoured sauce. 'A local speciality,' he explained. As they ate, he amused her with light conversation about Heldenburg. When the talk turned to equestrian activities he seemed surprised – and, she suspected, pleased – to discover that she was a keen horsewoman.

'And what do your traditions say about women riding?' she asked, as the servant girl cleared the dishes away.

The count finished his wine. 'Nothing. And if they did, I'm sure you'd ignore them.'

'Oh?' She lifted her eyebrows in mock surprise. 'I'm *allowed* to disobey, am I?'

'Everyone is allowed to break a few rules,' he said. 'I intended to break one today.' His dark gaze assessed her again. 'But now I'm not so sure. Meeting you has changed my mind. Perhaps I'll follow tradition after all.'

The wine had made her feel relaxed. 'Not another tradition? You do seem to have a lot of them.'

'We do, don't we?' he murmured. 'But this is a particularly ancient one. I believe you once had a similar rule in England.'

'What rule was that?' she asked lightly.

He leant back in his chair and stretched out his legs, slightly apart. His tight riding breeches blatantly emphasised the bulge of his manhood, and she realised with a slight shock that he had adopted the position deliberately. 'The *droit du seigneur*,' he said. 'In our tradition it gives me the right to take your virginity.' He smiled. 'And to teach you enough to ensure that my son has an interesting wedding night.'

She stared at him for a full minute in silence. 'I don't believe you,' she said, at last. 'If that's supposed to be a *traditional* joke, I simply don't find it amusing.'

His smile disappeared. He looked at her with lazy arrogance. 'A joke? Certainly not. So far, I've followed the rules. I brought you out here to this discreet location. I had you dressed in costume. I have behaved like a civilised host, and now tradition dictates that, if I choose, I can claim my rights. In fact, it would be a pleasure.' His eyes moved down to her breasts. 'I can imagine what will happen when I unlace that bodice, which suits you very well, I might add. You have the right kind of body for peasant clothes. And when I lay you down and lift up those skirts, I'm sure the view will be equally delightful.'

She did not know whether she was more infuriated by his presumption or by the fact that his suggestions excited her. She imagined those amused dark eyes surveying her, enjoying the contrast of her white thighs and black silk stocking-tops, the V of her dark pubic hair, the whole erotic picture displayed against the background of white frilled petticoats. Her imagination tempted her onwards. After he had admired her, what then? He was undoubtedly experienced, and she was certain he would be inventive. In fact, he was everything she had ever wanted. My God, she thought, I should slap his face, but instead I'm hoping that he means to exercise his so-called rights.

He stood up suddenly, a tall, dangerous figure. 'The idea of making love to me excites you, doesn't it?' he said, softly.

Am I so transparent? she thought, angry with herself. 'Certainly not,' she lied. 'I might have a peasant's body, but you have a peasant's manners.'

He laughed then, an easy laugh of sheer amusement. 'You are far better than I ever expected. What a pity you have to be wasted on my son.'

Before she realised what was happening he swung her round and hoisted her, face downward, over his shoulder, holding her legs close to his chest. For a moment she was stunned by the unexpectedness of it. By the time she had recovered, and started to think of retaliating, he had reached a door, and opened it. From her upside-down position she could see a huge bed, with four carved posts in each corner. The next moment, she was tossed on to the bed, her skirts billowing out around her. The count sat down next to her and began to unbutton his jacket.

'Lie back,' he said.

She tried to sit up and he placed his hand against her chest and pushed her down. She felt his fingers touch the top of her breasts and repressed a shiver of excitement. Under his coat he wore a simple collarless shirt. He threw the jacket on the floor and opened the shirt. She saw that his tanned chest was hard with muscle. Could I use one of Jack Telfer's wrestling tricks to overpower him? she wondered. She rather doubted it, although she would have liked to try. The idea of tangling with that taut strong body was a very attractive one. A fight, she thought, with both of us naked. And if he let me win, what then? What would I do to him? The idea of having him at her mercy was also very appealing.

'What are you thinking?' He was leaning over her now. 'Of the games we will play together?'

It was so near the truth that she blushed. 'Certainly not,' she said, quickly. 'I was thinking that I suppose I will have to submit to your superior strength.'

'Very sensible,' he said. He began to unfasten her bodice. He worked swiftly and expertly. It was half-undone when she moved. She tried to hook her arm round his neck in a stranglehold that Jack had taught her, and because she took him completely by surprise she almost succeeded. Then he reacted, swift as a cat. He opened her grip with one strong hand and flipped her over on her stomach with a neat elegance that she thought Jack Telfer would have envied. He held her down, one hand under her, cupping her breast, the other holding her wrists. His fingers played with her nipple, and she felt it tingle and harden under his touch.

'You are full of surprises, aren't you?' She could hear the amusement in his voice. 'But now it's my turn.' Suddenly she was in darkness. He had tossed the full skirt and frilly petticoats up over her head. His hand slid out from under her body, and she felt his warm palm caress her thighs and move upwards. 'This is one game I like to play,' he said. 'I think you'll enjoy it, too.'

His hand landed flat and hard on her bottom. The blow stung, and she yelled, more from surprise than pain. More slaps followed, and she struggled to escape, both from the petticoats that billowed over her, and from his strong grip. But even as she did so, she knew that escape was the last thing she wanted. The spanking was intensely stimulating, and so was the thought that he was enjoying it. Each blow intensified the erotic sensations, and she realised that as she struggled he was also stripping her. The lacing on her bodice snapped and she felt his hand pulling the garment away. He untied the skirt and pulled that off roughly. She heard a seam rip. The petticoats followed. By the time she was gasping and out of breath from the delights of the spanking she was also naked, except for her stockings and shoes, and the tattered remnants of the white, full-sleeved blouse.

He turned her over, pulled her on to her knees, and knelt on the bed in front of her, his thighs close to hers. With one hand, he pushed her tangled hair back from her face. The other hand rested flat on her tingling bottom, holding her close. She felt the hard peaks of his nipples against her breasts, and the warmth of his body made hers glow. Then he kissed her.

It was a long kiss that grew more violent as she writhed against him. His fingers twisted into her hair, preventing her from moving away. At first his mouth touched hers in a gentle caress that slowly grew more insistent, until their tongues met in a dance of mutual pleasure. They parted through a need to draw breath. He kissed her once more, lightly, and then moved to her breasts, teasing each nipple in turn with his lips and his teeth. As he worked on her he pushed her backward until she was lying full length, and he was kneeling astride her. His breeches were half-unbuttoned now, and she realised that he was not wearing anything under them. She could see the dark line of his pubic hair, and the impressive bulge of his erect cock and balls straining to get free.

'Now,' he said, 'we will play some different games. But first, open your legs.' She realised that no one had ever asked her to do such a thing before. Jack had never wanted to look at her and, she thought, poor Will Shannon had never had the chance. She glanced up at the count's face. It was sheened with sweat and his thick hair had fallen forward and almost covered his eyes. 'Let me see how much you want me,' he said.

His voice was husky with excitement, and she obeyed him. It aroused her to know that she could affect him like this. And, she realised, it made her feel powerful.

His eyes lingered on the dark bush of her pubic hair.

'Wider,' he murmured. 'In Heldenburg, women shave, so we can easily see how pleased they are with us.' He reached forward and parted her secret lips. She moaned softly at his touch. 'Yes,' he said. 'You need me, don't you? Every bit as much as I need you.'

His fingers slid smoothly over her swollen clitoris, experimenting. She writhed and moaned under his touch. He was surprisingly sensitive to her needs and read her body language expertly. Soon he was pleasuring her with hands as effective as her own. His finger probed her and she gasped, pushing her hips up towards him. He withdrew one finger and inserted two. She felt her desire spiralling as she responded. She heard him laugh softly, then he pulled away. Before she could moan in protest, he had removed his breeches with surprising speed, and was astride her again. He penetrated her easily and smoothly, making his first thrust deep and strong.

'Beautiful,' he murmured. 'You are everything a man could want.'

He continued to thrust, with a slow rhythm, and she felt continually on the brink of being satisfied. It was an erotic experience, but also frustrating. Then she realised that he was deliberately demonstrating his control over her. She tried to speed his response by quickening her own hip movements, and heard him laugh.

'Ask me,' he whispered, close to her ear. 'Just ask. Let me hear you ask.'

'Now,' she gasped. 'I want to come ... I must ... Now.'

It only took a slight alteration of his movements to bring her release. Her orgasm was sudden and intense, and she felt his body share her pleasure. He lay on top of her for a few moments, as his breathing slowed, then rolled off and cradled her against his chest.

'Do you think Ruprecht will be pleased with me?' she asked lightly.

'I am pleased with you,' he said. 'That's all that matters.'

'But I didn't come to Heldenburg to marry you,' she commented.

He turned on one side and propped himself up on his elbow. 'No,' he said soberly, 'you didn't, did you?'

She turned to him. 'Exactly why *have* I come?'

'You've just answered that,' he said. 'To get married. To provide me with an heir. A son with the von Krohnenstein blood in his veins.'

'You have a son,' she said.

He looked away. 'I need another,' he said, flatly. 'To carry on the family traditions.'

'Deflowering poor innocent virgins?' she teased. 'Like me?'

'You were not a virgin,' he said.

'You didn't know that,' she objected. 'Until you explored me.'

'I knew it when I first saw you,' he said. 'You looked like a woman who knew what she wanted. And it did not take me long to realise that you wanted me.'

'Which is just as well,' she said. 'Since you intended to force yourself on me anyway.'

He laughed. 'I had no intention of doing any such thing. I have never forced myself on a woman in my life.'

'So it was all lies?' she challenged. 'There is no tradition of *droit du seigneur*?'

'There is,' he said. 'Or there was. But now it has degenerated into a simple social meeting. The wife-to-be dresses in national costume, and is entertained by her prospective father-in-law. He does have the right to cancel the wedding if he doesn't like his son's choice, but once again this right is rarely, if ever, enforced.'

'So you could forbid Ruprecht to marry me?' she asked.

'I could,' he said. 'But I won't.'

'Because you want a son?'

'That's one reason,' he agreed.

But you could give me a son, she thought. A better son than Ruprecht. A son that would look like you. She felt him stretch out beside her in the bed, and glanced sideways at his strong profile. He saw her looking at him and smiled.

'Go to sleep,' he said. 'We'll talk again in the morning.'

What about, she wondered? Were his thoughts mirroring hers? He was a widower, after all, and had been for nearly twenty years. What would it be like to be married to this man? She looked at him again. His eyes were closed, and he appeared to be sleeping, his mane of dark hair attractively tousled on the pillow. She let her imagination wander, then checked it, and tried to dismiss the thoughts that were crowding her mind. She had come to Heldenburg to be married out of a sense of duty, not love, although she was prepared to make the best of things. Now here she was, falling for her future husband's father. It was ridiculous to think of marrying him – wasn't it? She looked at him again. No, she decided, it wasn't!

Chapter Three

*K*atherine awoke lying on her face, the linen bed sheets light and warm on her naked flesh, her head half-buried in the huge pillow. She stretched, and sighed. Somewhere in the distance she heard a door opening.

'Good morning.' It was the count's voice. 'Are you awake?'

'No,' she said, snuggling into the feather bed and the soft pillow. 'I think I'm still dreaming.'

She felt the bed move as he sat down next to her. He touched her shoulder, lightly. 'What are you dreaming about?'

'Last night,' she said.

'It pleased you?'

'Umm,' she murmured.

'It pleased me, too,' he said. His hand slid under the sheet and found her leg. He smoothed the delicate skin behind her knee, sliding up the back of her thigh towards her bottom. Once there he stroked her gently, with circular movements, moving slowly towards the base of her spine. She tried to keep still but his light caresses were deliciously arousing. She wriggled, delighted with the sensations he was giving her.

She felt him move again. Through half-closed eyes she saw him slip off the dark silk dressing-gown. Cool air touched her skin as the sheets were pulled back. Before she could protest, he was kneeling astride her and his hands had slipped under her body to cup her breasts, and tease her semi-erect nipples with expert fingers. She felt the warmth of his body against hers, and the strength of his erection pressing between her buttocks. Then he lifted her into a kneeling position. She rested on her elbows while his hands opened her bent legs wider, and his fingers searched for her clitoris. He fondled it gently, confirming that she was wet and ready for him.

He entered her slowly, and his hands travelled back to her breasts again. He thrust slowly too, short movements alternating with deeper ones. With his palms flat against her nipples, he massaged her with strong, circular movements. His tongue caressed the sensitive skin at the nape of her beck. She turned her head, encouraging him to move to her shoulders, her ears, and then back to the top of her spine again. They rocked together for a few minutes and she felt as if she were floating on a spiral of sensation. Then his hands became rougher, more demanding. His hips moved faster. She heard his breathing quicken.

'Now?' he muttered. 'Tell me. Let me hear you ask.'

'Now,' she confirmed, because she was ready. 'Now, please.'

Her orgasm was violent and sudden. Her body bucked and shook under him against his, and she was only dimly aware that he was enjoying a similar release. When she fell forward, exhausted, she felt him still inside her. As he grew calmer he lay over her, careful not to pin her down with his weight, his face close to hers.

'Wasted,' he murmured softly, his mouth brushing her ear.

She turned towards him. 'Wasted?'

'On my son.' He rolled away from her then and lay on his back, staring at the ceiling.

'I hope he won't think so,' she said lightly.

The count grunted irritably. 'What Ruprecht thinks doesn't matter.'

'When will I see him again?'

'You want to see him?' He sounded surprised.

No, Katherine thought, I don't want to see him. Right now I really wouldn't care if I never saw Ruprecht again! 'Of course I want to see him,' she lied diplomatically.

She felt the bed move as the count stood up, and watched him as he loped across the room, pulling the silk dressing-gown over his shoulders. She felt a little stab of disappointment when his neat buttocks and slimly muscular thighs disappeared behind the dark silk. The count went outside and closed the door behind him.

So here I am, she thought, sent out here to marry a young man I hardly know, and now I'm lusting after his father. She lay back in the bed and half closed her eyes. And what's more, I don't feel in the least bit ashamed of myself. When she thought of Ruprecht, with his delicate, almost feminine, face it was difficult to accept that he was actually related to the virile and attractively masculine count. If the count is so anxious to have a son, she thought, surely he'd be interested in marrying again.

The door opened. The count stood there, still in his silky gown. 'Pin up your hair and come with me,' he said. 'Unless you intend to lie in bed all day?'

She padded across the floor after him, wondering where he was going. He led her through another door into a room full of steam. She saw a huge bath, with claw feet and brass taps, standing in the middle of the tiled floor.

'Get in,' he said abruptly.

'It looks scalding hot,' she protested.

'Of course it's hot,' he agreed. 'But not scalding.' When she still hesitated he added, 'Get in, unless you want me to help you. And I won't be too gentle, I promise you.' He slipped off the dressing-gown and pointed to the steaming bath. 'In!'

She still hesitated, mainly because she was enjoying the sight of him, naked and semi-erect, with the steam swirling round him. He took three quick steps to her side, swept her off the ground and carried her just as swiftly to the bath, where he unceremoniously dumped her in the hot, foamy water. 'When I tell you to do something,' he said, 'you do it. Try to remember that for the future.'

The water was, as he had promised, hot but not scalding. It also smelled of a sharply scented perfume.

'Do we have a future?' she asked.

He was in the bath with her in a matter of seconds, imprisoning her between his legs as he sat opposite her. 'I think we have,' he said. He leant forward and slid his soapy hands up over her breasts to her shoulders. His fingers kneaded her flesh, gently but firmly. She closed her eyes. 'Turn round,' he instructed softly. The water slopped over the side of the bath as she twisted and slithered until she ended up sitting between his out-stretched legs, her back against his chest. His fingers dug into her neck muscles, kneading them expertly. She could feel his penis swelling and moving against the cleft of her buttocks as he massaged her. She let her head fall back against his shoulder.

The warmth of the water and the strong rhythm of his fingers made her feel sleepy again. Her eyes closed. His hands moved to her breasts and down to her stomach. At first it was an undemanding exploration. She did not feel the need to respond, beyond wriggling a little closer to him as he grew harder. She kept her eyes half-closed and enjoyed the sensation of his body close to hers.

Then his hands pressed against her inner thighs, forc-ing her to open her legs. He found her clitoris and began to caress her expertly. She moaned with delight, and her body began to wriggle involuntarily as her pleasure mounted. He imprisoned her against him with one strong arm, so that her buttocks slid smoothly over his erect cock. With their bodies oiled by the scented, soapy water, they writhed together in a sensual horizontal dance, their movements swirling the white froth over the edges of the bath and onto the tiled floor.

Katherine tried to search between her own legs, and behind her back, in an attempt to offer the count the same pleasure that he was giving her, but she could not reach him, and he showed no inclination to help her, although he was obviously intent on pleasing her. As her own sensations mounted she heard his breath quicken, close to her ear, as if her movements and her little gasps and moans of pleasure were as stimulating to him as a physical caress. Then her orgasm finally overwhelmed her. Her limbs threshed the water, sending waves of foam over the edge of the bath. She heard him laugh softly, and felt his embrace tighten. His legs closed round her, holding her, until she was calm again.

'Was it good?' he asked finally.

'Yes,' she said simply. She tried to reach for him again. 'Now, let me please you.'

He laughed again. 'Soon.' He grasped the sides of the bath and stood up, soap suds still clinging to him. He reached out to her. 'Stand up,' he said. She allowed him to pull her from the bath. 'Over here.'

She followed him into another, smaller room. It was tiled from floor to ceiling, and over her head she saw coiled copper pipes. He reached for a lever on the wall, pulled it down and suddenly water cascaded over her like warm rain. It was so unexpected that she gave a startled yelp and instinctively closed her eyes. The water soaked her hair and sluiced the soap from her body. She gasped as it beat against her skin. The sensation was distinctly erotic.

She heard the count laugh, and felt his hand on her

shoulders. As he turned her round she opened her eyes. The water had polished his tanned skin like metal and flattened his thick black hair like a helmet against his head. 'Our own private rainstorm,' he said. 'Do you like it?'

'It's marvellous!' She spun round, laughing. 'Did you have this built for yourself?'

'No,' the count said. 'My father designed it. The story is that he believed cleanliness was next to godliness, but I rather think he had a more worldly motive. My father liked to make love in the rain, so I have been told. If there was no convenient rain, this was the next best thing.'

'So maybe you were conceived in here?' she suggested lightly.

He laughed. 'I doubt it. I'm sure I was conceived in the marital bed, and without any pleasure on the part of either of my parents. The games played in this room would have been a commercial transaction. My father believed that sex was a commodity, like food, and he was quite willing to buy it when he needed it.'

'How unromantic,' she said.

'Normal,' the count corrected. 'Marriage is for procreation. Whores are for pleasure.' He pulled her towards him and she felt the hard smoothness of his muscular body against hers. 'Don't try and tell me it isn't the same in England.' He smiled suddenly, but this time there was no humour in it. 'I know very well why you are here. It certainly isn't because you are in love with my son.' She started to protest and he pushed her back a little and tightened his fingers round her wrists so that she gave a little gasp of pain instead. 'Don't lie to me,' he said softly. 'I know more about you than you realise.'

Katherine stared up at him. She remembered the way Markus Bruckner had reacted at the mention of the von Krohnenstein name, and she suddenly understood the

67

young Leutnant's fear. But her blue eyes met the count's dark gaze coolly.

'So if I'm not in love, why am I prepared to marry Ruprecht?' she asked calmly.

'For money,' the count said. 'Your father is a gambler, and he is deeply in debt. His house and lands are forfeit. You are very beautiful, but probably the only marriage settlement he could expect to arrange for you in England would be with some elderly lecher who would be willing to pay for the privilege of bedding you. I'm sure he would not wish that for you. My son must have sounded a much better option.'

'But you agreed to it,' she said. 'If you knew I was penniless, why did you agree?'

'I have already told you,' he said abruptly. 'I need an heir. You are, in fact, eminently suitable. You come from a noble family. Your pedigree is possibly even longer than ours.' The trace of a smile touched his mouth, and again she felt a little tremor of fear, but this time it was mixed with excitement. The Count von Krohnenstein was an unknown quantity. A dangerous unknown quantity. He was like a jungle cat, waiting to pounce. 'And the fact that you are a pauper,' he added softly, 'means that you will do as you are told.'

She felt her temper rising. 'It does not!'

His smile twisted. 'You will obey me, Lady Katherine. And what's more, you will enjoy every minute of it.'

Without releasing his hold on her he reached out to the lever on the wall. The water slowed to a gentle cascade. She could feel his erection hard against her thighs.

'Service me,' he ordered.

Grasping both her wrists again he forced her downwards. She resisted half-heartedly, but ended up on her knees in front of him, her arms above her head. He held her wrists in one hand and pressed her towards him with the other. The warm water flowed over her. His erection was so strong that his penis was upright against his stomach, rising from his thick dark pubic hair. Suddenly she wanted very much to take it in her mouth. To gain control over him by giving him pleasure.

And it seemed the most natural thing to move towards him, and use her mouth to pleasure him. To feel how warm and taut his penis was as it strained upwards. To slide her lips over it, and use her tongue to circle and torment. He held her close, with his hand on her head, but seemed content to let her explore this new form of intimacy in her own time. To savour the size and taste of his sexual equipment while the cascading water drenched them and polished their skin with its warmth. Then she felt the muscles in his thighs begin to tremble and knew that he was slipping out of control. She tried to keep him in her mouth but as he came he pulled away from her, but still held her close, so that she felt his body shudder with pleasure as the water sluiced him clean.

He helped her to her feet and they stood together for a few more minutes. Then he slackened his grip on her wrists and gently touched her soaked hair. 'Beautiful,' he said softly. 'Touched with gold. Most Heldenburg women are dark.' His other hand strayed over the curve of her stomach and brushed her pubic hair. 'But shave, please.'

'Because it's traditional?' she asked.

'Because I am asking you,' he said.

She smiled. 'Asking? Not ordering?'

'Sometimes I ask,' he said. 'And sometimes I order.' His fingers caught her pubic hair suddenly, and he tugged. 'I think you like being ordered, Lady Katherine. It excites you.' He tightened his grip. Her body stiffened. 'Am I right?'

'Sometimes,' she admitted.

'To surrender control,' he said, softly. 'That can be arousing. I can understand that.'

For a moment she thought he was going to make love

69

to her again. Maybe pin her against the wall and explore her with his hands, or lay her on the tiled floor and use his tongue. But instead he reached out and turned the water off. She realised that she was disappointed.

'We will explore that path,' he said, 'later. But now, we dress. And then we eat.'

She enjoyed the meal. Once again the count was the perfect host, explaining the various local delicacies and introducing her to a hot spiced drink that he claimed was far superior to English tea.

'It's different,' she agreed. 'But then a lot of things are different in Heldenburg.'

'Different, and better,' he said. Then he smiled. 'I think you will like living here, Katherine.'

As long as I can continue to see you, she thought. Aloud she said, 'I'm looking forward to seeing your capital city. When will I be travelling to Grazheim? Today?'

His smile disappeared. 'No,' he said, abruptly.

'Tomorrow?'

He pushed his plate away. 'You must stay here until the day before your marriage.'

She stared at him in horror. 'But we haven't set a date yet. It could be *weeks* away.'

'So you will stay here for weeks,' he said.

She stood up, angry now. 'I will *not!*'

'You will.' He lifted one hand to silence her continuing objections. 'Perhaps Ruprecht should have explained the situation to you. It's considered bad luck for a betrothed couple to be seen together once the marriage plans have been announced.' He smiled. 'Another tradition, I'm afraid. I had no intention of upsetting you when I made arrangements for you to stay here. I thought you would be happy, with the women for company, at least for a few weeks.' He leant towards her. 'Katherine, humour me in this. As one of Heldenburg's leading families, we

70

have to be seen to observe the old ways, even if we sometimes find them inconvenient.'

'Perhaps you ought to tell me if there are any other inconvenient traditions that I am expected to adhere to?' she suggested crossly. 'It's possible that, when I hear them, I might decide not to marry your son after all.'

'There is nothing else,' he said. 'I promise you. In fact, as soon as you are married you will be free to go wherever you like, and you will be accepted in society, and at the Grand Duke's court.'

'As long as Ruprecht comes with me?' she countered.

'No, no,' he said. 'No one expects that. You will have to attend some social functions together, but for most of the time you will be free to live your own life.' He leant back in his chair. 'And you will not have to pretend that you are madly in love with Ruprecht. Arranged marriages are quite common among our aristocracy, and yours too, I don't doubt. My marriage was arranged for me. My late wife and I met for the first time at the altar in Grazheim cathedral. You, at least, have made a choice.' He reached forward and took her hand, and she wondered if any woman had ever said no to him, once he had decided to seduce them. 'And I shall visit you often while you're here, Katherine. I promise you won't be bored.'

But she was bored. The count stayed with her for another day, and they spent the time lazily together. He took her to the edge of the forest, but warned her against venturing any further. Later they ate together in a candlelit room, and later still he made love to her. When she finally slept it was the sleep of happy exhaustion. When she awoke, he had gone.

Despite his promise, he did not return as quickly as she had hoped. She was left with only the women for company, and the option of listening to them gossiping about people she had never heard of (they refused to

71

discuss Ruprecht or the count), or playing a very genteel game of cards, without the excitement of laying bets. She managed to force them to let her take a few short walks outside, but they always accompanied her, and spoiled the occasions by constantly nagging her not to go near to the surrounding trees.

By the end of the week she decided that she had to do something active and adventurous, or go mad. She spent the day yawning and claiming to be tired, and retired to bed early, having given strict orders that she was not to be disturbed. Once in her room she unlocked her leather-covered box. Inside, her male riding clothes were neatly folded, with her boots and the brimmed hat she wore to cover her abundant curls. She stripped off her feminine clothes and re-dressed herself quickly. With her figure disguised by her waistcoat and jacket, and her hair tucked away, she knew she made a passable young man. Going out without permission was only a small adventure, but at least it made her feel in control once more. She was making her own rules now.

She glanced at the pistol lying in the trunk, but decided against taking it. She knew there were wild boars in the forest, but she was certain that a pistol would not stop one if it charged. She would just have to take care. If she heard the sounds of a boar rooting for food she would avoid him. And the animal, she thought positively, would undoubtedly do the same to her.

It was easy to climb out of the window and drop to the ground. She knew that the servants slept on the other side of the lodge, and no one (including Frau Grussell) would be looking out of the windows at this time in the evening. As far as they were concerned there was nothing to see. They would all be busy sewing and chattering.

She felt a great sense of freedom as the trees closed round her and shut out the sight of the lodge. The forest was alive with noises, but they were familiar, natural sounds. They reminded her of her forays into the woods in England, and of the many times she had accompanied her father's head gamekeeper on his nocturnal duties. She was so busy reminiscing that, without realising it, she found herself moving out of the shelter of the trees and onto a well-beaten track. Instead of slipping back under cover again she decided to walk on the track for a while, convinced that no one would be out in the forest that late. She walked slowly, lost in thought, remembering her happy childhood days and the slow changes that came into her lifestyle as her father's gambling slowly eroded his fortunes. When she heard hoofbeats it startled her. She turned and ran for the cover of the trees, but it was too late. The horseman cantered round the bend, saw her and urged his horse onward in a sudden burst of speed.

She hoped to throw him off by diving into the undergrowth, but he rode with a madcap recklessness that under any other circumstances she would have admired, crashing through bushes and ducking low branches. Suddenly he swerved to the left and for a moment she lost sight of him. But before she had time to breathe a sigh of relief he appeared in front of her, his horse rearing, blocking her path. Obviously he knew the forest better than she did.

He dismounted swiftly, and she knew he was following her on foot as she plunged into the undergrowth again. She might have evaded him even then if she had not caught her foot and stumbled. She righted herself almost at once, but this brief accident had allowed him to catch up with her. She felt his hand on her shoulder, but instead of spinning her round he pushed her forward, tripping her at the same time, so that she sprawled face down on the ground. When she turned he was standing over her, holding his riding crop in both hands. Her first reaction was relief that this was not the count's dour-faced servant, Hecht. Her second, despite her apprehension, was interest.

Tall and slim, her captor wore knee-high riding boots, and white trousers so tight she could see the muscles tensing in his lean thighs when he moved. His jacket was tailored in a fitted cavalry style, but there was nothing else military about him. His jet-black hair was dishevelled, and cut with rakish sideburns that made him look more like a wild gipsy than a soldier. He was younger than the count and, although he lacked the older man's overpowering sensual masculinity, he had an elegance and self-assurance that was every bit as sexually attractive. In fact, she thought, he looked a lot like the fantasy man she had conjured up for her own enjoyment during her coach ride to the Grünholz hunting lodge.

'Stand up,' he said. She obeyed him, bowing her head, but he reached forward and placed his fingers under her chin, tilting her face up. He looked at her critically. 'You're only a youngster, aren't you? What are you after? One of the count's rabbits, for your stew?' Then he smiled. It was a devastatingly attractive smile, all the more so because it was unexpected. It transformed the taut Slavic lines of his face, removing the danger and replacing it with a dazzling charm. 'Don't look so worried. I'm not going to hand you over to the game-keeper. You're a local, aren't you? Maybe you can give me some information about this area, and the people who come here. I'd be willing to pay you. You could buy rabbits then, instead of chasing them. What do you say to that?'

Katherine bowed her head again. Maybe she could pass as a boy in the shadows of the forest, but she did not think she could fool this man for long if she had to keep talking to him. And she was not sure how he would treat her if he discovered that she was female. Despite his youthful appearance, there was something about him that made her feel he could be ruthless as well as charming. And who was he, anyway? His German was fluent, but his accent was different from the count's, and from

74

the women at the lodge. He was riding on the count's land. Was he a relative? A friend? Whoever he is, she thought, I don't want him to find out who *I* am. If I run he'll probably catch me again, but not if I slow him down a little. And she knew that the best way to do that would be to aim the hard toe of her booted foot at his knee.

She moved quickly, but he was quicker. He saw her leg swing back and twisted out of her way. At the same time he grabbed her roughly by the wrist and spun her round. Despite his slim frame he was surprisingly strong. He held her easily, her arm bent behind her back.

'You vicious little bastard!' His voice was hard and angry now. 'Try and kick me, would you? Now you're going to find out how unpleasant I can be.'

She heard the riding crop swish through the air and tried to dodge, but it landed sharply across her bottom. It was hard enough to sting, and it made her gasp, but she realised that she also found it arousing. The trouble was, she did not know how many of such blows he intended to deliver, and whether he would stop when they became genuinely painful rather than erotically exciting. She was not given the chance to find out. As she struggled, she realised her hat was slipping. She attempted to retrieve it, and felt it suddenly wrenched from her head. Her golden-brown curls tumbled to her shoulders.

For a moment her attacker stood frozen. Then he started to laugh. He twisted her round to face him. 'Well, now,' he drawled. 'This is an unexpected surprise. But a very pleasant one.' He reached out and stroked her hair with the whip. 'I think I'm going to enjoy spanking you.'

'You'll do no such thing,' she said haughtily, deciding that the best thing she could do was brazen it out. 'Let me go at once!'

'What a charming accent.' He still kept hold of her. 'But it makes things even more mysterious. You're

English, aren't you? An English rose in the Count von Krohnenstein's forest. An English rose dressed as a boy.' The warmth of his hand seemed to be burning her wrist. 'There has to be a most interesting explanation for all this. Please enlighten me.'

'I don't have to explain,' she said. 'I'm a guest at the count's hunting lodge. I can walk wherever I please. Wearing these clothes makes it more comfortable for me.'

'So why did you run like a thief?'

She tried to look meek. 'I didn't know if you meant me any harm.'

'Well, you still don't know, do you?' He sounded amused. The whip slapped rhythmically against the side of his boot. 'What will you do if I try to beat you? Scream?' He smiled again, the brilliant, attractive smile that had captivated her before. 'Or maybe you'd enjoy it? Many women do.'

Because it was so near to the truth she felt herself blushing. 'I'm sure you're a gentleman, sir. You wouldn't take advantage of a lady.'

'Don't be sure,' he warned. 'And anyway, I know you're not as inoffensive as you look. So – ' he took a step back, and stood with his long legs braced apart ' – you're staying at the Grünholz lodge, are you? Will you tell the Count von Krohnenstein that we met?'

'How can I?' she countered. 'I don't even know your name.'

He bowed. 'Sergei von Lenz, at your service. Like you, I am also a guest in this country.'

'Do you know the count?'

Von Lenz grinned lazily. 'I've heard his name mentioned. And I'm sure he's heard of me. The count knows nearly everything that goes on in Heldenburg.'

'Why should he have heard of you?' she asked.

'Because I've taken money from most of his acquaintances at the gaming tables. And more than money, from some of the ladies.'

'In Grazheim?' She was surprised. 'I didn't know they were so free with their favours in this country.'

'Like many outwardly respectable cities, there are illicit pleasures to be found if you know where to look.' His dark eyes held hers. 'And I know exactly where to look.'

'Then I hope I shall meet you when I go to Grazheim,' she said, holding his gaze.

'When will that be?' he asked. 'Soon?'

'In a few weeks.'

He treated her to his dazzling smile again. 'I don't think I can wait that long. I've found our conversation very stimulating. Let's meet tomorrow evening, here in the forest.' The whip gently tapped the side of his glossy riding boot. 'We'll allow ourselves plenty of time to get to know each other. Are you game for an adventure, English Rose?'

Katherine hesitated. She knew she should refuse. She was certain he had charmed a great many women into assignations before, and he probably saw her as just one more victory to add to his list. But she found his air of elegant sexual self-assurance hypnotically attractive. And I'm not married yet, she thought defiantly. If I agree I'll still have a day to reconsider. I can always back out.

'Very well,' she said. 'Until tomorrow.'

She was still undecided about the meeting until the following afternoon. Frau Grussell had brought her a message telling her to be ready for a visit from the count. He was planning to ride out to the lodge that evening and hoped she would dine with him.

Katherine suppressed a smile. 'I would be delighted to dine with the count. Does he expect me to wear the Heldenburg national costume again?'

'Oh no, no.' Frau Grussell fluttered her hands dismissively. 'You can wear whatever you wish, gracious lady. No doubt you have some pretty gowns of your own?'

As she prepared for the count's visit Katherine felt

almost relieved that she no longer needed to make a decision about meeting Sergei von Lenz. She had to admit that she had been tempted. His rakish charm and flashing smile had definitely attracted her, but she had wondered if she were being foolish to consider an illicit rendezvous. Foolish to do anything that might antagonise the count. Foolish to risk ruining her chance of marrying Ruprecht von Krohnenstein. As the count had correctly pointed out, the only other option for a penniless female in her position was the far less attractive choice of an older man who would, in effect, be purchasing her body for his private entertainment. She did not want to have to live each day with the thought that she was going to be pawed and prodded by an elderly lecher at night. Anything was better than that. At least Ruprecht was young and, she had to admit, pleasant enough in an inoffensive way.

She had come to terms with the idea of a loveless marriage. But the count had upset her resolve. She remembered the strength of his body, the impression it gave of controlled power. She remembered the size of his erection and the delicious sense of helplessness she experienced when he held her down, and made love to her. I could be happy with him, she thought. I know I could. I could delight him in bed, and out. I'd like to become part of his life. We could laugh and talk and ride. And I could give him a child, if that's what he really wants. Although I can't see why he needs an heir when he's already got Ruprecht to carry on the family name. She sighed with frustration. Why can't Ruprecht marry a nice Heldenburg girl? she thought, and I'll marry Count Werner von Krohnenstein.

She removed her heavy overskirt and sat down on the bed. She tried to think about what she would wear that evening, but her imagination showed her pictures of a wedding ceremony instead. She lay back on the bed, closed her eyes, and daydreamed, imagining herself in a beaded dress, so intricately embroidered that it felt like glittering armour. Her wrists and neck would glitter too, with diamonds. Enough diamonds to pay her father's debts ten times over. She smiled suddenly at this unexpected intrusion of reality into her fantasy. Father would be proud to see me looking like a lady for once, she thought, amused. And a wealthy lady, at that.

She imagined the count walking by her side, resplendent in a military uniform. Dark blue, she decided, with a tightly fitted military jacket enhanced with silver braid. Tight breeches with a silver stripe down the leg. And maybe a peaked ceremonial helmet emblazoned with the Heldenburg crest. She would glance at him as they walked towards the altar, noting the slight smile on his lips, proof that his mind was not on the coming ceremony, but beyond it. Beyond the solemnity of the cathedral service. Beyond the sumptuous reception, and the swirl of couples on the dance floor. They would dance together, of course, in a formal embrace, while he whispered to her the various things he was planning to do to her later, when they were finally alone together. When he would strip her of her dress and jewellery and stretch her on the bed, exciting her body until she moaned for release, both wanting it and yet not wishing to end the pleasurable frustration he was inflicting on her.

She imagined him in the collarless white undershirt and the tight dark trousers that so delightfully emphasised his bulging erection. He would have to remove her dress for her. It would have an intricate back fastening that would need to be unhooked. Each hook separately. And her corset would have be be unlaced. He would do it slowly, she thought. The bead-encrusted cloth would part, revealing the sweep of her spine. His thumbs would massage her as his hands moved downwards, with gentle pressure at first. She would feel the warmth of his body close to her back, feel the warmth of his hands, feel his breath on her neck. When his fingers reached the cleft of her buttocks they would linger, circling, rougher now. I would be quite naked under the dress, she thought. That would surprise him.

'What kind of woman have I married?' With his arms round her he would caress her stomach. She imagined the pressure of his palms, holding her against his body. 'A courtesan?'

'Is that a complaint?' she would murmur.

'Not if you have a courtesan's repertoire of tricks.' He would move downwards, searching for the warmth between her thighs.

'That's for you to discover,' she would answer.

Then, she thought, he would grasp the top of her dress and wrench it down. Tiny beads would scatter over the floor. The dress would be stripped off. She would feel the rough surface of his uniform breeches against her own legs, feel his erection against her buttocks. She imagined that she could see herself in a mirror, diamond jewellery glittering against her pale skin, and his strong brown hands holding her prisoner. She imagined his black hair, contrasting starkly with her golden brown, as his head bent close to hers, his tongue circled her ear and his fingers found her nipples. She realised that her body was responding to her thoughts, and her clitoris was uncomfortable with desire.

It was a simple matter to ruffle up her petticoats and begin to pleasure herself, slowly at first, her mind still conjuring pictures of the count. She wished she was lying naked on the bed, and his fingers were making her writhe with delight. She stopped caressing herself for a moment, reached above her head and grasped the carved bedposts with her hands, stretching her legs wide. She imagined herself secured with silver chains round her wrists and ankles. Imagined the count standing over her, his eyes exploring her body. Would he complain that she had not yet shaved her pubic hair? Maybe he would do it for her? The thought was surprisingly erotic. She stroked herself again, more urgently, and came with a sudden explosive jolt that made her gasp.

Far from satisfying her, her brief dalliance had made her even more eager to see the count again. She had decided to wear the wine-coloured dress with the low scooped neck, with her diamond choker emphasising the smoothness of her neck. It would glitter in the candle-light, she thought. She imagined the count sitting opposite her, the flickering light softening the strong lines of his face. Maybe he would look at the choker, and comment on it, then let his eyes stray down to the swell of her breasts. She would pretend to be shocked at his frankly sexual appraisal. Their conversation would grow increasingly lascivious as the meal progressed. She would watch his mouth as he ate, and mentally list the things it would be doing to her later. Maybe he would be fantasising too, imagining her mouth on his. And later, her lips on his cock.

When she heard a knock on the door she was already wet with anticipation. She took a deep breath and called out, 'Come in.'

Frau Grussell opened the door and as soon as Katherine saw the old woman's face she knew that something was wrong. 'I'm sorry, gracious lady.' Frau Grussell bobbed her head in greeting. 'A messenger has just arrived from the count. Urgent matters have compelled him to stay in Grazheim. He sends his apologies, but knows you will understand that State matters must take precedence over pleasure.'

Katherine stared at Frau Grussell dumbly. Her disappointment was so acute that she felt she had received a physical blow. She heard her own voice, as if from a distance, saying, 'I understand. Thank you for telling me, Frau Grussell.'

'Will you dine now, gracious lady?' Frau Grussell

asked tentatively. 'We have already prepared a meal. Shall I bring it to you?'

'No!' Katherine saw Frau Grussell flinch and realised her voice had sounded unnecessarily sharp. She softened it, and even managed a smile. 'No, thank you, Frau Grussell. I don't really feel like eating.'

Frau Grussell turned to go, hesitated, then turned back. 'I am so sorry to bring you this news, gracious lady. The count has many duties at court. It is often very difficult for him to find time for social events.'

It was then that Katherine realised Frau Grussell was well aware of the nature of her relationship with the count. But there was no condemnation in her tone. If anything, she looked sympathetic. She bobbed her head again, closed the door behind her and left Katherine alone.

Suddenly Katherine's disappointment turned to anger. State matters took precedence over pleasure, did they? What exactly did that mean? What kind of State matters took place in the evening? The kind that involved being charming to a woman over a candlelit table of food?

The image infuriated her. She tugged the diamond choker from her neck and threw it on the bed. Well, your lordship, she thought furiously, two can play at games like that! She summoned her maid to help her undress, and gave orders that she was not to be disturbed until the morning. When the maid had left she opened her small leather box and took out her male clothes. In less than half an hour she had transformed herself into a passable young man. She climbed out of the window and headed for the forest, walking down the track until she knew she was near the spot where she had first encountered Sergei von Lenz. But there was no sign of him this time. For a furious moment she thought he had also decided to let her down. Then the trees moved and she saw him. He stood with his long legs apart, his dark clothes blending with the shadows.

'Good evening, English Rose.' His face was in shadow too. 'I wondered if you'd be brave enough to keep your promise.'

'Brave?' she repeated, surprised. 'That's an odd word to choose. You know I'm not afraid of the forest at night.'

'Not the forest,' he agreed. 'But what about the Count von Krohnenstein? You certainly should be just a little bit afraid of him.'

She masked her total surprise and stared at him coolly. 'I have no idea what you're talking about.'

'Of course you have,' he said. 'It really wasn't difficult to find out all about you. Your marriage is quite a talking point in Grazheim.' He stepped forward and treated her to his dazzling smile. 'But how do you think your future father-in-law would react if he knew you had come out here with the intention of making love to me?'

She tipped her chin up defiantly, letting her anger mask her disappointment. 'So that's your plan, is it? You'll tell him, unless I pay for your silence? I trusted you, and now you're going to try and blackmail me? Well, you won't get any money out of me.'

He stared at her for a moment, then threw back his head and laughed. 'You certainly have spirit, English Rose. But that doesn't surprise me. Anyone who wants to marry Ruprecht von Krohnenstein has to be unusual.' Suddenly he was serious again. 'I don't want your money. I have plenty of my own. But I *am* curious. Why choose to marry Ruprecht, of all people? I would have thought the pretty daughter of an English baronet would have had a dozen better proposals.'

'My marriage plans are my own affair,' she said coolly.

He stepped forward, and she realised for the first time how tall he was. Her head only came up to his chest. 'I could beat you.' His voice was hard. 'You'd tell me then.'

'I wouldn't,' she said.

He laughed softly. She actually felt her body tingling when she looked up at the angular lines of his face. 'No,

83

maybe you wouldn't,' he agreed. 'In fact, I think you'd probably enjoy it.' He reached out and touched her face lightly with one slim hand, his fingers tracing a line round the curve of her jaw to end up resting on her lips. 'I think you'd like it if I held you down, and used my hand on that very attractive bottom of yours. Or maybe used my whip? The whip would sting nicely.' His voice was soft and seductive. 'A little bit of erotic pain, Lady Katherine? Have you ever experienced that before? Has any man ever tied you up and whipped you? Maybe I would be the first. Does that idea appeal to you?'

She looked at him with mixed emotions. He was reading her thoughts far too accurately. She was amazed at herself for finding his suggestions exciting. And even more amazed to realise that she was growing damp at the thought of them becoming reality. He put his hands on her shoulders. She felt their warmth through the thick cloth of her riding jacket. 'Shall I teach you how to please me, English Rose?'

'Isn't that why you asked me to meet you here?' she responded.

'Well, partly,' he agreed. 'I thought you were a guest at the lodge. A bored guest, with a husband too stupid to appreciate you. I meet women like that all the time. But you're much too promising to waste on a quick seduction.' He put his fingers under her chin and tipped her head up. 'When I start instructing you I want us both to enjoy it in comfort. We must arrange to meet in Grazheim. I have a house there. When are you going back to the city?'

'Not until the day before my wedding,' she said.

He laughed. 'Don't be absurd. You'll have to go into Grazheim to be part of the wedding plans.'

'I've no doubt the count and his family will take care of all that,' she said. 'I'm not allowed to see Ruprecht until the wedding. It's a stupid Heldenburg tradition.'

He stared at her for such a long time without comment

that she began to feel uncomfortable. 'Who told you that?' he asked, at last.

'The count,' she said.

Another long, silent stare. Finally, he asked: 'How well do you know Ruprecht von Krohnenstein, English Rose?'

'I'm *marrying* him,' she said, crossly.

'Yes,' he agreed. 'But that doesn't answer my question.'

She hesitated for a moment, then remembered that the count had already told her that Heldenburg society understood and accepted the arrangement she had with Ruprecht. She decided there was no harm in telling Sergei von Lenz the truth. 'I've only met Ruprecht twice,' she admitted. 'But such marriages are arranged all the time, and they can be very successful.'

'By why choose to come to Heldenburg?' he persisted. 'Are they all blind in England? Can't they recognise a beauty when they see one?'

She had no intention of explaining her financial position to him. 'The von Krohnensteins are a very ancient and noble family,' she said. 'I was honoured by the proposal.'

He stared at her for what seemed like a very long time, and when he spoke again the humour had gone from his voice. 'Listen to me, English Rose. The count has been lying to you.' She was about to speak, but he silenced her by putting his fingers against her lips. 'I admit I'm a visitor to this little duchy, and I know the people here have some peculiar ways, but I can assure you there's no tradition that says you have to hibernate out here until you walk down the aisle to be wed.' He stood in front of her, his long legs braced apart, the night wind tousling his jet-black hair. Once again she was reminded of a wild gypsy, an adventurer. And once again she felt a thrill of sexual desire. 'I like you, English Rose,' he said. 'So I'm going to do you a favour. Come to Grazheim with me. I want to show you something.'

'The interior of your bedroom, no doubt?' she commented.

'That comes later.' He smiled his winning smile and she knew she was going to let herself be persuaded. 'First let me show you why the count wants to keep you shut away at his hunting lodge. Then you can decide if you still want to marry Ruprecht. You make a passable young man, at least at night. I'll bring you a student's cap. You can keep that on all the time to disguise those curls of yours. You'll be my cousin, taking a break from your university studies.' His smile was both dangerous and inviting. 'I'll show you the sights, English Rose. I think you'll be surprised at some of them. Very surprised indeed.'

It was much easier than Katherine expected. Frau Grussell was unexpectedly sympathetic to her wishes. When she complained that she felt tired, and needed to retire early, Frau Grussell nodded reassuringly. She would see to it that the gracious lady was not disturbed.

Katherine knew she was taking a risk. If an emergency occurred and one of the women came for her, they would find an empty bed and an unfastened window. But she did not care. I'm not married yet, she thought. I can go where I like. And if Sergei is right, and the count has his own reasons for keeping me closeted away out here, I want to know why.

Sergei von Lenz met her in the forest, and led her to the road, where he had a small carriage waiting. He drove the carriage himself. It was a bumpy ride, and she was glad when she heard the wheels rattle on cobbles and they came to a halt. When she stepped down she was in a narrow street, lit only by a dimly flickering lamp.

'Exactly what kind of sights are you going to show me?' she asked.

'The kind that the good citizens of Heldenburg like to

pretend don't exist,' he said. 'I'm taking you to the Peacock Club.' He linked his arm in hers and escorted her down an alleyway. She realised that she was now totally at his mercy. She had no idea where she was, and she certainly had no idea how to get back to Grünholz again. But far from alarming her, she found her situation invigorating. It was a long time since she had felt so alive. Suddenly von Lenz stopped by a large, anonymous door. He knocked sharply and after a moment a small flap opened and she heard a voice ask abruptly: 'Yes?'

'It's Sergei,' von Lenz said. 'And a friend. Let us in.'

The door creaked open. Katherine followed him into a grubby-looking passage. A lamp swung suddenly, momentarily blinding her.

'For God's sake, Heini,' von Lenz said irritably. 'You know who I am.'

'Just checking your friend.'

Katherine blinked as the lamp flashed in her face.

'My cousin,' von Lenz explained.

The man stared at Katherine. 'He's safe?'

'As safe as me,' von Lenz said. 'He's an innocent lad. I'm teaching him some vices.'

The man laughed. 'I believe you.' He loomed over Katherine. 'Pretty, isn't he?'

'And he likes girls,' von Lenz said, pushing Katherine forward.

'So do I,' the man called after them. 'Sometimes.'

The passage ended in another door. Von Lenz pushed it open, and Katherine gasped in surprise. She was on the threshold of huge room, its dark-red walls heavy with gilded cherubs and garlands of golden flowers. A small orchestra sat on a dais, and in the centre of the room couples danced, embracing far more intimately then they would ever dare to do at a formal ball. She noticed that the men, in uniform or evening dress, were from a wide age range, but all of the women looked stunningly beautiful, and young. Around the walls were numerous alcoves furnished with padded seats and small tables. Red velvet curtains framed them, some pulled back and fastened with gold ropes, others drawn, giving the alcove's occupants complete privacy. Arches opened into anterooms where Katherine could see gaming tables, and hear the muted click of counters. The air was heavy with cigar smoke, and other aromas that she did not recognise, sweetly scented and heady.

Von Lenz escorted her to one of the alcoves. As they sat down a distinguished-looking man, with his arm round an elfin-faced dark-haired girl, walked past. The man stopped and turned. 'Von Lenz, old fellow, didn't know you frequented this sort of place. Come to gamble?'

'Just showing my cousin the sights,' von Lenz said smoothly.

The girl looked at Katherine, and smiled. Her companion slapped her on the bottom. She gave a squeal that sounded more like delight than protest. The man smiled, wolfishly. 'Now then, my dear, behave yourself, or I'll get very cross with you.' His hand stayed where it was and began to fondle the girl's buttocks, his fingers probing at the cleft between them. The girl snuggled up to him.

'And how is Berthilde?' von Lenz enquired.

'Swollen up like a pumpkin,' the man said. 'Won't be long now. Hope it's a boy this time. Five girls are too much for anyone.'

Katherine watched the couple walk towards one of the alcoves and sit down. After a few moments the girl stood up and drew the curtains. As they closed she smiled seductively at Katherine.

'I think you've made a conquest,' von Lenz drawled.

Katherine sat down on one of the soft plush-covered seats. 'Exactly why did you bring me here?' she asked politely. 'To show me that married men come to gaming clubs with their mistresses? I knew that already.'

'Of course you did.' Von Lenz snapped his fingers at a

passing waiter. 'Wine,' he ordered. Then he lounged back in his seat, and gave her an amused look. 'You're quite a woman of the world, aren't you, English Rose?' In the semi-darkness of the alcove, his long legs stretched out in front of him and his lean body relaxing, she thought he looked irresistibly attractive. She wished he would pull the curtains across their alcove and make love to her. Instead he accepted the tray of wine from the waiter and poured two glasses. 'Good health,' he said, in English. And then, in German again, 'Relax, English Rose. Look around. What kind of club do you think this is?'

Katherine sipped her wine and watched the dancers. The couple nearest to her seemed to be swaying to a rhythm of their own. As they moved away she realised that the woman had her hand inside the man's trousers, and the trembling of his body had nothing to do with the tune the orchestra was playing.

She turned to von Lenz. 'This isn't a gaming club at all. It's a whorehouse.'

He grinned. 'Actually, they do gamble here. That's why I come.'

'Just for the gambling?' she agreed. 'Of course!'

'Believe me,' he grinned. 'It's the truth.'

Another couple swayed past. This time both dancers were actively fondling each other. The woman, a statuesque beauty with long red hair, had her eyes closed as the man's hands roamed over her satin-covered bottom, pinching and probing. Suddenly there was a loud cheer from one of the gaming rooms. Katherine heard the sound of hands pounding on the table and a cry of 'Forfeit! forfeit!'. Several of the dancing couples altered direction and made their way over to the open door.

'What's happening over there?' Katherine asked.

'I believe someone's lost a bet,' von Lenz said.

'And the loser pays a forfeit?' she enquired. 'Don't they gamble for money here?'

'Some do,' he said. 'Some prefer forfeits.' He stood up. 'Come and look.'

Inside the gaming room a crowd had gathered round a man and a woman. The man was distinguished looking, with wavy grey hair. The woman, Katherine had to admit, was exceptionally glamorous. A green satin dress swathed her slim figure, and her auburn curls cascaded to her bare shoulders. She wore satin gloves that covered her arms almost to her shoulders, and her wrists glittered with diamonds. Her lips were full, expertly painted, luscious and pouting. The grey-haired man held her by the arm. She was pretending to struggle with him, but it was quite clear that her protests were not genuine. Katherine heard someone shout, 'You made the bet, Magenta. You lost. Now pay the forfeit.'

There was more cheering and shouting as the older man undid his jacket.

'Now this is a stroke of luck, English Rose,' von Lenz said softly. 'The famous Magenta is about to perform.'

The auburn-haired woman reached for her partner's trouser buttons and unfastened them. Amid shouts of encouragement she moved closer, and slid down elegantly to her knees in front of him. Katherine heard someone shout, 'How long do you think you can last, Manfred?'

The grey-haired man leant back against the gaming table. He put his hand on the woman's glossy curls and pulled her head closer. 'It'll take this bitch all of ten minutes. Maybe more.'

'Your self-control isn't that good,' someone shouted. 'Five minutes. Two hundred marks that Manfred can't last five minutes.'

'Have you tried that slut's mouth?' another voice yelled. 'He won't last five.'

The auburn-haired woman turned to the speaker and smiled. She stuck out her tongue, licked her lips lewdly, then pantomimed a kiss in his direction. 'Thank you, darling.' Her voice was low and husky. 'I remember your lovely cock. It danced very nicely for me.'

'And then it made you dance!' another voice yelled.

Magenta laughed throatily. 'But I *love* dancing. You all know that.'

There was another cheer, and more laughter as bets were exchanged.

'Three minutes!'

'Two! He's practically come already, just thinking about it.'

The woman pouted and smiled as the bets were laid.

'If you don't let the bitch get on with it,' someone said, 'we won't have time for another game.'

After more jostling and betting among themselves, the crowd calmed down. One man took out a pocket watch. The auburn-haired woman turned her attention to her partner. She took his cock in her mouth. Her hands cupped his balls. The crowd seemed to be holding its breath. Then there was a sound like a collective sigh as she began to move her head, slowly and rhythmically, her lips sliding up and down. After about a minute, the grey-haired man began to look a little less controlled. He shifted his position, but the woman slipped her hands round his hips and grasped his buttocks, pulling him close. 'Don't try and escape, darling.' She looked round at the crowd, licked her lips again, and added, 'I've bet that you won't last five minutes. And I need the money.'

She had her hands round his hips, her long fingers digging into his bottom as she embraced him. Her head moved faster now. The crowd began to shout encouragement. Katherine glanced sideways at Sergei von Lenz. She found the sight of him far more sexually exciting than Magenta's performance. Her eyes travelled up his long legs to the edge of his dark military-style jacket. It was cut longer than usual, and made it impossible for her to check if he was physically excited by the exhibition in progress. She looked at his face, its angular lines softened by the flickering candlelight. She was surprised to note that, unlike the other men in the room, he looked bored. Either he's a very good actor, she thought, or he really isn't a voyeur. Perhaps he simply did not find the auburn-haired Magenta exciting. Maybe he preferred golden-brown curls?

But if he wanted to make love to her, why hadn't he taken her straight to his house? she thought. Why bring her to this dubious club? And what did the tawdry exhibition she was witnessing have to do with her marriage? Nothing at all, she thought. He's playing some kind of game with me. Perhaps it's exciting him to think that he's shocking me. There was another burst of noise from the gaming room. Magenta and her companion were now writhing on the floor, surrounded by a raucously cheering crowd.

Suddenly Katherine wanted to leave. She turned to von Lenz and realised that he was watching her, and not Magenta's performance. 'Is this what you brought me here to see?' she asked coolly.

'I brought you to see the club,' he said. 'The performance is a bonus.'

'If you're trying to shock me,' she said, 'you've failed. I already knew places like this exist, and if you're going to tell me that the count plans to bring Ruprecht here to educate him, that won't shock me either. I'm well aware that things like that go on.' She suddenly remembered Yvonne Tressilian. 'I dare say some of the women here are really quite nice.'

He lounged back elegantly in his seat. '*All* the women here are nice,' he said. 'If a little naive.' She stared at him. 'Haven't you guessed what's going on yet, English Rose?' He smiled. 'Haven't you realised that you're the only woman in this room?'

She stared at him, for a moment not really understanding what he was telling her. Magenta's audience was still cheering as she actively serviced the grey-haired man, but another man had pushed her dress up to her waist. Straddling her from behind, he was making obscene thrusting movements, accompanied by shouts of encouragement from his audience.

Von Lenz glanced at the mêlée, and then back at Katherine. 'And I really don't think Ruprecht needs educating, do you? He seems to be doing quite well without any help.' Katherine looked at the heaving bodies on the gaming-room floor. Von Lenz produced his sudden irresistible smile. 'In case you're still confused, English Rose, your future husband is the one in the auburn wig.'

'Everyone knows about Ruprecht,' von Lenz said. He was sitting with Katherine in the back of the carriage, having driven from the club to the side of the wide, dark river that bisected Heldenburg's capital city. 'He's certainly not the only man in Heldenburg to enjoy such activities, as you've just observed, but whereas other people do their duty at home and indulge their sexual preferences in private, Ruprecht is suicidally indiscreet. Of course, no one in Heldenburg society wants him as a son-in-law. You must have seemed like a gift from heaven. An innocent from England. Young, beautiful, and single. The count's only problem was making sure you didn't find out any unsavoury details about Ruprecht before the wedding ring was firmly on your finger. But I still don't understand exactly what you hoped to gain from the marriage. Why come to Heldenburg? And why choose Ruprecht? Even wearing trousers, and on his best behaviour, I don't believe for a moment that he'd attract you. So why did you agree to marry him?' He looked at her quizzically. 'You're not pregnant, are you?'

'No, I'm not,' she said, crossly. The shock of the recent revelations was wearing off. Her brain was beginning to work again. She had no intention of explaining her financial position to Sergei von Lenz, much as she liked him. 'I've already told you why I agreed to marry Ruprecht. It was an honour to be asked.'

He laughed. 'Are you still trying to tell me you were impressed by his ancient family name? I'm sorry, but I don't believe you.' He reached out and removed the student's cap, then loosened her pinned-up hair. 'Not that it matters.' His dark face was very close to hers now, his eyes glinting in the moonlight that slanted through the carriage window. 'I'd like to make love to you right now, English Rose, but waiting will make it sweeter. Once you've told the count to cancel the marriage plans, you don't need to see him, or pretty Miss Ruprecht, again. You can rent a house in Grazheim. I know several that would suit your needs. And then – ' he ran one finger gently over her lips, probing them open ' – I'll begin your education. You'd like that, wouldn't you?'

'Yes,' she said.

That, at least, was true. She wanted an affair with Sergei von Lenz, but she also wanted to marry Count Werner von Krohnenstein. Although Sergei did not realise it, he had probably offered her an opportunity to fulfil both those ambitions. She suddenly felt better than she had done for months. She could look forward to the future now. She was about to take control of her life again.

Chapter Four

Katherine watched Count von Krohnenstein pace about her bedroom like a dark panther. She had confronted him coolly with her new knowledge, and refused to divulge her informant. So far he had managed to keep his temper under control. But for how much longer? she wondered. Unanswered questions obviously infuriated him.

'It was one of the servants!' he insisted. 'I'll have them beaten. I'll dismiss them all!'

'It was not any of the servants,' Katherine said. 'And I won't have them blamed – or beaten.'

'Do you think you could stop me?' He rounded on her furiously. 'I'll punish them all unless you tell me who has been gossiping to you.'

'I heard rumours about Ruprecht in England.' She was surprised at how easy it was to lie. 'He has not exactly been discreet about his activities.'

The count laughed derisively. 'Do you expect me to believe that? If you suspected that my son was a lover of men, you would never have agreed to marry him.'

'I don't necessarily believe rumours,' she said. 'I was at least willing to give Ruprecht the benefit of the doubt.

But when one of the women mentioned that there was no tradition that I should stay here until the wedding, I assumed that you were trying to hide something from me.' She smiled at him demurely. 'It seems I was correct.'

The count stopped pacing and flung himself down in a chair. 'So what happens now, dear Lady Katherine? I'm sure you have some kind of ultimatum for me.'

She smiled. 'As you very well know, my financial position precludes me from returning home.' She moved over to him, and stood in front of him. He stared up at her, his dark eyes unreadable, his body still tense with anger. She said calmly, 'I am quite willing to continue with our previous arrangement, but I am no longer willing to go to the altar like a stupid sacrificial lamb.'

'And what exactly does that mean?' he enquired.

'The marriage date must be put in abeyance,' she said. 'I want a house in Grazheim, and some time to get to know the city and to socialise. Time to enjoy myself, as a free woman.' She move closer to him until she was all but standing between his outstretched legs. 'Surely you can have no objection to that?'

'I have never given any of my mistresses a house in Grazheim,' he said. 'Why should I do it for you?'

'Because you want a grandson to carry on your family name,' she said. 'I can give you one. And I will, if you agree to my terms.'

He stared at her for a long moment, and then he began to laugh. It was such a genuine burst of laughter that she was momentarily startled by it. 'My dear Lady Katherine,' he said, at last, 'you are either very brave, or very ignorant. Or perhaps a little bit of both. Very few people who know me well would ever attempt to blackmail me.'

'Oh, I would hardly call it blackmail,' she protested innocently.

'Then what would you call it?'

'Negotiation?' she suggested. 'I have something you

want, but you also have something I want. We should be able to reach an amicable agreement.'

His eyes shifted from her face and moved down to her breasts. Pushed upwards by her laced corset, they swelled provocatively. She had chosen the rather revealing, scoop-necked gown deliberately when she dressed for this meeting.

'Is that your second line of attack?' he asked, amused. 'If you can't win by negotiation, you'll try to use – what? Your body?' He moved his legs abruptly. His foot swept behind her knee and he knocked her off balance. As she fell he caught her arm and pulled her forward so that she tumbled into his lap. She was briefly angry at being taken unawares. Jack Telfer would be ashamed of me, she thought. Then the count's lips brushed her neck and moved downwards. 'How very feminine of you.' His tongue found the cleft between her breasts. The light touch of his mouth and the closeness of his body was already arousing her. 'Did you think it was that easy to seduce me?' Suddenly he twisted her round and tipped her off his lap. She fell in an undignified heap on the floor and her carefully pinned hair was partially shaken loose. It was so unexpected that she gave a little yelp of surprise. 'More experienced women than you have tried that trick,' he said coldly. 'And failed.'

'Indeed?' She stood up. 'But did they offer you as much as I can?'

His expression changed abruptly. Now there was no humour in it. He looked suddenly dangerous, and for the first time since meeting him she felt a little chill of real apprehension. 'You are not the only woman in Europe who can be bought,' he said, cruelly. 'Or even the only woman in Heldenburg. You are simply my first choice. But there are others. Never forget that, Lady Katherine.' She stared at him defiantly. He was still seated, leaning back in his chair. His long legs were stretched out and slightly apart, but she could see no evidence that he was sexually aroused. He surveyed her with half-closed eyes. His pose was so arrogantly self-assured that she knew it ought to infuriate her, but all she felt was a rush of desire. 'Although I have to admit,' he added lazily and, she thought, with a hint of amusement, 'I probably would not have enjoyed the *droit du seigneur* so much with any of the other candidates.'

'I'm sure you wouldn't,' she agreed.

'You think I find you irresistible, don't you?' His voice was mocking. 'You think you can flaunt your nipples, and open your legs, and I will offer you anything, like a lovelorn boy.' His expression changed. 'I'm afraid not, Katherine. I am not that easy to seduce.' He smiled, without humour. 'Although you're welcome to take off your clothes and try.'

'Perhaps you'd like to make it worth my while?' she parried.

'A challenge?' He looked interested now. 'You're a gambler? I like that.' His smile changed to one of genuine amusement. He leant back in his chair and crossed one long leg over the other. 'Very well, I'll make you a wager. Try to seduce me and, if you make it interesting, and bring it to a satisfactory conclusion, I will provide you with a house in Grazheim and defer the wedding date.' He paused. 'If you fail to arouse me sufficiently, you will stay here, and marry Ruprecht when I tell you. Agreed?'

'Agreed,' she said, lightly.

He suddenly uncrossed his legs and stood up. 'There is, of course, a time limit. Even my self-control is not inexhaustible. I'll allow you fifteen minutes.'

'That's unfair,' she protested.

He put his hands on his hips and stared down at her. 'Those are my terms. Accept them, or the deal's off.'

She only hesitated for a moment, then bowed her head in mock humility. 'Very well. I accept.'

'Good,' he said. For a moment they confronted each

other, each waiting for the other to move. Then the count said pleasantly, 'Aren't you going to undress?'

Katherine's expression changed. She surveyed him imperiously. 'No. You are. And be quick about it!'

For a moment he looked startled, and she thought he was going to refuse. That she had made a mistake. Then he smiled. 'Unusual,' he murmured. 'But then you're an unusual woman.'

He stripped slowly. She wanted to hurry him up, but the sight of him removing his clothes was compulsively watchable. His riding jacket came off first. Then he unwound his cravat and unbuttoned his collarless undershirt, still taking his time. She was aware of the clock ticking. He dropped the shirt on the floor. Once again she reflected that he had the kind of body a younger man would envy. Muscled like an athlete, with his chest tapering to a narrow waist and narrow hips. Half naked, he stretched like a lazy panther, and watched her with amused eyes.

'If you deliberately waste time,' she said briskly, 'we'll extend the limit.'

'I make the rules,' he said, 'not you.'

'You're cheating,' she argued. She gave him the same kind of sexual assessment that he had once given her, letting her eyes linger on the slight bulge of his partial erection. She smiled. 'I wonder why.'

He laughed softly, flattened the palm of his hand against his stomach and smoothed in downwards. 'Don't be misled by this,' he said, grasping himself briefly. 'I can control it.'

'Just strip,' she said. 'And stop boasting.'

He walked over to the bed. Sitting down, he began to take off his boots. Although he was still obviously tantalising her by refusing to hurry, he was watching her more intently now. Standing again, he unbuttoned his tight military-style trousers, and removed them quickly and without any attempt to tease her. He waited by the bed, and with his legs slightly apart, smiling. 'Well, Lady Katherine,' he said. 'What now?'

It was difficult not to be excited by his overpowering masculinity. The dark hair on his chest thinned into a line that pointed directly to his impressive cock and balls.

'Face down,' she said, pointing to the bed. 'Take hold of the bed rails.'

He obeyed instantly, without any comment. She saw his muscles tense and then relax as he stretched full length on the bed. For a brief moment she admired his lithe body and the taut shape of his buttocks. Then, without thinking, she lifted her hand and brought it down with all her strength on the curving, unprotected flesh. When her palm landed it sounded like a pistol shot.

His body jerked and he gave a yell of surprise. She was almost as surprised as he was, both by her own action and the pleasure it gave her. It was totally unplanned. She had intended to try and arouse him with more orthodox caresses. But the sight of him lying face down on the bed changed her mind. She wanted to show him that she was in control. She wanted to command, and see him obey. She had never thought of playing such a role before, but as soon as she acted on it she knew that she had discovered a new facet of her sexual personality. And when the count stayed exactly where he was, his arms above his head and his hands still grasping the bed rail as firmly as if they had been tied there, she realised that he enjoyed this kind of role reversal too.

Encouraged, she slapped him again, just as hard, three times in succession. This time he groaned, but it was a groan of pleasure. And still he remained lying submissively on the bed. She rested her palms flat on his buttocks and felt him quiver. Sliding her hands between his thighs she reached for him and inspected him, confirming her suspicions. Her finger squeezed his swelling cock. 'I thought you could control this,' she murmured.

'I thought so too,' he muttered. And then, 'You ride, don't you? Have you a whip?'

'Yes,' she said.

'Use it!' She saw his hands tightened on the bed rail, and saw his muscles tighten.

'Use it . . . *Please,*' she corrected.

'Use it . . .' His face was muffled against the bed clothes. 'Please.'

She kept her riding crop in the leather-covered box with her masculine clothes. It took her only a moment to find it. She walked back to the bed, swishing it against her palm. As she watched the count she could see his body begin to tremble with anticipation.

She whipped him hard enough to give him a pleasurable amount of erotic pain, but without cutting his skin or drawing blood. His body jerked and quivered under the assault, but he made no attempt to evade the welcome punishment. She was amazed at the pleasure it gave her, both to beat him and to hear his stifled groans of rising sexual pleasure. She was equally amazed that it did not diminish her respect and desire for him.

'Enough!' He rolled over. His erection was so strong she was surprised he had controlled it for so long. He reached for her. 'I need you. Now.' She backed away. 'You've won, damn it,' he said.

'But I still have some time left.' She pointed to the clock with her whip, and then tapped his massive erection. 'I will allow you to make yourself comfortable.' His eyes met hers. She smiled. 'Do it,' she said. 'That's an order.'

He took hold of himself with unselfconscious need. She had hoped to gain some insight on the kind of techniques he enjoyed, but his orgasm came so quickly, and so violently, that all she could remember afterwards was her surprise at the roughness of his movements.

When his body had ceased shaking she leant over him, her lips brushing his damp forehead. 'Well,' she said. 'Was that conclusion satisfactory?'

'It was for me,' he said. Suddenly he reached out and caught her round the waist, tumbling her down beside him. Bunching up her skirt, he explored between her silk-stockinged, ribbon-gartered legs. His searching fingers stroked her swollen clitoris. 'And it's obvious,' he observed, 'that you enjoyed it too.' She was surprised at how aroused she had become. His light touch made her groan. She opened her legs wider, encouraging him. 'This,' he said, 'was not part of our wager.'

'It's my reward,' she murmured. 'For winning.'

Closing her eyes she surrendered to the pleasure his fingers were giving her. And within a minute she felt her climax building and overtaking her. It was a lengthy orgasm, rising and falling in waves of sensation, leaving her pleasantly relaxed rather than exhausted. They lay side by side for a few more minutes, then the clock chimed four times, and the count sat up.

'I have to attend a dinner this evening,' he said. 'And I have to ride back to Grazheim.' He reached for his breeches and pulled them on carefully. She saw him wince. 'You have a heavy hand, Lady Katherine Gainsworth,' he commented.

'You made the wager,' she replied.

'I was interested to know how you would go about seducing me,' he said. 'I suspected that you might be inventive, and you certainly didn't disappoint me.' He reached for his shirt and pulled it over his head. Once again she experienced a thrill of pleasure at watching him move. 'Tell me, have you played the dominant mistress many times before?'

'Heavens, no,' she said. 'That was the first time.'

'Well, you certainly have a talent for it,' he said. He stopped buttoning his shirt and turned towards her. 'Did it surprise you to realise you enjoyed it?'

'Yes,' she said, truthfully. 'But I was even more surprised when you enjoyed it too. I did it on impulse. If I'd thought about it, I probably wouldn't have dared.' He was watching her with amused eyes. 'You did hint at it in one of our conversations, some days ago,' she remembered. 'But I didn't take it seriously. You didn't seem like the kind of man who would submit to a woman.'

He laughed. 'I don't do it very often. It has to be the right woman. A strong woman. Not only physically strong, but a woman with character, with a mind of her own. And it has to be someone who enjoys the pleasures of the whip as much as I do. I don't want favours. There is no satisfaction for me unless the enjoyment is mutual. It's rare to meet such a woman. It doesn't happen often and, when it does, it is something to be savoured.' He let his eyes move over her body, slowly. 'We must explore those fascinating pathways again.' He paused. 'The thought of having you at my disposal in Grazheim is a very attractive one.'

'The thought of having a house in Grazheim is a very attractive one,' she countered. 'I honestly didn't think I'd get it.'

'You didn't think you'd win the bet?' He smiled. 'You underestimate your talents, Lady Katherine.'

'I didn't think you'd honour the bet,' she said.

'That's the second time you've insulted me this evening,' he said. 'First you try to blackmail me, and now you imply that I don't keep my word.' He took a step towards her and placed his hands on her shoulders. She felt the strength of his fingers gripping her. 'I *always* keep my word, Lady Katherine,' he said, softly. 'Just remember that.' Then he turned away from her, and picked up his military-style riding jacket. 'You will be in Grazheim within a week.'

Grazheim was much more attractive than Katherine expected. Crowded along the banks of a rather sluggish river, it was a mixture of wide, tree-lined avenues, and ancient winding alleyways filled with tiny shops and noisy coffee houses. The grand duke's palace was a gothic-style castle protected by ornate wrought-iron gates and a guard of Heldenburg Hussars, clad in blue and silver. The Heldenburg flag, with its tusked golden boar snarling against a blue background, fluttered from the main flagpole.

The house the count had given her was spacious, beautifully furnished, and on the outskirts of the town. He also provided her with a carriage, two good riding horses (and a side saddle, she noted) and a personal staff of four, including Frau Grussell.

Katherine was quite pleased to see Frau Grussell again, despite suspecting that one of the old woman's duties probably included that of a benign spy. She had managed to evade Frau Grussell before, and was confident that she could do so again. But she soon discovered that subterfuge was not necessary. She was allowed to come and go as she pleased. Several shopping trips enhanced her wardrobe at the count's expense, and she also discovered an excellent seamstress who was willing to make gowns and provide tailored riding habits.

From the day of her arrival in Grazheim she received a succession of formal invitations to visit members of Heldenburg society. Although she guessed that most of these invitations were prompted by curiosity – everyone wanted to meet Ruprecht von Krohnenstein's future wife – she did not care. Her unexpected notoriety amused her. She mixed with representatives of Heldenburg's aristocracy, all of whom treated her with rather formal, but apparently genuine, friendship. But Frau Grussell, who was a never-ending source of gossip, warned her that there were certain families who had not yet invited her, and would not do so until they knew her forthcoming marriage was approved by the grand duke.

'I thought the count's family were friends of the grand duke,' Katherine said. 'Surely that is approval enough?'

'The count's family have always *served* the grand duke,' Frau Grussell emphasised. 'I serve the von Krohnensteins, but I would not presume to call them my friends.'

At each dinner and dance that she attended Katherine hoped to see Sergei von Lenz, but she never did. Neither did anyone ever mention his name. She was sometimes tempted to ask about him, but a quick look at her companions always persuaded her to keep silent. These upstanding pillars of Heldenburg society did not look as if they would know a man who frequented the Peacock Club, even if he only went there to gamble. In contrast, the count's name was frequently mentioned. The comments were always flattering, as if her companions were deliberately feeding her with compliments in the hope that she would report them to the count. She would have been happy to do so, if he had visited her. But he did not do so.

Then, one afternoon, she heard the clatter of wheels outside and saw the familiar black carriage outside, its doors emblazoned with the von Krohnenstein crest. She checked her appearance quickly in the mirror, turning with a smile when the door opened.

'My *dear* fiancée.' Ruprecht stood in the doorway. He was wearing male clothes, but they were ornate and theatrical: a heavily embroidered waistcoat over a shirt with billowing sleeves, and a pair of formal fitted trousers, the decorated front flap clearly designed to draw attention to his crotch. He stood with one hand on his hip, posing. 'Please don't bother to greet me with the traditional kiss.'

'I had no intention of doing so,' she said coolly. Looking at him she could not recognise the shy young boy who had proposed marriage to her in England. Or, she had to admit, the outrageous redhead from the Peacock Club.

'Well, that's a relief. Actually, kissing women makes me feel positively ill.' He inspected the room with exaggerated politeness, and then gave her a supercilious smile. 'You *have* come up in the world since I saw you last, haven't you? This is quite an improvement from your rather scruffy little ancestral home. My father must be *very* fond of you. He's not usually so generous to his mistresses.' She was about to protest, but he silenced her with a gesture. 'Oh, don't deny it. Do you think I *care*? With luck he'll get you pregnant, and save me the unpleasant duty.'

'Well, if I must have a child,' she said, 'I would rather know it had a *man* for a father.'

Ruprecht smiled. 'You do have a bitchy tongue, don't you, darling? And big ears too, I gather.' He wandered over to a chair and sat down. 'Enlighten me, please. How did you find out that I wasn't quite the little virgin boy you were expecting?'

'So that you can tell your father?' She smiled sweetly. 'I'm sure he'd like to know. Did he send you here to question me?'

'Are you suggesting my father would ask me a favour?' Ruprecht laughed harshly. 'That's the last thing he'd do. And I wouldn't oblige him, either.' He lounged back in his chair. 'I'm just curious, that's all. Someone out there is meddling in my private affairs. I find it irritating.'

'From what I've heard,' she said, tartly, 'your affairs are far from private. And informing me about them can hardly be construed as meddling in your affairs.'

Ruprecht crossed his legs, elegantly. 'Then let me put it another way. In two weeks we could have been married. Thanks to your little arrangement with my father, I may have to wait two months, while you enjoy yourself in Grazheim at my expense.'

'At your father's expense,' she corrected. 'And I was not aware that you were so anxious to become my husband.'

'I'm not,' he said. 'But I am anxious to be married.' He smiled coldly. 'Does that confuse you, dear? It's quite simple really. My father keeps a very tight rein on my allowances. When I'm married he'll have to be more generous. He can't let people say that the Count von Krohnenstein's only son and his pretty young wife are living in virtual poverty, can he?'

'And what if I decide not to marry you?' she challenged.

'We both know you don't have that option, dear.' He stood up, wandered over to the mirror and posed for a moment, patting his hair. 'You need the money too, don't you?' He turned on her suddenly and viciously, and she realised that the effeminate Ruprecht von Krohnenstein would make a vindictive enemy. 'So unless you want to be packed off home to your father's dilapidated mansion and his pile of unpaid bills, I suggest you get over this little rebellion of yours as quickly as possible, and start doing as you're told. We *are* going to be married, and the sooner the better, whether you like it or not!'

Frau Grussell held a silver plate with a plain white envelope on it. 'Gracious lady, look at this.' She thrust the plate at Katherine, her face alight with excitement. 'Look at the crest. This is from the Countess Montrossi.'

Katherine took the envelope. 'That doesn't sound like a Heldenburg name.'

'Oh, it isn't,' Frau Grussell agreed. 'The countess comes from Italy, I believe. I've heard that she gives the most wonderful parties, and everyone in Grazheim wants to be invited, but of course most of them never will be. The countess has the most extraordinary guests. Actors, artists and strange people like that. Even courtesans, so I've been told. She cares nothing for convention.

In fact – ' Frau Grussell assumed an appropriately shocked expression ' – I have been told that the countess was once a courtesan herself.'

'So how did she acquire a title?' Katherine asked.

'By marrying an old Italian count, a paramour,' Frau Grussell said. She added conspiratorially, 'And later poisoning him in order to get his money. Or so I heard.'

Katherine laughed. 'You really shouldn't listen to gossip, Frau Grussell. The countess may be a widow who acquired her title by marrying an older man, but that doesn't mean she murdered him.' She added, 'Perhaps he merely died of exhaustion.'

'Oh, my goodness,' Frau Grussell giggled, clearly delighted with the implication. 'What a dreadful thing to say!'

Katherine looked at the invitation again. It was couched in formal language: Francesca, Countess Montrossi, requested the pleasure of her company. But at the bottom there was a footnote: *gambling for the brave.*

What exactly does that mean? Katherine wondered. Gambling for very high stakes? If that was the case, she could not participate. The count allowed her to purchase clothes, but she was certain he would not finance her at games of chance. It would be frustrating to see others enjoying themselves at the gaming tables and not be able to participate. Maybe she should refuse the invitation. But what if Sergei von Lenz was also at the party? She had a feeling that he might be the kind of guest the countess would enjoy. It would be even more frustrating to think that she had missed seeing him again.

Later that evening, when she tried to decide what dress she would wear, she began to wonder if Sergei had anything to do with her invitation. Perhaps this was his way of arranging a meeting. And from this meeting, what would follow? Despite her feelings for the count, Sergei von Lenz frequently haunted her thoughts and her fantasies. He was a mystery. He talked as if he gambled regularly. Did he have inherited wealth? Strangely, there was something about him that reminded her of her father's more dubious friends. The ones that made their living at the gaming tables. The ones who could manipulate the cards and make them perform dishonest miracles. The ones who lived on the edge of danger, but who always seemed to survive against the odds. She could certainly imagine Sergei von Lenz smiling his flashing smile, talking his way out of any tight corner. And, she realised, she could also imagine him charming his way into any woman's bed.

But hadn't he already admitted as much? He had not made any false promises. He was clearly not interested in a long-term commitment to marriage, or in fidelity. What he seemed to be offering her was an exciting affair. And why not? she thought. There are a lot of erotic pathways I want to explore before I finally settle down.

The more she thought about it, the more she became convinced that Sergei had arranged this invitation for her. He undoubtedly knew by now that she was still involved with the von Krohnenstein family. He could not call at her house, and he was clearly not on the guest list of any aristocratic hostesses. How else could he meet her? A party given by an unconventional woman like the Countess Montrossi was the obvious choice. And if the countess did not consider Lady Katherine Gainsworth particularly interesting, no doubt he could find ways of persuading her to issue an invitation anyway.

But what kind of ways, Katherine wondered, feeling a sudden stab of jealousy. She imagined the two of them together. She was sure the countess would be beautiful. A fortune hunter who ensnared a rich, elderly aristocrat would have to do it with her looks and her body. She would probably have an olive complexion and black hair tumbling to her shoulders, glossy and curled. She would be tall and voluptuous, with a magnificent bosom. And

Sergei von Lenz would certainly be on very intimate terms with her.

Katherine sat down on the bed, surprised that the thought of him charming another woman with that irresistible smile was actually making her jealous. She imagined them together. Imagined them at one of the countess's famous parties, the centre of a crowd of laughing friends and admirers, with Sergei dressed as she remembered him, in tight breeches and boots, his tailored military-style jacket accentuating his narrow waist and slim hips, his black hair brushing the back of his collar, and the jagged fringe and sideburns framing his tanned face. A wild gipsy, dark and exciting, with that sudden, unexpected smile lighting up his face. No wonder Francesca, Countess Montrossi, had fallen for him.

And the countess herself? How would she dress? Katherine lay back on the bed and imagined the courtesan countess as a peasant girl, which was probably, she thought bitchily, how Francesca Montrossi had started out in life, anyway. A peasant girl, now wearing a provocative version of her traditional costume. A blouse with embroidered sleeves, and a low scooped neck gathered by a ribbon that could be quickly undone. A skirt flared into a crinoline by layers of white petticoats. And she would be holding onto Sergei's arm possessively. Despite herself Katherine could not help imagining Sergei returning the countess's smile, his eyes straying to her cleavage, and then maybe one hand entangled in her thick, curled hair as he pressed his fingers against her scalp, turned her head, and leant towards her, his mouth ready to claim her red painted lips.

No! Katherine thought. Even in a fantasy she did not want him to have eyes for anyone else. In her imagination she voiced her protest loudly. The noisy room was suddenly quiet. All eyes turned to her. She stood facing Sergei and the countess. In her mind's eye she decided how the scene would look. She would be imperious, a direct contrast to the carnal Francesca. She clothed herself in a cream satin dress, with a close-fitting bodice and a low décolletage, a neckline that made her breasts as interesting as her rival's. She added ivory combs to hold up her piled hair, and pearls round her neck.

But which one of us would Sergei prefer? she wondered. I would be an unknown. He would not know what I was capable of until he sampled me. Surely that would excite him? He had already told her that he wanted to take charge of her erotic education. She could not believe that he would prefer an over-ripe woman like the countess. But what if he did?

Lying back on the bed she closed her eyes. She imagined the countess tightening her grip on Sergei's arm. Whispering in his ear. Trying to tug him away from the crowd, to the privacy of an upstairs room. But Sergei would hesitate. He would look at this new contender for his favours. She would stare back, challenging him. His dark eyes would meet hers, then travel lazily down the curve of her neck to the swell of her breasts. She knew he was curious. Maybe he already knew that sex with the countess would be passionate and noisy, energetic and demanding. But what would it be like with the unexplored body of the intriguing English Rose? Katherine smiled to herself. Once the countess suspected that she had a serious rival she would argue and threaten, and soon the whole room would be impatient to know who was going to end up in Sergei von Lenz's bed that night.

She rearranged the scene in her mind. Now Sergei was reclining in a chair, like a king surveying his court, with his friends in a large circle round him. She stood in the centre of the circle, next to the countess. Sergei would look straight at her, tempting her with that sudden brilliant smile. 'Are you willing to fight for me, English Rose?'

'Yes,' she said.

Another smile. 'And you, countess?'

Countess Francesca Montrossi put her hands on her hips and stared contemptuously at Katherine. 'It hardly seems fair. I will strip this skinny English flower of her fine petals, and then maybe I'll spank her and send her home.'

'Don't be too sure,' Sergei drawled. 'The English are full of surprises.'

'I bet on the countess!' It was a voice from the crowd. 'Ten crowns that the countess has the Rose naked in five minutes.'

'Oh, it'll take longer than that,' another voice objected, 'Ten minutes, at least. Five crowns that it takes ten minutes.'

They haggled briefly. Other men stepped forward to place bets. Someone suggested that maybe Katherine would win, but he was laughed into silence. Most of these men had seen the countess fight before. They were confident that her heavier build, and her experience, would prove superior.

'It seems no one will bet on you, English Rose,' Sergei observed. 'Except me.' He threw down a handful of coins. 'Ten crowns on the English beauty.' His voice sounded mocking. His eyes held Katherine's for a moment. 'Don't disappoint me,' he said, softly. 'If I lose I'll expect to be reimbursed.'

Katherine stared at him. 'So you'll win, either way?'

Sergei still smiled. 'I always play to win,' he said.

'That's interesting,' she replied coolly. 'So do I.' She held his gaze. 'What exactly are the rules of this charade?'

He stretched out his legs. 'The first one to end up completely naked loses. And we don't expect to see blood. No biting, no scratching, no punches. Remember – you're both ladies!' The crowd laughed. 'And no jewellery,' Sergei added.

The countess began to remove her earrings and finger

112

rings. Katherine removed her combs and pearls. Her hair fell to her shoulders. The countess stood opposite her, her hands on her hips. 'I'm ready for you, my fragile flower,' she sneered.

Katherine could not imagine herself fighting in a full-skirted dress. She quickly redressed herself in her imagination, so that her legs were free. Then she kicked off her silk shoes with their tiny heels. Turning towards the countess she mimicked the other woman's aggressive stance. 'I'm ready for you, too,' she said, softly.

Would Sergei really enjoy seeing two women fighting over him, each one trying hard to strip the other? She had a strong suspicion that he would! How would the countess fight, she wondered? Using strength to try and pin her opponent down, then ripping at her chemisette and corsets? Well, maybe I'd do the same, Katherine thought. I'd have that blouse off her in no time at all. She imagined the tearing cloth, and then the sensation of the countess's swelling breasts under her hands. The crowd would cheer, delighted to see the Amazonian Italian half-naked. Maybe they would shout encouragement to the countess, anxious to see her return the compliment. And I think I'd let her, Katherine decided. Not for the crowd, but for Sergei. There's nothing wrong with my breasts. I'd let her rip off my underclothes and my corset – but that's all!

Because she was used to Jack Telfer's hard bulk, Katherine found it difficult to imagine what it would be like wrestling with a woman. But it wasn't difficult to imagine the audience watching them both, enjoying the sight of two very different female bodies entangled together – the dark, tigerish countess and the slim Englishwoman, with her golden hair and long legs. Watching them and waiting for more of their clothes to come off. Shouting encouragement, making more bets if it looked as if the countess would certainly be the winner.

113

Looking forward to the sight of the countess holding her victim down and spanking her.

But Katherine had no intention of including that in her fantasy! The idea of being man-handled by a woman did not appeal to her at all. She felt certain that in a real fight she could beat another woman, even one as healthily statuesque as she imagined the countess to be. The only decision would be when to make her move. She wanted Sergei to see enough of her body to tempt him into wanting more. But she did not like the idea of exposing too much of herself to the other watching men. Being stripped to the waist was acceptable, but nothing more. When that happened she would use the skills Jack Telfer had taught her. As they struggled she would wait until the countess was off balance. Then she would use the woman's own body weight to topple her, tugging her forward and kicking at her ankle. It was not strictly a wrestling move – but the painful arm lock she would then apply certainly would be.

Unable to struggle, the countess would find herself stripped of her remaining clothes. The skirt and the petticoats and the remains of her blouse would be tugged and ripped and tossed aside until all she was wearing was her dark stockings and her shoes. No doubt she would look exotically dishevelled and probably wouldn't mind over much at being exposed to the cheering crowd. After all, plenty of men had seen her naked before, and probably would again.

And then, Katherine thought, I would claim my prize. She imagined Sergei walking towards her, holding out his hand, smiling. 'Congratulations, English Rose, I knew you'd be full of surprises.'

She took his hand. 'I have more,' she promised.

'I do hope so,' he said. He lowered his voice. 'Put your dress back on, English Rose. It makes you look innocent and fragile.' His fingers tightened round hers. 'But you're not fragile, are you? Or innocent?'

'Oh, but I am,' she protested. 'You once promised to educate me.'

'I've a feeling that you could also educate me,' he murmured.

Maybe I could, Katherine thought. The thought of stripping him and tying him down was suddenly appealing. It surprised her. She had always wanted her men to be dominant and authoritative. In fact, she thought, I still do. But the idea of reversing the roles was exciting, too. She remembered the erotic thrill it had given her to see the count stretched out on the bed as she whipped him. Hearing the sound of the leather as it landed on his taut buttocks. Hearing him gasp with pleasure. If anyone had told her previously that she could still find a man intensely desirable after seeing him in that position, she would not have believed them. But taking the dominant role had definitely not diminished the count's masculine appeal. If anything, it had increased her desire for him.

Would it be as satisfying to see Sergei von Lenz stretched out like that, his lean body spread-eagled, his wrists and ankles tied or chained? She was certain that it would, but less certain that he would acquiesce. He was every bit as masculine as the count, but much less easy to categorise. She knew now that the count had very real power in Heldenburg although she still did not really understand the basis for it. He was close to the grand duke, that much she had learned from gossip at the various parties she had attended. Many people respected him, some feared him. Once they knew her own connection with the von Krohnenstein family, some of the people she had met had been polite to the point of a sycophancy.

But Sergei von Lenz was still a mystery. All she knew about him was that he did not come from Heldenburg, and that he gambled. He was obviously not Prussian either. His German was fluent but accented. He had come into her life suddenly and unexpectedly, and she had a feeling that he would disappear from it in the same way. The thought depressed her and destroyed her fantasy. She wanted to see him again. It seemed ridiculous to desire him so much, when she was still so attracted to the count. Maybe when she did meet him again she would recognise him simply as an adventurer, out to take advantage of her. Perhaps then she could banish him from her fantasies, and her life. She thought about it, and doubted it. She had a feeling that the next time she saw him he would only have to smile and she would be helplessly beguiled again.

Frau Grussell seemed as excited about Katherine's acceptance of the countess's invitation as she was at any proposed visit by the count. She fussed round Katherine, checking her pale-blue dress with its tight bodice, off-the-shoulder neckline, and puffed sleeves. Katherine was wearing a necklace of diamonds and sapphires, a piece of von Krohnenstein family jewellery loaned to her by the count. There was a matching bracelet on her gloved wrist. Her hair was held in place with tortoiseshell combs and decorated with fresh flowers. Sapphire earrings completed the ensemble.

'You will have to tell me everything that happens,' Frau Grussell hinted hopefully. 'All the naughty details.'

Frau Grussell had frequently surprised Katherine by her interest in salacious gossip. She felt sure that, despite her genuine respect for her employer, the old lady would have thoroughly enjoyed a description of her exploits with the count.

'There won't be any naughty details,' she said, pretending to be shocked at the idea. 'I'm sure the countess's reputation has been greatly exaggerated.'

When her carriage stopped outside the gates of the countess's town house, and she saw the light streaming from the windows and heard the sounds of music, Katherine had a feeling that her light-hearted remarks might well turn out to be true. A distinguished-looking servant took her cloak and another took her card. She was ushered into a large ballroom. Although a small group of musicians were playing, no one was dancing. Most of the guests were standing in small groups, talking and laughing. When she was announced, a tall woman in a dark and slightly old-fashioned high-waisted gown broke away from one of the smaller groups and came towards her.

'Lady Katherine?' Hooded eyes surveyed her, and Katherine felt that this woman was mentally assessing the worth of her jewellery and the cost of her dress. 'I am the countess Montrossi. You don't mind if we talk in English while we're together, do you? I like to keep in practice.' She slipped her arm through Katherine's. 'I'm so glad you could come. So many people here would like to meet you.'

For a moment Katherine was genuinely startled. Whatever she had been expecting it had not been this angular, middle-aged woman, whose face, with its high-bridged aquiline nose, was striking rather than beautiful, and whose dress was decorous to the point of being matronly. The Countess smiled regally, and Katherine realised that she had probably been quite striking in her youth, but she almost laughed at the thought of indulging in a half-naked wrestling match with her.

'I see you haven't brought your future husband with you,' the countess added. 'I shall have to find you a companion.'

A companion? Katherine looked quickly round the room. Had she been correct in assuming Sergei had arranged this meeting? Was he there? She could not see him. The countess was watching her, her face a mask of polite attention.

'Ruprecht and I do not socialise together,' Katherine said carefully.

The countess surprised her by laughing. 'That's a droll

way of putting it,' she said. She took Katherine's arm and led her to a double door that opened into the garden. 'I'll introduce you to everyone quite soon, but first I want you to myself for a few moments. You must answer the question that I'm sure most people are probably too well mannered to ask you: why in God's name did you agree to marry Ruprecht von Krohnenstein?'

The question startled Katherine. The countess was right. No one had actually put their curiosity into words. She had a feeling that none of her standard lies would satisfy the countess. She was right.

'The boy is a disgusting, selfish little swine,' the countess added. 'And what's more, you know it.'

A young man suddenly appeared at the double doors. He was dressed in tight white trousers and a loose, half-unbuttoned shirt, and for a heart-jolting moment Katherine thought it was Sergei. Then she realised that the newcomer was little more than a boy, and obviously drunk. The countess turned towards him. 'Alfons, darling, I'm busy right now. You'll have to find someone else's shoulder to cry on.'

The young man staggered slightly, then nodded and wandered off again. 'Poor dear,' the countess said. 'He has the same sexual preferences as Ruprecht, but he's so sweet that everyone loves him.' She smiled regally. 'And quite a lot of them fuck him, too, of course, but that's their business. I'm quite open-minded about sexual preferences. It doesn't bother me at all if Ruprecht wants to dress up like a whore, or behave like one, either. But as a person, his character is slightly less savoury than a pig's arsehole. I can't imagine any sensible woman wanting to be in the same room with him, let alone allowing him to try and get her with child.' She stopped suddenly and turned to Katherine. 'The count isn't blackmailing you into this marriage, is he?'

'Heavens, no,' Katherine said, startled.

'That's good,' the countess said. She looked at Katherine

intensely and Katherine suddenly felt uncomfortable. 'You're much too beautiful for Werner to use you like that.' She sighed. 'I suppose that means you're servicing him because you like it, eh?' For a moment Katherine was speechless. The countess laughed good humouredly. 'Oh, don't look so surprised. Everyone knows. No one thinks any the worse of you. Werner has never had any trouble getting women to fall at his feet. Or maybe I should say, into his bed.' She thought for a moment. 'Then it has to be for money.' She turned impulsively to Katherine. 'My dear girl, tell me the truth. If it's money you need you don't have to marry into the von Krohnenstein family to get it. With a face and figure like yours, you could make a fortune.'

'If you mean prostitution,' Katherine said coolly, 'I don't think my father would approve of that.' Remembering the gossip she had heard about the countess's early life she not not think it would be polite to add that she would not like it either.

'Don't tell him,' the countess shrugged. 'Invent some story. Say you'd been lucky on the gaming tables.'

'I'd need money to begin with for that,' Katherine said.

'You mean you haven't anything? No money at all?' That silenced the countess for a moment. 'Well, it's no secret that I started with nothing, but I went on the streets. There wasn't any other choice for a girl of my class. Except marriage and constant childbirth, of course, and I certainly didn't want that. Most of the silly bitches I worked with spent as fast as they earned it, on their pimps or on some fancy paramour. I was sensible. When I had saved enough, I started to get myself seen in the right places. I became a mistress instead of a common whore and, whenever I changed men, I always moved up the ladder. It was slow, but I was lucky. I met Paolino Montrossi before I got too haggard to attract anyone. His prick wasn't up to much, but he knew how to use his tongue. I didn't mind that. It saved me from bringing any unwanted brats into the world. When he died I was lucky again. I inherited everything.' She gave Katherine a sympathetic look. 'Perhaps what you need is a protector, my dear.'

There was something in the countess's eyes that disturbed Katherine. 'The count seems concerned about my welfare,' she said cautiously.

The countess laughed. 'I think you'll find that all that charming bastard is concerned about is that you open your legs for him whenever he asks you. But all men are the same.' She took Katherine's arm and led her back into the ballroom again. 'Has Werner talked politics to you yet?'

'No,' Katherine said. 'Is he involved in politics?'

'He's involved in anything that affects his future,' the countess said. She gave Katherine a lingering look, and once again Katherine felt uncomfortable. 'But then, if I had you for a toy, I wouldn't talk politics either.'

'I didn't think there was much to talk about,' Katherine said. 'The duchy seems quite stable, and the grand duke seems very popular.'

'That's what people are supposed to think,' the countess agreed. 'And in some ways, it's the truth. But there are also those in Heldenburg who would like to see changes. To be blunt, they would rather have the Prussians in control than the grand duke.'

'Union with Prussia?' Katherine said. 'I didn't know it was even being discussed.'

'It isn't,' the countess said. 'At least, not in public. But underground it's a different matter. A lot of people would like to see the grand duke deposed, and Werner von Krohnenstein with him.' She laughed harshly. 'Idiots! Keep the devil you know, I always say. And as long as you don't talk treason in Heldenburg, the count will leave you alone.'

'And if you do talk treason?' Katherine asked.

The Countess Montrossi drew one finger lightly across

her throat. 'The von Krohnensteins have always been patriots. Being Werner's mistress wouldn't save you if he thought you were threatening Heldenburg's neutrality.' She smiled. 'But you're not likely to do that, are you? I'm sure you're much more interested in enjoying yourself.' She took Katherine's arm again, pulled her closer than Katherine really wanted, and led her back into the spacious ballroom again. 'I know you've met some of Heldenburg's dull aristocrats. Let me introduce you to a more exotic circle of friends. There are some quite influential people here.' She pointed to a man standing in the centre of a laughing crowd, a man who stood out from the rest because of his shaven head and pugnacious stance.

'That's Oskar von Hohlmann,' she said. 'And no doubt you can guess his nationality.'

'He looks like a Prussian officer,' Katherine said.

'Well, you're nearly right,' the countess agreed. 'He was an officer, but he transferred to the diplomatic corps.'

'Do many Prussians come to your parties?' Katherine asked, thinking that von Hohlmann looked like the last person she would have expected to see in what was supposed to be a gathering of bohemian pleasure lovers.

'Quite a few.' The countess shrugged. 'It depends on what they're looking for.'

'Gambling?' Katherine asked, lightly. 'But only for the brave?'

The countess laughed. 'That's just a little harmless fun,' she said. 'I have a reputation for providing naughty amusements. We play for forfeits. Sometimes rather wicked ones, especially if one of the gentlemen players is interested in one of the ladies.' She gave Katherine another unfathomable look. 'That doesn't shock you, does it? You didn't run home in tears when you discovered the kind of man you were expected to marry. You didn't refuse to jump when Werner cracked the whip, I imagine?' The countess's unexpected choice of phrase brought a sudden erotic image to Katherine's mind. She vividly remembered the sight of the count's naked body lying on the bed, the red welts from her riding crop only too visible on his backside. She felt herself blushing, and turned her head away from the countess. The countess put her fingers under Katherine's chin, and turned her head back again. 'Or did you get Werner jumping to your commands?' She laughed, suddenly. 'My dear girl, don't be embarrassed. I have heard the rumours. But I'm unshockable. And discreet. That's why I'm so popular. That's why people like Oskar are willing to visit me.'

She escorted Katherine to Oskar von Hohlmann's group and introduced her. Katherine felt von Hohlmann's supercilious pale blue eyes assessing her, but it was a politely disinterested evaluation. Several other members of the group looked more interested.

One woman held on to her hand for much longer than necessary, her bright green eyes animated. 'You're to be Ruprecht's wife?' She made a sympathetic moue with her full lips. 'How perfectly dreadful for you. Can't we persuade you to change your mind?'

'Maybe we will,' the countess said, lightly. When they moved away from the group she said, 'Poor Oskar would not be happy if Heldenburg lost its autonomy. Where else would he feel safe to indulge himself and play?' She smiled conspiratorially. 'Oskar likes to be bound tightly with thin little straps. The longer it takes to buckle him up, the better he likes it. He has a special piece of equipment that he designed himself, to truss up his cock and balls. Can you imagine? Narrow straps made of leather, six of them round his cock, and longer straps to pull it back against his stomach and hold it there. When he gets excited he swells up, and it must be agonising – which is what he loves, of course. He pays his pretty boyfriends to excite him, and the longer he can stand the pain, the happier he is. And before you ask, I haven't seen him wriggling, although I'd certainly like to. When Oskar plays, it's boys only. He doesn't care for girls. But then, girls can entertain themselves without a man, can't they?' She gave Katherine another speculative look. 'Don't you agree?'

For the first time Katherine realised exactly what the countess had been hinting at ever since they met. Even her suggestion of a protector made sense now. No doubt the countess would have been happy to 'save' her from Ruprecht by offering her a home. But there would obviously be a price. Katherine had never even thought about another woman as a sexual partner. The idea did not disgust her; it simply did not interest her.

'Women understand each other,' the countess added softly. 'They are less selfish than men. And their bodies are far more interesting and beautiful.'

'Not to me, I'm afraid,' Katherine said crisply.

The countess looked at her, and sighed. 'Oh, you are *so* English. So conventional. So boring.'

'It's just that I prefer men,' Katherine said.

'So you'll marry Ruprecht von Krohnenstein?'

'Maybe,' Katherine murmured. 'Maybe not.'

The countess gave her a long, steady look. 'You must realise that no other man in Heldenburg would dare court you as long as you are under the count's protection,' she said. 'No one with any sense would offend the von Krohensteins.'

Katherine shrugged. The thought that she might actually marry the count, and not his son, did not seem to have occurred to the Countess Montrossi. But she had to admit that at that moment the man uppermost in her thoughts was not Werner von Krohnenstein, but Sergei von Lenz. Where *was* he? Had she misjudged him? Had he simply been amusing himself by suggesting an erotic liaison? Was he afraid of the von Krohnensteins, too?

Somehow she could not believe that he was afraid of anyone. Either he had not arranged her invitation to the countess's party at all, and did not even know she was there, or he intended to arrive later. She was longing to ask the countess about him. But she did not want to make her interest too obvious, or supply her hostess with any more titbits about her private life. The countess was clearly a collector and a purveyor of gossip. If Sergei was genuine in his desire to see her again, and they did start a clandestine relationship, the countess would undoubtedly get to know about it before long, anyway.

After some more introductions, the countess left Katherine to socialise on her own. For the rest of the evening Katherine moved from group to group in the ballroom, and she certainly found most of the conversations more stimulating than those she had listened to at the more formal parties she had previously attended.

As Frau Grussell had predicted, many of the guests had unconventional occupations and opinions. She met writers, artists and actors, and quite a few guests who were secretive about their daily lives. She was also aware that at certain times people would break away from the general crowd and go off together. No one commented on these comings and goings, and although she was welcomed with a relaxed and open friendliness, no one suggested she joined in any activities that might have been taking place away from the ballroom.

After a while she realised that most of the conversations she was having started quite innocently but ended up heavy with veiled sexual innuendo. She frequently felt that she was being tested. Remarks were made, and her reactions checked. It became a game that she found quite amusing to play. By the end of the evening she thought she had made her sexual orientation quite clear, although it was self-evident that had she wanted to pursue a same-sex affair she could have had her choice of several partners.

But what she wanted, she thought in frustration as the carriage took her back to her house, was an affair with Sergei von Lenz. Not only had he not appeared at the party, but no one had mentioned his name. She felt a sudden surge of frustration. And anger. Now that she had freedom of movement, she could meet him at his house any time she liked. It would be easy to make excuses to Frau Grussell, and the count seemed to be far too busy to worry about her activities. He had not visited her since she arrived in Grazheim, and she had no idea when she would see him again.

If only I could make love to Sergei once, she thought, maybe this infatuation would be assuaged. Then I could concentrate on persuading the count that I would make him an excellent wife. But I want one exciting affair first. The more she thought about Sergei's tall, slim figure, and that sudden smile that lit up his dark face and charmed her so effortlessly, the more she wanted him.

She leant back on her seat as the carriage rattled through the darkness, and imagined undressing him, slowly, as they relaxed on a bed. She would unbutton his jacket and feel the warmth of his body as her hands touched his skin. She would help him tug off his shirt, pressing herself close to him. While he tangled with the white cotton, his arms above his head, she would run her tongue round each of his nipples in turn. He would fall back, his arms still trapped, enjoying it. Her mouth would play with him, sucking now, feeling him respond. Her hands would move down over his flat stomach, to the buttons on his tight breeches. She would undo them, pull down the front flap, maybe explore a little. Feel him swelling as her hand closed round his cock. She would tug, and stroke and tantalise. He would struggle to get free of his shirt, to grab her and turn her over, and take control.

But she would be too quick for him. She would wind the loose sleeves round his wrists, wind them round the bedposts. Do anything to keep him captive, because she wanted to see him completely naked and fully aroused. Wanted him to need her desperately, but know that he was unable to get at her until she allowed it. She would tease him still further by undressing slowly in front of him. She would enjoy his discomfiture. She would make him regret that he had kept her waiting for this pleasure for so long.

She imagined him stripped and spread-eagled – his ankles would be tied as well, she decided – his long legs stretched out and slightly apart so that she could inspect and handle his aching erection more easily. And she would handle him for a long time, she thought, applying just enough erotic torture to make him beg for release. Finally she would have mercy on him. She would give him that release, with her hands, or her mouth. And then untie him. And then he would certainly repay her in kind. She wriggled in her seat, preparing to imagine it, already feeling aroused at the idea of being his helpless prisoner.

The carriage jolted to a halt and brought her back to the present. She experienced a feeling of intense disappointment. Her fantasy had made her delightfully uncomfortable. She wanted to lie back and relax and enjoy a satisfactory release. But instead she had to straighten her skirts, go inside and, she thought, probably fend off a hundred questions about the countess's party from Frau Grussell, whom she knew from past experience would certainly be waiting for her.

She opened the front door to find the hallway in half-darkness, which surprised her. There was no one there to take her cloak, or offer her the usual glass of spiced wine that Frau Grussell always said promoted a good night's sleep. She walked towards the bell pull to summon one of the servants and a tall figure appeared out of the shadows, caught her in a strong grasp, and twisted her round so that her back was against the wall.

It happened so suddenly that she was taken completely by surprise, and yet instinctively she felt herself react by twisting round and making an attempt to escape. When this failed she reached for her attacker's throat. Fingers grasped her wrists in a grip of steel.

'Fight me, would you?' She recognised the count's voice, amused, but authoritative. 'You won't find me so compliant this time, Lady Katherine.' She was unable to prevent him from pushing her through the door into the drawing room. He held her tightly, his face shadowed by moonlight. 'I've been waiting for you,' he said. 'A long time.'

Suddenly she felt herself lifted up and tipped backwards. In a moment she was lying on the thick carpet, her skirts around her waist. The count was astride her. She struggled with him, more for the pleasure of feeling him using his strength against her than from a desire to escape. Her skirts were up near her chin and partially covered her face. She felt him part her legs and then, without any preliminary caresses, enter her with powerful, deep thrusting movements that were almost like an attack.

Although she was already wet, his man-handling had aroused her even more. She almost sighed with relief as she felt him inside her. She needed him then as badly as he needed her. His urgency stimulated her. She matched his demanding rhythm instinctively. He made no attempt to adapt to her needs, but she found that exciting, too. His orgasm was violent and sudden, and triggered her own. She clung to him as her body shook, and felt his own spasms rocking her. Afterwards they lay together on the carpet, still joined.

It was the thought of being discovered in this position that finally caused Katherine to suggest moving. The count withdrew from her then, gently, and laughed softly. 'No one will come in here,' he said. 'I sent everyone to bed.' She saw him stand and adjust his clothing. Pushing down her skirts, she stood up next to him. 'Go up to your room,' he said. 'I'll follow you shortly.'

When he did appear at the door of her bedroom she was amazed to see that he was carrying a basket. In it were bottles of wine, several traditional cakes, seasoned with spices and rich with honey, and some fruit. The count sat down near a small table and began to unpack the food.

'Are you hungry?' he asked pleasantly. 'Or did you actually find time to eat at Francesca's party?' He held out a glass. 'I'm sure you had plenty to drink. But try this wine, anyway.'

'I didn't drink much,' Katherine said, wondering who had told him where she had been. Frau Grussell, she guessed.

As she walked to the table the count stood up suddenly. 'But first,' he said, 'take off that dress. I'm sure Francesca's eyes have crawled all over it.' He took her by the shoulders and turned her round. 'I'll help you,' he said. He unhooked the dress expertly. 'Has anyone else done this to you this evening?'

'Certainly not,' she said, indignantly. 'What a disgusting suggestion!'

'I believe you,' he said, obviously not in the least contrite. 'But I know all about Francesca's parties.'

'Nothing indecorous went on,' she said, sitting down again and helping herself to one of the spiced cakes.

'Not in the main ballroom,' he agreed. He looked at her, amused. 'Obviously you resisted going upstairs, or to one of the gambling rooms. Congratulations.'

'I couldn't gamble because I didn't have any money,' she said.

He gave her a quizzical look, then laughed. 'My dear Katherine, you don't need money to gamble at the countess's parties.' He poured her a glass of wine. 'Francesca cannot forget her roots. She feels happiest in a brothel. But I'm glad you resisted.'

Katherine sipped her wine. 'The countess surprised me. She speaks excellent English. And she was very honest. She told me she started life as a prostitute.'

'She was only telling you something that's common knowledge,' the count said. 'Although it was a long time ago, and most people are too polite to mention it now. And as for her English, it should be good, it's her mother tongue.' He smiled at Katherine's obvious surprise. 'I see she didn't tell you that? Not many people know. She likes to be thought of as an Italian.'

'But you knew?' Katherine observed.

He shrugged. 'I know a great many things. About a great many people.'

Katherine bit into one of the spiced cakes. 'How long had you been waiting for me?'

'Long enough to begin to wonder whether I should take myself in hand, or call one of the servants.' He lazed back in his chair and smiled. 'There are several here who would come quickly enough, I can tell you. In more ways than one.'

'Well, isn't it lucky that I arrived when I did?' she said demurely.

'Lucky for you,' he said.

'You're not angry with me for attending the party, and not being here when you wanted me?'

'Of course not,' he said. 'You wanted to enjoy yourself before you married, didn't you? I don't expect you to stay at home all day.' He finished his wine and poured himself another glass. His dark eyes watched her. She was expecting a compliment, but instead he said casually, 'You were beautifully wet when I took you. Who were you thinking of, to arouse you that much?'

She was startled enough to almost choke on her cake, and was glad that at least her red cheeks would be ascribed to her quick bout of coughing. 'Hasn't it occurred to you that I was thinking of you?' she said.

He leant back in the chair and laughed softly. 'You're

such a delightful liar, Katherine. That's what I like about you.' His eyes strayed down her body, over the swell of her breasts to between her legs. 'That, and other things, of course. But there is still one thing I want to change. Wait here.'

This time he was gone for some time. She finished another spiced cake and licked some honey from her fingers. When he returned he held two bowls of steaming water on a tray. He put it on the floor by her feet, and she saw that there was also a razor and soap, and a folded towel. He pulled a chair forward and sat opposite her.

'Shave,' he said. For a moment she did not understand what he meant. 'And try not to cut yourself,' he added. 'The razor is very sharp.'

'But ... I don't know how,' she stammered. She actually felt embarrassed. This seemed such a private thing that she was not sure she could do it while he was watching.

'You're blushing,' he said, amused. 'You're not ashamed of your female parts, are you? You English! It's a wonder you manage to reproduce.'

'I'll do it later,' she promised. 'Tonight.'

'You'll do it now,' he said.

'And if I refuse?'

'You'll stay in this room until you obey. I'll have food sent in to you.'

She looked at him. The determined lines of his face convinced her that he was speaking the truth. She fumbled with the razor, opened it and put it down. Then she picked up the shaving brush and soap, and put them down again too.

'Heldenburg women do this every few days,' the count said. 'If they took as long as you, they wouldn't have time to do the cleaning and the cooking.'

She gave him a furious glare, and then picked up the brush again. Trying to ignore his amused look she sat back in the seat, drew up her legs and parted them. Taking the brush she lathered it, and soaped herself. Handling the razor was more difficult. She was so intent on not cutting her soft flesh that she almost forgot he was there, watching her intently, enjoying every move she made. She bent her legs and splayed her knees, smoothing the razor gently over her skin. When she had finished and rinsed off the remaining suds, she put the razor back on the tray.

'Wipe the blade,' the count said. 'That's Solingen steel. Treat it with respect.'

'You sound like a swordsman,' she said.

'It's one of my many accomplishments,' he admitted.

'Are you good?' she asked, lightly.

'I'm unpredictable,' he said. 'Which always gives me an advantage.' He stood up, and stood over her. When she attempted to close her legs he leant forward and held them apart, his palms flat against her inner thighs. Then he knelt down, still holding her legs open. His hands slid upwards, his fingers searching. 'Most Heldenburg women have dark hair,' he said. 'It hides one of their most attractive assets. Your brown curls were very pretty, but I still prefer to have you shaved.' His fingers tantalised her clitoris with quick, light strokes. She felt herself swelling with desire. 'That's what I like to see,' he murmured. 'Proof that you want me. Whores can give you pretty words, and roll about like cats in heat, but it's all fake. They're probably thinking of their girlfriends.' He leant forward and kissed her knee, then continued travelling up her leg until his lips met his lightly moving fingers, and mimicked their caresses.

The warmth of his mouth sent a shudder of delight through her. She opened her legs wider to make it easier for him. The sensation of his tongue made her groan with pleasure. Its teasing movements built up a crescendo of sensation that made her body shake with uncontrolled need. She grasped his head, and pulled him closer, her fingers entwined in his thick hair. Her climax came almost too quickly. She both wanted it and wanted to prolong it. When it overtook her, her back arched and her body stiffened. The overwhelming rush of pleasure forced her to give an uncontrolled cry of delight.

As the sensations subsided she knew she should give the count the same kind of pleasure in return, but for the moment she simply wanted to drowse sleepily. She saw the count stand up and go back to his own chair. He poured himself another glass of wine.

'So,' he said. 'You went to one of Francesca's famous parties, and all the time you thought of me?'

'There was very little else to think about,' she said. She shifted contentedly in her chair, pulling her knees up to her chest. 'I'm not sure what I was expecting, but everything I saw was very decorous.'

'And you were disappointed?'

'Well, no,' she said, awkwardly. 'But I believed there would be some genuine gambling.'

'And I'm sure your father has schooled you well in that activity,' the count said. He sipped his wine. 'Did Francesca introduce you to Oskar von Hohlmann, the soldier turned diplomat?'

'We exchanged a few words,' Katherine said cautiously.

'He didn't respond to your charms?' The count smiled briefly. 'If he knew how well you could handle a whip, he might change his opinion.'

'I was told he didn't care for women,' Katherine said.

'So Francesca did gossip a little? What else did she say?'

'Nothing,' Katherine said uncomfortably. The count stared at her. 'Really, nothing,' she repeated. 'I neither saw nor heard anything worth recounting.'

'Your reticence is admirable,' the count said. 'But unnecessary.' He leant back in his chair and smiled. It was the smile of a lazy predator. 'You could not incriminate any of Francesca's guests. I know everything about them. The important ones, the not so important, and the dregs from Heldenburg's so-called artistic underworld.'

'Perhaps that's why I was treated with such caution?' she suggested. He looked at her quizzically. 'Because of my association with you,' she elaborated.

He laughed. 'I don't think so. I do not have a reputation as a moralist. Once you have established that you are a free-minded woman, you may well get other invitations of a more exciting nature.'

'And you don't mind if I accept?'

'I promised you freedom,' he said. 'I simply ask that you are discreet. In fact, I will be interested to hear of your progress along the more exotic byways of Heldenburg's hidden society.' His expression hardened. 'But always remember, Lady Katherine, in the end you are promised to my son. That does not change. When I decide that you have had enough little adventures, you will marry Ruprecht. And you will bear him a son.' His dark eyes were suddenly cold and dangerous. 'That is your ultimate future. Don't ever forget it.'

Chapter Five

*T*he invitation card was small, cream coloured and embossed with a snarling golden boar. It said simply that the Grand Duke Ferdinand Gustav requested the pleasure of the company of Lady Katherine Gainsworth and Ruprecht Wilhelm von Krohnenstein at the Grand Military Ball.

The count looked at it and smiled. 'So, it has come at last. This is the final seal of approval. If the grand duke likes you, you will be received by every family of any importance in Heldenburg.'

'I thought you'd be pleased,' Katherine said. She faced him across a candlelit table. Elegantly dressed in evening clothes, he had refused any food, but had accepted a glass of wine. 'I have already made arrangements for a new ball gown. I hope you'll find it acceptable.' She smiled at him, sweetly. 'If you visited me more frequently, you could have indicated your approval before I spent your money.'

'My dear Katherine,' he said. 'I am a very busy man. I have duties to perform.'

She let her eyes travel slowly over his dark suit, with its cutaway coat, and starched white shirt, and the red-lined opera cloak that he had tossed over the back of a chair. 'I can see you've been working,' she observed.

His eyes made a similar assessment of her clothes: a silk wrap that she had pulled on hastily when his arrival summoned her from bed. 'I don't listen to opera through choice,' he commented.

She glanced at the ornate clock. Its hands said ten to one. 'And certainly not such a long one,' she observed.

He finished his wine and put the glass down. 'Well,' he said pleasantly, 'having socialised in the line of duty, I felt I was entitled to a little personal indulgence. There was a young lady in the party, the niece of my host I believe, who found it difficult to take her eyes off me for the entire evening. And I have to admit that as she was young, and I suspected she was probably a virgin, I found it equally difficult not to respond.' He leant back in his chair and stretched out his legs. 'I spent the first act wondering what her neat little untouched breasts were like, and whether her nipples were already erect from the thoughts she was clearly having about me. I progressed from there, and kept myself amused throughout the entire opera by imagining myself guiding this sweet young girl through a series of entertaining tableaux, during which she lost all of her clothes and was obliged to assume some very interesting positions. By the end of what could have been a very tedious evening I was more than prepared to be of service to the young lady, and I was confident that she was equally ready to please me.'

'Despite being a virgin?' Katherine asked, not sure whether she believed this story or not.

'You can't be a virgin forever,' the count said. 'I thought she seemed bored with her condition. And she presumably felt that it was better to have her first experience with me, rather than with a fumbling boy of her own age who had probably never seen a naked woman before, let alone handled one. I believe all young women should be apprenticed to an older tutor. Someone who knows there is a little centre of pleasure between a woman's legs that needs arousing. I was offering this young lady an invaluable education.'

'And I suppose she eagerly took advantage of it?' Katherine agreed acidly.

'Of course,' he said. 'We went through the usual ritual of arguing about who would accompany her home, but my host really wanted to attend his club for some gambling, and so it wasn't difficult for me to persuade the young lady to let me escort her. Naturally she directed me to her house, and naturally I took her to mine. She pretended to be annoyed, rather unconvincingly, and she was equally unconvincing when I made it plain that I had not taken all this trouble to get her on her own simply for the pleasure of her conversation. As I stripped her she protested about her modesty, and her honour, and all the other ridiculous excuses you ladies like to produce, but I didn't really notice her struggling too hard to evade me, and I had her naked on the bed before very long, still telling me that she was an innocent, and begging me to leave her alone, and not ruin her.' He smiled. 'A quaint phrase. And a lie. Her nipples were as hard as little berries. I spent some time on them, and I had the impression that when I made a move downward she wanted me to stay where I was. But I was certain she would taste just as delightful when I explored her more deeply, and I was right. Being a well-brought-up Heldenburg woman she was beautifully shaven, and beautifully ready for me. I encouraged her a little more with my tongue and then I took her, and probably gave her the best orgasm she'll ever have in her life.'

'Don't be so sure,' Katherine said, still trying to decide whether he was telling her the truth. 'For many women the first time is a disappointment.'

'Not when I'm the tutor,' he said. 'And the proof is that after she had recovered her breath she wanted me again. What else could I do but oblige?'

'How terrible for you,' Katherine said acidly. 'And how many times did you have to oblige, before she let you go?'

'I lost count,' he said. 'I gave her one last pleasant memory before coming straight here.'

'I don't believe you,' Katherine said.

He stared at her in mock anger. 'You don't?' Then he smiled lazily. 'You're correct. I'll tell you the truth. I wanted to leave early, and save a little of my strength for you, but this young woman was so enamoured with me that she wouldn't let me go. She found some straps from somewhere and tied me to the bedposts.' He shrugged. 'You know my tastes. She was very persuasive. I simply could not force myself to struggle. And when she found a riding crop from somewhere and told me what she'd like to do with it, I just couldn't resist letting her oblige.'

'So you let her whip you?' Katherine asked.

'The opportunity was too good to miss,' he admitted. 'She wasn't as strong as you, but it was very satisfying, all the same. Afterwards she turned me over and, after a little verbal instruction from me, she used her mouth like an expert.' He grinned. 'She was a very fast learner, for a virgin.'

Katherine stood up and walked over to him. 'You,' she said, 'are a liar.'

He lifted one eyebrow quizzically. 'Really? I'm surprised to hear you say that. You don't think I'd have enjoyed that kind of disciplinary treatment?'

'I've learned quite a lot about you since I came to Grazheim,' she said. 'I simply don't believe you'd risk it with someone you hardly knew.'

He looked at her steadily. 'Why shouldn't I trust her? I trusted you.'

'I'm dependent on you, aren't I?' she said.

He smiled. 'I'm glad you accept that.'

'The whole story was a lie, wasn't it?' she persisted.

'If you want it to be,' he said agreeably. He reached

out, grasped her wrists, and pulled her down on his lap. His hand slipped under her silk robe and found her breast. His thumb brushed her erect nipple, gently. 'But you found it arousing, didn't you?'

She shifted her position until she could search between his legs. She put her lips close to his ear. 'So did you,' she said.

'I had to imagine something interesting to keep myself awake during that interminable singing,' he said. 'And when it was over I thought I would pay you a visit, and my host insisted I went with him to a rather dismal club, where I let him win a few games, to make him feel good.' His withdrew his hand and kissed her lightly on the cheek. 'Now make me feel good, Katherine. I deserve it. Stand up and let that robe fall to the ground. Very slowly.'

She smiled, and stood up. Bunching the robe under her breasts, she shook herself so that it slipped off her shoulders. She had pinned her hair up hastily when she knew he was waiting for her, and now some of the pins dislodged themselves and fell on the floor, and her golden-brown curls tumbled to her shoulders. Slowly, teasing him, she gradually revealed her breasts, feeling her nipples protruding under the silk as she let it slide over them. With the robe swathed round her waist and legs, she turned her back on him, let the silky cloth drop to below her buttocks, and then to the floor.

'Come closer,' he instructed. She started to turn round, but he stopped her, his fingers lightly touching her curving rear. 'No, just move backwards.' His hands moved to her waist and he guided her until she straddled his lap.

'Do you feel good now?' she asked softly.

'Yes,' he said, equally softly. He let go of her for a moment, and she felt his cock moving. Then he grasped her thighs and pulled her downwards. She realised that

138

he was guiding her onto his waiting erection. As he entered her, he added, 'But this feels even better.'

She leant forward and bent her legs in order to accommodate him more easily. He moved slowly, almost lazily, pushing deeper and then withdrawing a little, teasing her with gentle thrusts until she felt frustrated by his lack of force and began to take control, contracting her muscles to pull him deeper. She heard him laugh and felt him respond to her urgency. Suddenly his body began to shake with pleasure, and she heard him groan with relief. Her own orgasm was close, but did not coincide with his. Instead she felt a sense of disappointment as he withdrew.

Because she was in such an awkward position, she moved away from him almost at once and picked up her fallen robe. He watched her as he adjusted his clothes again. 'It was good for me,' he said. He paused. 'But perhaps not so good for you?'

'Yes,' she said. 'It was. It's always good with you.' He stood up, elegantly composed now, in his black evening suit. 'It's good just to be with you,' she added truthfully.

He laughed, but she suspected he was pleased. 'You're a diplomat. You are going to need your skills when you attend the grand duke's ball.'

'Why?' She sat down opposite him. 'Is the grand duke difficult?'

'The grand duke is never difficult to beautiful women,' the count said. 'But he doesn't like Ruprecht, and he might well try and persuade you to marry someone else.'

'Who else?' she asked, curiously.

'God knows,' the count said. 'He could even propose to you himself. If he does, you'll have to be diplomatic again.'

She glanced at him mischievously. 'Maybe I'll accept his proposal.'

The count smiled briefly. 'Please don't. It would be

very inconvenient if our Head of State died of exhaustion.'

'Who would take over?' she asked curiously. 'You?'

He laughed in genuine amusement. 'Good God, no. I am not even distantly related to the grand duke's family.' Then he was serious again. 'There are no direct heirs. The grand duke's only son died of smallpox when he was seventeen, and although His Excellency made commendable efforts to father more children, nothing happened. As things stand at present, he would probably be succeeded by his nephew Georg.'

'An eventuality that doesn't appeal to you?' Katherine guessed.

'Georg favours union with Prussia,' the count said abruptly. 'I would prefer the grand duke's second cousin Otto to take control. He has far more sensible ideas. But for that to be possible, there would have to be constitutional changes.'

'And they'd be difficult to implement?'

'At present. Given time, the people of Heldenburg could be persuaded to accept Otto.'

'Do you need the people's approval?' She was surprised. 'Can't you just tell them who is going to be Head of State?'

'If the people are happy, the country is secure,' the count said. 'Most of my countrymen respect the grand duke. It's my job to maintain that situation. Then, if the grand duke eventually tells them to accept Otto, they'll do it, and Georg's supporters won't be able to persuade them otherwise.' He looked up at her. 'Why are we discussing politics? I have to think politics all day. When I'm with you I want to relax.'

'I'm interested,' she said. 'After all, this is to be my country too, and I've been hearing talk of a proposed union with Prussia. Obviously you don't think it would be a good idea.'

'It would be a disaster,' he said, abruptly. 'There are

140

idiots who believe that it would make us prosperous, but small countries are always swallowed up by larger ones, and that's what would happen to us. We need to preserve our neutrality and our independence.' His voice hardened. 'I would sacrifice anything to that end. Including my life.' His dark eyes held hers. 'Or even yours.'

'You mean you'd kill me, if you thought I was a traitor?'

His eyes were dark and cold. 'I would do whatever was necessary to protect the stability of my country.'

Looking at him, with the candlelight throwing shadows on his face, she believed him. Once again she was reminded of a jungle predator, remorseless and cruel. She thought, I don't know him at all. I've shared his bed. I've enjoyed his body. I believe I'm in love with him. But I don't know him. I really don't know him at all.

Katherine watched the count chatting amicably to two elderly, heavily bejewelled ladies, seated on gilded chairs on the edge of the grand duke's ballroom. She found it hard to forget her last conversation with him. She admired his loyalty, but it also disturbed her. He looked as elegant as ever in the dress uniform of the Imperial Heldenburg Hussars. The buttons on his tightly fitted, heavily braided jacket winked in the light from the huge chandeliers that hung from the ballroom ceiling. He was charming the two old ladies, but he still reminded her of a beautiful jungle cat. As dangerous, and as unpredictable. He's nothing like any man I've ever met before, she thought.

Somewhere to her left she could see Ruprecht, drinking yet another glass of wine and looking sulky and uncomfortable in the dress uniform of a cavalry regiment. He had hardly spoken a word to her during their ride to the palace, and looked as if he intended to keep up his glacial indifference for the rest of the evening. Not that I mind, she thought. But she wished the count would come over and talk to her. He had arrived in a separate coach, and so far he had been polite, but distant. Did he mean to ignore her all evening? She watched him with irritation and mounting anger.

'Lady Katherine Gainsworth?' Katherine turned at the sound of a female voice close behind her. A bright-eyed young woman with dark curly hair smiled at her. 'You look at a loss. Can I introduce you to my friends?'

'That would be delightful,' Katherine said, returning the smile. 'But you have me at a disadvantage. Have we met before?'

'No, but I've heard of you. I'm Marie Holzmann.' She linked arms with Katherine and guided her to the side of the dance floor. 'Tell me, are you really intending to marry Ruprecht von Krohnenstein?'

'That was why I came to Heldenburg,' Katherine parried.

'But now that you're here,' Marie countered, 'haven't you changed your mind?'

'Why should I do that?' Katherine asked innocently.

Marie laughed. 'Because I'm sure you would prefer the count!' As Katherine was about to protest, Marie added: 'Don't deny it. If it wasn't already common knowledge in some circles that you're his mistress, the way you've been looking at him ever since you arrived would confirm it.'

'But not the way he's been looking at me.' Katherine was unable to keep the anger out of her voice.

'Oh, is that what's worrying you?' Marie said. 'Don't give it a thought. Haven't you realised yet that we are very traditional people? We all obey the rules in public.' She pointed discreetly to a tall, grey-haired, distinguished-looking man dancing with a dignified woman of his own age. 'That's Baron Theo von Kreuss,' she said, 'dancing so prettily with his wife. Watch and see if he glances this way when he passes.' The couple moved by sedately, apparently with eyes only for each other. 'I've been Theo's mistress for over a year,' Marie said. 'And he didn't even glance at me, did he?'

'You are remarkably indiscreet,' Katherine said. 'How do you know I won't gossip? Maybe to the baron's wife?'

Marie giggled. 'I'm sure you won't. Theo's wife knows all about me, anyway. I was with her for several months before I decided that I preferred to be serviced by a man.'

'That's an even more indiscreet admission,' Katherine said. 'What makes you so sure of me?'

'There are two kinds of people in the world,' Marie said. 'The boring ones, who abide by convention, and those who love to make life an adventure. It's quite clear which one you are.' She smiled at Katherine. 'You are enjoying the attentions of one of the most powerful, and dangerous, men in Heldenburg, and yet I believe you would not be averse to a dalliance with a charming mutual acquaintance, whose name I don't think I need to mention.'

'I really don't understand you,' Katherine said, stiffly.

'Of course you do,' Marie said. 'You must trust me, you know. If you want to see this person again, you must accept an invitation to dine with me next week. Then we'll go to a special gaming house together. I know you love to gamble.'

Suddenly the band stopped playing, leaving the dancers stranded. They hastily moved to the side of the floor. There was a murmur of anticipation among the guests.

'Oh dear,' Marie said. 'The old dears are about to appear. I must find my husband.' She leant forward and kissed Katherine lightly on the cheek. 'Don't forget,' she whispered. 'A personal invitation to dine. Next week.'

She was gone before Katherine had a chance to question her further. Just as unexpectedly she realised that Ruprecht was by her side.

'Time to display our two ancient monuments,' he said, waspishly. 'What a bore this nonsense is.' He offered her

143

his arm. 'Try and look as if you're pleased to be with me.' He smiled stiffly. 'And I'll try to reciprocate. After all, we're supposed to be engaged.'

Before she realised what was happening, he encouraged her forward. The orchestra began to play a rousing march. Katherine looked round for the count, but could not see him. Then the double doors at the end of the ballroom opened. Two people appeared, a tall man in a uniform resplendent with medals and gold braid, and an elderly woman who glittered even more resplendently with diamonds. Katherine did not have to be told that the man was the Grand Duke Ferdinand, although she could not identify the woman. The orchestra changed immediately into a solemn tune. Several of the older men in the crowd pulled back their shoulders and saluted. The grand duke and his companion, flanked by servants who seemed to have appeared out of nowhere, moved forward into the ballroom to greet their guests.

Katherine felt Ruprecht encourage her forward. 'Let's get this charade over with,' he muttered.

'Who is that with the grand duke?' Katherine asked as they edged through the crowd.

'The Dowager Duchess, Helena,' Ruprecht said. 'Old Ferdi's auntie. And don't bother talking to her. She's stone deaf.'

As she moved nearer to the grand duke, Katherine realised that he must have been a commanding figure in his youth. His bushy, snow-white moustache did not disguise the strong lines of his face, and although he was slightly stooped his height was still impressive. The dowager duchess had a face so lined that it was difficult to judge her previous looks. But she looked kind, Katherine thought. Her bright blue eyes gazed round vaguely, and she held the grand duke's arm tightly as if afraid of falling. Given her age and obvious frailty, Katherine thought that this might be a distinct possibility.

She was in front of the grand duke before she realised

it, and her curtsey was slightly awkward and hasty. She saw a white kid glove stretched out to her and, without thinking, grasped the proffered hand and rose to her feet again.

'And who are you, my dear?' The grand duke's dark eyes held hers, and for a moment Katherine was reminded of the count.

'May I present my future wife, Your Excellency?' Ruprecht stepped forward. 'Lady Katherine Gainsworth.'

The grand duke smiled at Katherine. 'Of course. Our visitor from England.' He looked at her with an intensity that she found rather disturbing. She felt his fingers tighten round hers. 'They didn't tell me you were a beauty.' He turned to the dowager duchess. 'This is Sir Henry's daughter,' he explained, loudly. 'From England.' The dowager duchess smiled sweetly at Katherine. 'Lovely girl, isn't she?' the grand duke shouted.

'Delighted, delighted,' the old lady said, clearly not having heard a word. 'So nice to meet you again.'

The grand duke gave Katherine another intense, appraising look. 'Tell me, my dear, is Werner looking after you?'

'The count has been more than kind,' Katherine said.

'Good, good.' One of the servants was trying unobtrusively to urge the grand duke to move forward. The old man seemed to realise for the first time that he was still holding Katherine's hand. He let go of her fingers rather reluctantly. 'I must get Werner to bring you to see me,' he said. 'I visited England, you know, many years ago. We must talk about it.'

Katherine curtsied again as the two of them moved away. It was only afterwards that she realised the grand duke had not spoken a word to Ruprecht.

'What a charming man,' she said. 'I'm rather surprised that he knew my father's name.'

'You shouldn't be,' Ruprecht said ungraciously. 'My

father has obviously been busy currying favours, as usual.'

'I really can't imagine the count doing anything of the kind,' Katherine said, disdainfully.

'Why else do you think we were invited here?' Ruprecht sneered. 'Old Ferdi certainly wasn't anxious to see me. Now that everyone has seen the grand duke fawning over you, you'll be accepted in any house in town.' He laughed harshly. 'Congratulations. You're now a respected member of Heldenburg society.'

'If the count arranged all this,' she said sweetly, 'perhaps I should go and thank him.'

Ruprecht grinned. 'Perhaps you should, dear,' he said. 'And later you can give him his reward.' He tightened his grip on her arm. 'But don't start looking for him now. We have to play by the rules. As long as the grand duke is here, you stay with me.'

It was the last thing Katherine wanted, but she knew she had no choice. She was beginning to understand Heldenburg society. Its superficially conventional veneer masked a hidden underworld of pleasure. A world where a variety of sexual games were played. A world that she knew she was about to enter. A world where she was going to meet Sergei von Lenz again.

Marie Holzmann's invitation arrived two days later. Frau Grussell looked unimpressed.

'The Holzmanns? They're nobodies. He made his money in trade, and she thinks she is special because one of her cousins married a foreign aristocrat, whose name I've quite forgotten. You don't need to associate with such people.'

'Frau Grussell, you are a terrible snob,' Katherine teased. 'I really want to dine with Marie.' She thought for a moment. 'I think I'll wear my new cream satin gown.'

'Such a beautiful gown, for a nobody,' Frau Grussell lamented.

'But I might meet someone important at the dinner,' Katherine said.

'No one important will be at a nobody's dinner,' Frau Grussell sniffed.

Oh, but they will, Katherine thought. She wondered what Frau Grussell would say if she knew about Sergei von Lenz. The old woman seemed to accept her liaison with the count. But would she be so tolerant if she knew I was planning to take another lover? Katherine asked herself. She had a feeling that Frau Grussell would see this as a betrayal, although she clearly accepted the count's lifestyle. Why is it permitted for him to make love to any woman he chooses, but not for me to sample another man? Katherine brooded crossly. She was certain the count was not faithful to her. What did he do with his evenings, when he wasn't visiting her? He certainly wasn't at the opera, or sitting at home with a cigar and a glass of wine.

As she bumped towards her destination in her carriage she felt almost nervous at the thought of meeting Sergei again. It seemed such a long time since that revealing visit to the Peacock Club and yet, she realised, it was less than a month since she had arrived in Heldenburg. She had certainly fantasised about Sergei often enough. Or, at least, about a dark, tall attractive man that looked a lot like Sergei, and also a lot like the count.

Is it possible to be in love with two men at once? she wondered. What would happen if I had to make a choice between them? Luckily, she told herself, that eventuality would never arise. She had not even considered spending her entire life with Sergei. Her relationship with him was going to be an adventure. Something she could look back on with pleasure when she was married to the count.

The Holzmanns lived in a town house near to the

river, set back from the road. An ornate double door led into a wide hall where Marie Holzmann greeted her effusively. 'Dear Katherine, what a magnificent dress. I'm so glad that you could come.' Katherine could hear the sound of laughter from a nearby room. 'Come and meet my husband.'

She led Katherine into a dining room that glowed warmly with candlelight. Several men turned towards her as she came in. The first thing she noticed was that Sergei von Lenz was not among them.

Marie's husband was a portly, vague-looking man, much older than his pretty wife, and the other guests were also middle-aged, and accompanied by women who looked too respectable to be anything other than their wives. Not the kind of people she would expect to frequent a gambling club, she thought, and wondered if Marie had brought her to the dinner under false pretences. Did she really know Sergei von Lenz at all? After the requisite introductions, and an exchange of small talk, they sat down to dine.

It was an excellent meal, but Katherine found it difficult to concentrate on the exchange of gossip. It was obvious that these worthy couples were acquaintances of Marie's husband, and all of them were excited to meet Katherine. 'A friend of the grand duke's', as Marie had shamelessly called her.

Bored and frustrated, Katherine did her best to be sociable but, after the meal and a little more polite talk, carriages began to arrive and soon everyone had gone home.

'Thank goodness for that,' Marie said, as the door closed behind the last departing couple. She smiled apologetically at Katherine. 'You must have been terribly bored, but as soon as my carriage arrives we'll go to the gaming house, and then I hope you'll find that the evening has been worthwhile.'

'I admit that I was rather surprised at your choice of dinner guests,' Katherine admitted.

'Oh, they weren't my choice.' Marie sounded horrified. 'They're all little shop-keepers, people that my husband likes to be nice to so that they buy his goods. They were so anxious to meet you, and I owe Karl a few favours, so I'm afraid I rather used my knowledge about our mutual friend to entice you here.'

'That was rather presumptuous of you,' Katherine said, angry now.

'Don't be cross,' Marie apologised. She moved forward and took Katherine's hands impulsively. 'Karl married me because of my society contacts, and I married him because he was the richest man to ask me. I know he looks stupid, and in lots of ways he is stupid, but he knows all about buying and selling bread and cakes and things. He makes a great deal of money. And he isn't very demanding. About once a month, and then it's over very quickly.'

'Does he know about your lover?' Katherine asked.

'Oh, probably,' Marie admitted. 'But, of course, he doesn't ask questions. And I don't tell. That way we're both happy.' She smiled at Katherine. 'As long as one is discreet, one can do almost anything.' She added slyly, 'Even deceive a man like Count von Krohnenstein.'

'The count has no moral rights to my body,' Katherine said. 'I'm still unmarried. I'm free to do as I please.'

'I'm sure that Werner wouldn't agree with you,' Marie said. 'He's very dominant, isn't he? Very possessive?'

'He's always been a gentleman with me,' Katherine said. She had no intention of offering Marie any titbits of gossip.

'Really?' Marie hinted. 'That's not what I've heard. Unless by gentleman you mean he acts like a stallion. I've been told that he had some unusual tastes.' She hesitated. 'A friend confided in me that he allowed a

149

woman to whip him.' She glanced at Katherine expectantly. 'I have to say that I didn't believe a word of that.'

'Quite right,' Katherine said. 'Can you imagine such a thing?'

But later, travelling with Marie in her elegant carriage, Katherine realised that her companion was not going to give up so easily. She badgered Katherine continually during the journey, obviously hoping for a juicy piece of scandal about the count that she could later spread among her friends. Katherine refused to oblige, but she was glad when the carriage clattered to a halt and she was free from Marie's constant questioning.

It was difficult to see what kind of house they had arrived at. The carriage was close to a door that opened immediately when Marie knocked, and Katherine only had a brief glimpse of a narrow street before she was inside again, her cloak was taken and she was ushered into a large room, lit by a magnificent central chandelier. Under the chandelier men and women sat at a large green-covered table and seemed to be playing a betting game, although there was no money on the table, and the game was not one that Katherine recognised.

But she did recognise one of the players. Sergei von Lenz was in close conversation with one of the women. Whatever he was whispering, she was obviously finding it highly amusing, and seemed reluctant to move away. In fact, Katherine thought with a stab of jealousy, she was moving her head seductively, her light-brown hair ruffling against Sergei's glossy black, and although Sergei's mouth was hidden Katherine was certain that his lips and tongue were caressing the girl's ear.

She stood by the door waiting for him to look across and acknowledge her. She knew he had seen her come in. Most of the the other men had looked up, and several had given her an approving smile. Sergei, looking relaxed and rakish in his black evening suit, seemed determined to ignore her.

'Do you want to play?' Marie sidled up to Katherine.

'I have no money,' Katherine said. 'I didn't come here to gamble.' She felt like adding, 'I came because you implied that I'd meet Sergei. In fact, I believed that he had asked you to arrange the meeting.' Now, as she watched him allowing the brown-haired woman to drape herself round his shoulders and rub her lips over his face, she was not so sure. Confused and angry, she wondered if he had asked Marie to arranged this meeting, or whether Marie had simply done it without consulting him.

Suddenly, amid laughter, Sergei threw down his hand in disgust. The brown-haired woman's mouth formed a little circle of surprise and disappointment. A young man with a bushy moustache stood up and smiled. Sergei elegantly disentangled the girl's arms from his shoulders. She seemed reluctant to let him go.

'Your luck's deserted you, you Russian magician,' the moustached man crowed. 'Run out of tricks to make the cards jump to your commands, have you?'

He came round the table and, as he did so, Sergei caught the girl by the wrist and twisted her away from him. 'I'm simply feeling generous,' he said.

The girl fell against the other man, who caught her and pulled her close. She opened her mouth to protest and he kissed her, forcing her head back at an uncomfortable angle. The kiss lasted a long time. The men at the table began to count and beat the table with their hands. When she was finally released the girl's face was flushed, but Katherine thought she looked far from unhappy with the situation

'Come on, sweetheart.' Her companion spun her round. 'Show them what they've lost, and what I've gained.'

Amid cheering he unhooked the back of the girl's dress, then slipped his hands under her armpits and fumbled for her breasts. With her help he lifted them out of the now loosened bodice and displayed them like two ripe fruits. The girl pretended to protest, but Katherine could see that her nipples were tight with pleasure. The man spun her round, and bent his head to take one nipple in his mouth. His friends applauded. The girl put up a token struggle, but her expression indicated that she was enjoying being the centre of attention.

Katherine glanced at Sergei. He had turned away from the exhibitionistic couple, and was gently shuffling a pack of cards. She watched his hands, hypnotised by the easy elegance of his movements. Then she glanced up. Sergei was looking at her, his dark eyes unreadable. As she stared back at him, he made the cards dance once more, then gathered them into a pack and placed them deliberately on the table.

'Time for another game,' he said loudly. He fixed his dark eyes on Katherine. 'Won't you join us?'

The table rearranged itself in some sort of order. The man with the moustache was still nuzzling the girl, but when he realised he was no longer being watched he patted her on the behind, and tugged her with him over to the door. A ragged cheer followed him, but the men and women at the table had now turned their attention to Sergei and Katherine.

'I have no money,' Katherine said. 'I didn't come here to gamble.'

'But if you had, you'd have come well prepared?' Sergei's voice was harshly sarcastic. 'With English guineas, no doubt?'

She stared at him angrily. This was definitely not the kind of welcome she had been expecting. 'I can look after myself at the tables, sir!' she said tartly.

'I'm sure you can,' he said smoothly. His dark look challenged her. 'So sit. And play.' He shuffled the cards again, in an elegant flurry. 'We're playing for forfeits now,' he said. 'You don't need money.'

The group parted to give Katherine room to sit down.

Brief introductions were made, quickly and informally, using first names only. Katherine did not recognise any of the people present.

'You bet on a full hand,' Sergei explained. 'Four aces overrule everyone. The Royal Family are almost as important, especially if they're all in the same suit. Or four pip cards of the same number. You'll soon remember the combinations. It's all pure luck, so everyone stands the same chance.'

She looked at his deft fingers working with the pack, and wondered if they were his own cards. He noticed her gaze and smiled. Suddenly he looked like the man she remembered. The dark, wild gipsy who could make her forget the count, and any thoughts of marriage.

'I use the cards provided by our host,' he said. His smile was suddenly a personal challenge, and she knew he was well aware of what she had been thinking. 'If it would make you feel more comfortable, I'll use any pack you care to give me. Have you brought one with you?'

'No,' she said, wishing that she had. 'I told you, I didn't expect to gamble.'

'Then you'll just have to trust me,' he said. 'Like everyone else.'

'And you'll have to trust me to make good any losses,' she said, wondering how she would be able to pay if she lost a large sum of money. Would the count meet her debts? She rather doubted it.

'You don't need money.' Marie said. 'Forfeits means exactly that. If you win you can ask anyone here to give you something.'

'In this game,' Sergei said, 'it will be an item of clothing.' Again he smiled at Katherine. 'Are you happy with that?'

'As long as you are,' she said.

She watched him deal, with the fast practised movements of an expert. The game started light heartedly. Cards were inspected, single cards discarded, others 'bought' on payment of small articles like rings, a fan, or a kerchief, which were dropped in a common pile and were obviously intended to be recovered at the end of the evening. The discarded cards were placed face upwards on a separate pile, and could not be reused during that game. One player finally decided to call and laid down a winning hand; his forfeit demand was his companion's jacket, which was surrendered willingly enough. The next few games had equally innocuous results.

Katherine noted that despite joining in the light conversation and responding to the often suggestive remarks of the other players, Sergei was watching the pattern of play intently. She was certain he always had a fair idea of each player's hand. After a few games, she had a similar knowledge. A friend of her father's had once taught her an effective method of memorising each card in the pack by associating it with a simple but foolish mental image, and then linking them in similarly absurd groups. Although it was by no means an infallible method, it was a good memory aid and enabled her to keep better track of her opponent's various hands than simply relying on chance.

To begin with, it wasn't really necessary to use her method. She 'lost' a ring in one game, and her fan in the next. More bottles of wine were brought, and as the players became more inebriated the winners became more reckless in their demands. Coats and shirts were discarded, and then one woman was obliged to give up her dress. The winner had the pleasure of unhooking her bodice and helping her out of the garment. He performed with drunken gallantry, rather spoiling the effect by also attempting to expose her breasts at the same time. A light but stinging slap discouraged him, although Katherine felt certain it was only a token gesture. Without thinking she turned her head and found herself looking directly at Sergei.

He was watching her with a very faint smile of anticipation. As she held his gaze, ignoring the raucous disruption going on around her, he picked up the cards and performed a complicated shuffle with a controlled elegance. 'As you can see,' he said, 'the game is getting more interesting.' He paused. 'If you wish, you can retire.'

She tilted her head defiantly. 'Why should I want to do that?'

The cards danced in his hands. 'All forfeits have to be paid,' he said.

'I'm glad you realise that,' she countered.

The other players stopped their horseplay and glanced at each other, and then at Katherine and Sergei, sensing the sudden tension between them. Katherine suspected that a duel of wits was something they understood, and if one of the partners was going to end up stripped, that was even better. She remembered that the moustached man had called Sergei a 'Russian magician', implying both that he was lucky with the cards and that maybe his companions suspected his luck was not always pure chance. She had a feeling that the men might like to see Sergei lose. And she did not doubt that the women would like to see him stripped.

Very well, she thought, watching him deal. You've manoeuvred me into this situation, Herr von Lenz, and I'm certain now that for some reason you want to embarrass me by getting me to pay some kind of humiliating forfeit or other. But you've picked the wrong victim. I'm not as innocent as you might think. And, she realised, not as drunk as almost everyone else round the table, either. Sergei, she knew, was sober. Professionals always stayed sober. She watched his long fingers handling the cards with the skill of a lover, and despite her anger she could not help imagining them touching her with the same degree of expertise.

He won the first game, helped partly, she thought, by

the carelessness of the other players. She wondered how much money he had won before she arrived. The cards lay fanned on the table, three aces and a king.

He pushed his chair back and stretched out his long legs. 'Well now,' he asked, softly. 'What are you prepared to give me, Katherine?'

'It's up to you to choose,' she said, tartly.

'In that case, your stockings,' he said. 'I'm sure they're best-quality silk. Count von Krohnenstein is known for his generosity to his ladies.'

There was a ripple of laughter round the table, and to her own annoyance Katherine felt her cheeks flush. 'I buy my own clothing, sir!' she said sharply and untruthfully.

Sergei stood up, and she was reminded of a lazy cat stretching after sleep. Preparing, she thought, to hunt. She realised that he exuded the same kind of controlled danger she found so attractive in the count. He walked round the table and stood in front of her.

'Then let's see if your taste is equal to his,' he said, agreeably. She lifted the hem of her skirt just far enough to reach her garter and was about to release one stocking and roll it down when he leant forward and stopped her. His long fingers touched hers, very lightly. 'I won,' he said, very softly. 'Remember?'

The sensation of his hands on her skin sent a shiver of pleasure through her. She did not mind him fumbling deliberately with her garter, his thumbs caressing her inner thigh. She did not mind him pushing the garter out of the way far higher than necessary, or the exciting touch of his fingers smoothing round the top of her stocking to loosen it. She enjoyed the slow way that he rolled the silk down, teasing the hollow behind her knees, circling her ankles, removing her shoes, brushing the soles of her feet and briefly massaging her toes.

She did mind that she found it very difficult to sit still and pretend that she was oblivious to his deliberate fondling. Her heart was beating faster than normal, and her nipples – thankfully hidden – were tight with desire.

'Best quality,' Sergei said, when he had removed the second stocking. He held them both up, but his eyes were on her. 'Very best quality.'

She wondered if she had misjudged him earlier. Perhaps he had arranged this meeting after all. But surely he did not intend to strip her in public? When he won the second game, and claimed the removal of her dress, she was not so sure. Once again he unhooked her bodice slowly, but when she attempted to lower the dress herself he grasped her hands and pulled them behind her back, holding her wrists with one hand and loosening the bodice with the other. She wanted to lean back against him, close her eyes and enjoy it, but her pride forbade her to be so obvious. Instead she held herself rigidly while his fingers brushed the swell of her breasts and took much longer than necessary to remove the dress completely.

'You'd make a good lady's maid, Sergei,' a man commented.

'You can have a position in my house,' Marie offered coquettishly.

'Yes, and we know what kind of position,' someone else laughed.

Sergei smiled at Marie. 'Any position would be delightful, with you,' he said.

Katherine was irritated to realise that she felt a stab of jealousy. All right, she thought. You've had your fun, Herr von Lenz. Now it's my turn.

She forgot that she was sitting in her underwear in a room full of strangers. If you want to be successful at the gaming tables, a friend of her father's had once told her, avoid anything that depends solely on luck, concentrate, and never underestimate your opponents.

She had no intention of underestimating Sergei. This time she played to win. When she finally laid down her hand, two aces and two kings, she was confident that no one else at the table could beat it, including Sergei. The fleeting look of surprise on his face confirmed it, and was the best reward she could have asked for. She walked round the table as proudly as if she was still fully dressed, and stopped in front of him. He stared up at her, his face unreadable.

'My choice this time, I believe?' she said sweetly.

'Take his trousers,' someone suggested. 'Let's see what all the ladies find so exciting.'

'Next time, maybe,' Katherine said. She held out her hand. 'This time I'll have your coat, if you please?'

She knew she had surprised him again. He stood up and took off his black cutaway coat slowly. Taking it, she slipped it on. She felt the warmth of his body still in the cloth.

'She looks better in that coat than you did,' someone commented.

'She'll look even better in your trousers,' someone else said.

Sergei shrugged, apparently unconcerned, and shuffled the cards again lazily. But Katherine knew that she had alerted him now. Her comments had implied that her win was not the result of sheer luck, and also that she intended to repeat her success. She wondered if she had been foolish to boast. But the gambling fever had gripped her, and she wanted to know if she could outwit him on equal terms.

She knew he was taking her more seriously during the next game. But she also knew that he wasn't sure exactly how she had gained her previous advantage over him. She had to admit that she was equally unsure of him. What kind of tricks did he use to ensure his success? She hoped she had eliminated any sleight-of-hand advantages by getting him to remove his jacket. Even so, by the time she called and laid down her cards she found she had only beaten him by a queen. This time he looked less blasé about his defeat.

She was tempted to humiliate him by asking for his trousers, but the drunken requests of the other women round the table discouraged her. Much as she wanted to strip him, it was for her personal pleasure, not theirs.

She looked at him coolly. 'Your shirt, sir,' she said.

'Oh, you have no imagination,' one of the women lamented, laughing. 'Shirt, indeed. She's treating you far too leniently, Sergei.'

'But she hasn't finished with him yet,' one of the men predicted. 'Soon we'll get to see what appeals to all the ladies. Eh, Sergei?'

Sergei smiled rather stiffly, and began to unbutton the evening shirt, with its starched front and cuffs. He wore nothing underneath, and his chest, with its dark body hair, was as tanned as his face. He was not as obviously muscular as Jack Telfer, whose bulging biceps were the product of physical labour. Or as solidly built as the count, who was beautifully proportioned and powerful. But he had a sinewy elegance that hinted at both strength and agility. She could not imagine him as a wrestler or a pugilist, but she could see him as a swordsman. A man who would move with deadly grace, and strike with the speed of a cobra. He bunched up the shirt and handed it to her, across the table. She took it and tossed it casually over the back of a chair.

'Luck does seem to be favouring you tonight, Katherine,' he said. 'But luck is a fickle mistress.' His mouth twisted into a brief, and not particularly friendly, smile. 'Perhaps you should give up now, while you are still winning.'

Was that a challenge? Katherine wondered. Or a warning? Either way she had no intention of backing down. And she hoped he would not do so, either.

'I'll take my chances,' she said, lightly. 'The same as everyone else.'

'So let's make the game more exciting,' he said. 'We'll play for something more valuable than an article of clothing. I suggest one thousand marks?'

'I don't have that sum of money with me,' she said.

'I'll trust you to procure it,' he answered. He fanned the cards on the table, and gathered them together again. 'Unless everyone would like to agree to another kind of bet?'

'What do you suggest?' she asked, wary now.

'A personal service? The winner can claim from anyone here. And they will agree on their honour to perform.'

There was a sudden silence round the table. Then Marie laughed. 'I'm willing to bet my personal services. I'm sure they're worth more than a thousand marks!'

Sergei was staring intently at Katherine. She was certain now that she would end up in bed with him, but winning a game in front of these people had obviously become a point of honour for him. Did he think she was going to back down and give him the game? If he did, she thought, he would very soon discover his mistake. She had her pride, too!

'Done,' she said. She watched the cards moving through his fingers. 'But I'll shuffle.'

'She doesn't trust you, Sergei,' one of the men commented with a grin.

Sergei handed her the pack of cards. 'Don't drop them,' he said politely.

She gave him a cool smile. 'I'll try not to.' She had learnt to handle the cards from her father and some of his friends, and now she demonstrated her skill with fluent ease. Sergei watched her expressionlessly. Then he leant back in his chair. He smoothed the palms of his hands against his thighs, then pulled his chair in closer to the table.

They began to play, but Katherine knew that there was a tacit acceptance that this game was a duel between her and Sergei. She expected it to be a lengthy game, but he called, far sooner than she expected. She still only had a queen and a jack coupled with some lower value pip cards. She looked at him in surprise, and he smiled briefly, then laid down his hand slowly. Three aces and a jack. She could not believe it. She knew that he had cheated, but she could not imagine how.

He tipped his chair back, and glanced round the table. 'I believe,' he said, 'that I've won.'

'They say the Devil looks after his own,' one of the men said, tossing down his cards. 'And he certainly seems to look after you, you Russian conjurer.'

'He does, doesn't he?' Sergei agreed softly. His dark eyes fixed on Katherine. 'You did agree to the terms of my bet,' he reminded her.

Katherine met his gaze imperiously. 'Are you suggesting that I'm going to refuse to honour it?'

He stood up, and walked round the table. 'I wouldn't dream of implying such a thing,' he said. He picked up his shirt and slung it over his shoulder. 'My coat, if you please,' he requested.

She slid the coat off and handed it to him. 'What exactly do you want me to do?' she asked.

'Come upstairs,' he said, 'and I'll tell you.'

She picked up her dress, retrieved the jewellery she had used to 'buy' cards in the earlier games, and followed him out of the room, ignoring the ribald comments that accompanied them both. Sergei said nothing to her until they reached an upper room. He pushed open the door and preceded her inside. The room was furnished with easy chairs and a large four-poster bed. Heavy curtains blanked out the windows. Several lamps were burning, giving a welcoming glow. But there was nothing welcoming about Sergei's first words when she closed the door behind her.

'You lied to me, English Rose,' he said. He walked towards her, and all she could think of was how attractive he looked. Lean and half-naked, his skin burnished gold in the lamplight. 'I don't like that.'

'Lied?' she repeated, genuinely confused. 'When?'

'When I first met you,' he said. 'You had no intention of breaking your association with Count von Krohnenstein.' He moved closer to her, his face shadowed now. 'You couldn't buy a house in Grazheim, even if you wanted to. All that talk about the honour of marrying a von Krohnenstein was nonsense. You're a penniless fortune hunter. You have to marry – anyone who'll have you.'

She stared at him defiantly. 'You've been busy asking questions,' she said. 'But just remember that I never made any false claims. You were the one who offered to find me a house in Grazheim, if I remember? I never said I had money. You simply assumed it.'

He reached out and caught her shoulders. His strong fingers dug into her flesh. 'You let me assume it,' he said, harshly. 'And don't flatter yourself that I wasted time asking questions about you. I didn't need to. You've already become quite a talking point in Grazheim society.'

'The kind of society you mix with, you mean?' she threw back at him. 'Gamblers and whores?'

He gave her a long, dark look. She could feel the heat from his body as he stood close to her. She tried hard to keep her expression form revealing how much she wanted him.

'You're a rose with thorns, aren't you?' Suddenly he stooped down and picked her up. Turning, he carried her to the bed and threw her unceremoniously on to it. It happened so quickly that she did not have time to protest. All she could think of, absurdly, was that Jack Telfer would have scolded her for her lack of attention. But then, she thought, as she lay with her legs apart, looking up at Sergei von Lenz, it's difficult to concentrate when a man who looks like a wild and exciting lover is

162

staring down at you as if he's planning to take you by force.

'Not only are you a liar,' Sergei said. 'You're a cheat.'

'Because I beat you at cards?' She laughed in delight. 'I didn't cheat. That was skill.' She sat up on the bed. 'You cheated! If you hadn't, I'd have won that last game too.'

'A liar.' He caught hold of her and flipped her over on her stomach. She tried to struggle but, for the first time, she realised just how strong he was. He held her down easily, her arms crooked behind her back. 'And a cheat.' She felt her skirts being tugged up to her waist, and then his hand landed on her bottom and she yelled both with surprise and a strange kind of relief at the physical contact.

The next blows were hard, and rapid. She wriggled and kicked, but her flailing feet only struck air. When her underskirts got in the way of Sergei's relentless hand, he dragged them higher up her body, and then tossed them over her head, muffling her cries and leaving her naked from the waist to the top of her gartered stockings. She could feel her flesh glowing, each new slap bringing a fresh wave of delightfully welcome, stinging pain. She also felt her corset loosening and, when he finally stopped spanking her and turned her over again, her breasts were exposed and her taut nipples showed clearly that she was far from displeased at the treatment she had received so far.

He sat down on the bed next to her, and placed the tip of his finger on one nipple. She felt a thrill of pleasure shoot through her body and gave an involuntary gasp. He smiled then, and pressed harder, rubbing in a circular movement, then sliding his finger up the slope of her breast until his hand cupped her. Pushing her back he leant over her, and kissed her.

The pressure of his mouth was light at first, and his tongue touched her lips gently, probing them apart. As

163

she responded, his kiss became more demanding, and his mouth forced hers open. Their tongues met, and caressed. It was a long kiss and ended only when they were both breathless. When he let her go Katherine fell back on the bed, her heart pounding.

'A liar,' he repeated, 'and a cheat.' He laughed then, and tugged at her corset, opening it wider. 'Rather like me, I suppose. Perhaps that's why I like you so much, English Rose.'

'You admit that you cheated,' she challenged.

'Of course,' he said. 'I palmed the aces while I was bunching up my shirt, and then hid them between my legs when I pulled my chair closer to the table. Simple.' He struggled with the back laces. 'Much simpler than undressing you.'

She laughed and helped him, undoing the ties that fastened her underskirts. In a few minutes she was completely naked except for her shoes, which she quickly kicked off. He propped himself up on one elbow and looked at her with an expression that was as exciting to her as the touch of his hands and mouth.

'Quite beautiful,' he said.

He reached down to unbutton his trousers but she stopped him. 'Let me,' she said.

He smiled then, and lay back on the bed, linking his hands behind his back and stretching his body luxuriously. 'Take your time,' he said.

She wished then that she had not already forced him to remove his coat and shirt. She had intended to explore him slowly and comprehensively, and undress him with the same pleasure that one took in unwrapping an exciting parcel. Feeling the movement of his body as he grew progressively more aroused. Tasting his skin, enjoying the sensation of his nipples growing hard in her mouth. Turning him over and tracing the path of his spine down to the cleft between his neat buttocks. Smoothing her hand over the long line of his thighs, imagining the bulge of his erection, hidden from her, then turning him over to see his cock springing up, hard and ready. Maybe hearing him groan as she took him in her mouth and teased him with her lips and tongue. Frustrating him with her deliberate slowness.

She had intended to enjoy herself for a long time, but suddenly she found she could not contain either her curiosity or her desire for him. She tugged at his trousers and, when the buttons refused to open, almost ripped them in her haste. His erection was everything she had imagined. In fact he was bigger than she expected, but now all she wanted, with erotic urgency, was to feel him inside her. Feel his body warm and strong against hers. Feel him thrusting deeply, and to know that she was giving him pleasure.

She straddled him quickly and guided him into her warm depths. If he was surprised at her aggressive directness he showed no signs of it. His hands circled her waist, and then slid to her buttocks, and he pulled her close. As she began to move her hips he adapted to her rhythm and moved with her. She looked down at his glossy hair, dishevelled on the white pillow. Then his dark face twisted into a spasm of mounting sexual need, and she felt his body stiffen, felt him push harder and deeper, losing control.

She was amazed and delighted to feel her own orgasmic pleasure corresponding with his. In fact, it outlasted him in its intensity, and receded gradually, leaving her lying against him, breathless and damp with sweat, but fulfilled and relaxed. She enjoyed the sensation of his lean body still stretched out under hers, until he gently withdrew from her and rolled over onto his back.

'That wasn't quite what I planned,' she said.

'Really?' He laughed softly. 'It was almost exactly what I planned.'

'I wanted it to be slower,' she explained. 'I wanted to enjoy it longer.'

'There'll be other times,' he said.

'You want to meet me again?'

'Of course.' He sounded surprised. 'I promised to educate you, remember? I've been looking forward to it.'

'Then why did it take you so long to arrange this?' she asked. 'And why do it this way?'

'Because I was angry,' he said. 'You deceived me. I intended to punish you. To force you to strip in front of those drunken idiots downstairs.' He propped himself up on one elbow, his face close to hers. 'In the end, I couldn't do it.' His finger traced the outline of her lips and then strayed down to the line of her throat. 'I don't know what came over me. I'm not usually so kind.'

'Well, I wanted to do the same thing to you,' she admitted. 'But then I decided I didn't want to share any part of you with those other women.'

He grinned lazily. 'You mean you expect me to be faithful to you?'

'Of course,' she said.

He rolled over to face her. 'While you're servicing the Count von Krohnenstein? And don't deny it, it's common knowledge. He certainly didn't set you up in a house of your own because he has a kind and generous heart.'

'As you've already pointed out,' she said, 'I'm a penniless fortune hunter. He's my future father-in-law. I have to be polite to him.'

Sergei gave a snort of laughter. 'Polite? That's the first time I've heard it called that. But don't worry, I'm not jealous. In fact I would be disappointed if you weren't accommodating the count.'

She put her hand on his chest and smoothed it across to his nipple. 'Why?' she asked.

'Because I like to think I'm having the pleasure of something he thinks is exclusively his.'

'You don't like him?' she guessed.

166

'Nobody likes the Count von Krohnenstein,' he said. 'It's difficult to like someone and be afraid of them at the same time.'

'So you're afraid of him?' She played with him gently, and felt his body responding.

'I'm not afraid of anyone,' he said. 'I simply don't like the way he plays God. But he makes a lot of people nervous, although most of them wouldn't admit it.'

'He's always been perfectly charming to me,' she said.

'Of course he has,' Sergei agreed. 'Just don't ever cross him.' He grinned, and stretched out on the bed. 'And don't stop doing that,' he added, glancing down at her hand.

'The count wouldn't harm me,' she said, but there was a faint doubt in her mind. 'Why should he?'

'You don't sound absolutely certain,' Sergei said. 'Just remember that the count is dedicated to keeping Heldenburg out of Prussian hands, and keeping that silly old fool the grand duke in power. If you threaten that, you'll see another side of him. An unpleasant side. And being a woman won't help you. Neither will the fact that you've shared his bed. The count has arranged for women to disappear before.' Sergei drew one finger lightly across her throat, and made a slicing sound. 'Believe me,' he said. 'It's the truth.'

Katherine remembered discussing Heldenburg's neutrality with the count. She remembered his words: *I would sacrifice my own life. Or even yours.* And she remembered the expression on his face. She had believed him then, and she believed Sergei now.

'Don't forget, this isn't England,' Sergei added. 'And Werner von Krohnenstein certainly isn't an English gentleman. Don't get involved in his politics, English Rose. Stay innocent, and you'll be safe.' He caught her hand and lifted it to his mouth, kissed her fingers lightly then guided them down between his thighs. 'But not too innocent,' he added.

He lay back on the bed, relaxed again, and she admired the sleek lines of his body, his narrow hips and flat abdomen, the silky darkness of his body hair. She wanted to smooth her hands all over him, feel the texture and warmth of his skin and the movement of the muscles and bones beneath it. She wanted to taste him, taste the salty tang of his sweat and the warmth of his mouth. She wanted to watch his nipples harden and see his penis engorged and straining upwards with desire for her.

She could feel it swelling now, under her caresses. She bent down and closed her mouth over its tip, running her tongue round its sensitive rim. She heard him groan. He opened his legs wider and she slipped her hand under him to cup his balls and massage them gently too. She wanted him inside her, and he was certainly stiff enough to enter her now, but he groaned again and murmured, 'Don't stop.'

She felt him grow even harder in her mouth, and his body began to shake. 'Not yet,' he muttered hoarsely. 'Too soon.' She attempted to move her mouth elsewhere, but his body bucked with sudden violence as his orgasmic tremors surged and exploded. His hands held her, crushed her head roughly against his groin, and she tasted him intimately. To her surprise, experiencing his orgasm like that was equally as satisfying as having him enter between her legs.

She moved away when she felt him subsiding. He lay back on the bed with a satisfied smile. 'I love that,' he said. 'There are women who won't give a man that pleasure, God knows why.' He turned towards her with his familiar, brilliant smile. 'You must let me return the favour, sometime.'

The thought of his mouth on her, and his tongue delighting her, made Katherine feel aroused again. No one else has ever made me feel like this, she realised. Not even, she thought, rather guiltily, the count. She could have happily made love to Sergei again and again.

And, she thought, with a secret smile, again! She hoped he was going to make good his promise there and then and felt a pang of disappointment when he sighed, stretched and said, 'It's been delightful, English Rose, but I must go downstairs again.'

She leant across him and kissed him. 'Why? Am I boring you?'

He laughed. 'No.' She reached for his nipple but he caught her hand and moved it away. 'I'd happily stay up here and exhaust you,' he said. 'But there are some plump birds here just waiting to be plucked.'

'Is that how you make your money?' she asked. 'I suspected it.'

'You're not going to tell me that you're shocked?' He swung his legs off the bed and stood up. Even in its relaxed state his cock was impressive. 'You're no stranger to the tricks of the trade yourself.'

'I've dabbled,' she said modestly.

'Taught by your father, no doubt?' When she looked surprised, he grinned. 'The Count von Krohnenstein isn't the only one with secret sources of information.' He reached for his trousers. 'I told you we were two of a kind.'

She watched him dress, and reflected that he was just as attractive with his clothes on. Then he helped her back into her dress, hooking her up expertly.

'You've done this before,' she said.

He kissed the nape of her neck. 'And I'll do it again,' he promised. 'Next time, at my house. I've rented one on Hochmeisterstrasse.'

'How will you contact me?'

He kissed her mouth this time, deeply, leaving her breathless. 'Don't worry,' he said. 'I'll do it discreetly. We belong together. Teacher and pupil.' He backed away from her and smiled again, and she felt her body tingle. 'The trouble is, after the way you've behaved this evening, I'm not sure now which one of us is which.'

Chapter Six

'This is an excellent wine.' The count put down his glass and smiled at Katherine. 'But you didn't ask me to come here just to tell you that.'

He was dressed formally and had already told her that he was on his way to dine with a friend. The knowledge that he continued his social life without ever inviting her to share it always angered Katherine.

'Everyone knows about us,' she had accused him once, 'so what does it matter?'

'What they know doesn't matter,' he had agreed. 'But what they see, does.'

'The wine was a gift from the grand duke,' she said. She took a small card from the table and handed it to him. 'With this invitation.'

He glanced at the card. 'A personal invitation to visit His Excellency tomorrow night?' He shrugged. 'Why consult me? It's addressed to you.'

'I want to know the correct procedure,' she said. 'What will be expected of me if I accept?'

The count looked at her in surprise, and then burst out laughing. 'My dear Katherine, what do you think will be expected of you? That you'll have to bed the grand duke?' His laughter stopped abruptly. 'Would that worry you so much?' His voice was suddenly cold. 'I don't believe you had similar objections when asked to perform for a liar and a cardsharp?' The accusation was so unexpected that she felt her cheeks flush. He added softly, 'Did you really think I didn't know about your little dalliance? I know everything you do, Katherine. Haven't you realised that by now? I know all about the gambling parties where women who should know better are happy to take off their clothes and pay forfeits. And I know all about men like Sergei von Lenz, who are equally happy to relieve them of their money, and anything else they care to offer.'

Katherine tilted her head up defiantly. If this was going to be a confrontation, she felt ready for it. The sight of Sergei von Lenz, naked on the bed, was burned into her mind. She still found the count both desirable and exciting, but if he forced her to make a decision, at that moment she knew who she would chose.

'So what are you going to do?' she asked. 'Send me back to England?'

For a moment he looked at her intently, his dark face unreadable, and then, to her surprise, he burst out laughing again. 'You English! I'll never understand you. Why should I send you home? You came out here to marry my son, and that's what you're going to do. I'm willing to be lenient with a few little indiscretions. Providing, of course, that you're always here for me when I need you. After all, I am paying for this house.' He leant back in his chair. 'I've never been over-possessive about my mistresses. At times I've even shared them with my friends.' He smiled, sardonically. 'Would you like that, Katherine? Would that excite you?'

'No,' she said, stiffly.

'But Sergei von Lenz was different, eh?'

'I had drunk too much wine,' she said.

'If you're going to lie to me,' he advised, 'try to be

more imaginative than that.' He pointed to the humidor. 'Good wine should be followed by a cigar. Get me one, please.'

She brought him a cigar and watched as he lit it. 'What exactly do you know about von Lenz?' he asked.

'I know he's a gambler,' she said.

The count blew a thin stream of blue smoke towards the ceiling. 'Is that all?'

'What else is there to know?' she countered.

'I hope you don't find out,' he said cryptically. 'But I also hope you don't think that the charming Sergei can be persuaded to save you from marrying Ruprecht. Acting like a knight in shining armour is not the kind of behaviour that men of his kind indulge in.'

'I don't need anyone to save me from anything,' Katherine said.

He stood up. 'No,' he said. 'I don't think you do. You're an independent woman, aren't you, Katherine? And an adventurous one as well.' He put the cigar back in his mouth and drew on it. The end glowed bright red. He was close enough for her to feel the warmth on her skin. When he removed the cigar, he held it as if he was about to touch her with it. 'Tell me,' he asked softly. 'Did you play games with your new friend Marie Holzmann?'

'Games?' she repeated, genuinely mystified.

'Did she proposition you?'

'Certainly not.' The accusation was so unexpected that she did not even feel angry.

'Don't pretend you didn't know Marie likes to bed women,' he said.

'I did know,' she admitted. 'She was quite open about it, in fact. But I don't care for that sort of thing.'

He laughed, and blew a stream of sweetly scented blue smoke towards the ceiling. 'You've never tasted a woman, Katherine?'

'No, I haven't,' she said, sharply.

'You sound angry. Does the idea shock you?'

172

'No.' She shrugged. 'It simply doesn't interest me.'

He tapped the ash delicately off the end of his cigar. 'Accept the grand duke's invitation,' he said. 'You might find it educational.'

Katherine had reviewed her conversation with the count several times during the previous day, and she remembered it again now, as the grand duke's carriage took her to the palace. What exactly had the count meant by this visit being educational? And what was it that he had implied she did not know, and would not want to know, about Sergei von Lenz?

She had, at first, been surprised and pleased at his easy acceptance of her 'dalliance' with Sergei, although she wondered if he would have been quite so sanguine if he could guess how deeply she had been affected by the incident. But later she realised that his relaxed attitude towards her could be construed as an insult. He had treated her as if her behaviour did not matter much to him. It forced her to reassess her position.

It was clear that he still saw her simply as Ruprecht's future wife. She felt sure he would be far more possessive if he had considered the possibility of marrying her himself. And what was she to make of that comment about sharing his mistresses? She did not see herself as his mistress, although she supposed that to others that might well seem to be her position. She had not considered it before, but suddenly it seemed grossly unfair that the only status a sexually active single woman could aspire to was mistress or whore. In other words, someone who was owned or bought. Why are there not similar insulting categories for single men? she thought angrily.

The carriage stopped outside the grand duke's palace. She heard the staccato exchange of recognition words, and then the metal-bound wheels clattered over cobbles and halted. She was helped down and realised that she had not come in through the main gates, but through a small side entrance that she heard being bolted behind her.

Once inside, an obsequious footman led her to a large comfortably furnished room and asked her to wait. She looked round the room. There was a huge oil painting over the fireplace: the grand duke, probably aged about thirty, in the full ceremonial regalia of a Heldenburg Hussar.

'I was a handsome figure of a man in those days, if I say so myself.'

She turned. Grand Duke Ferdinand Gustav stood in the doorway, casually dressed in an embroidered smoking jacket and pale trousers. He came towards her with his hand outstretched. She took it and curtsied but he tugged her gently to her feet.

'No, no, my dear. This is informal. I see too much damned bobbing up and down during the day.' He led her by the hand to a chair. 'Just sit there, and talk to me.' He sat opposite her, and smiled. She saw his eyes travel over her face and then down to the creamy swell of her breasts, where they stayed far longer than politeness allowed. She suddenly wished she had chosen a more discreet dress, with a higher neckline. The grand duke might not have been capable of servicing a woman, but from the expression on his face he certainly had not stopped thinking about it. 'Tell me – ' he indicated the portrait ' – would you have been attracted to that young fellow? Handsome, eh?'

'He's very handsome,' she said, deliberately avoiding a straight answer to the first part of his question. 'But I'm sure many women told him that, over the years.'

'True,' the grand duke agreed. 'But not so many lately.' He picked up a small hand bell and rang it. 'Perhaps it's just as well. Couldn't take advantage of the compliments these days.' He winked at her slyly. 'If you understand me?' A footman came in pushing a trolley loaded with silver dishes full of cakes, and several bottles of wine.

'Thought you might be hungry,' the grand duke said. 'Eat up, and tell me how you're enjoying my country.' He paused. 'And if you intend to stay?'

'I'm to be married, sir,' she said.

'To that little swine Ruprecht, eh?' The grand duke snorted impatiently. 'A damned waste. I told Werner.' He poured her a glass of wine. 'You don't harness a thoroughbred to a cesscart. That's what I told him. Plain and straight.'

'And what did he say?' Katherine asked.

'He wants a son,' the grand duke grunted. 'A real son. You understand me? Someone to carry on the tradition. Can't talk him out of it.'

'I thought maybe the count might have remarried,' Katherine suggested. 'Instead of forcing Ruprecht to do so,' she added, rather lamely.

'The boy ought to marry,' the grand duke said. 'Looks bad if he doesn't. If he marries and has a son, then he's done his duty. Looks good. You understand me?'

'So it's all to do with masculine pride?' Katherine said.

'Tradition,' the grand duke corrected. 'Very important to Werner. He's a good man. They've always served us, you know? The von Krohnensteins. He has the country's interests at heart.'

'I understand he opposes any union with Prussia,' Katherine said. 'He's very emphatic about it.'

'Oh, politics,' the old man muttered, peevishly. 'That's all I hear these days. Didn't used to be like that. The people knew their place, and I knew mine. Everyone was happy, and there wasn't all this talk of change.' He leant forward and pushed a plate of sugary cakes towards her. 'No politics tonight. Hate to hear a pretty woman talking politics, anyway. Leave that to men like Werner. They thrive on it.' His eyes brightened again. 'Eat your food, my dear. I've arranged a little show for you afterwards.' He patted her knee. 'Not easily shocked, are you? You enjoy a gamble, so I've heard.' He smiled. 'And a good fucking from the gentlemen.'

She was so surprised she nearly choked on her cake. As it was, her coughing brought tears to her eyes. The grand duke was obviously delighted with her reaction. He leant closer, his eyes bright. 'Now, don't pretend you're an innocent. Werner keeps you happy, eh? Women seem to like him. Mind you, I was more than a match for him at one time. Not any more though.' He sat back and let his eyes stray over her again. 'When I was younger I'd have stripped you by now. I'd have inspected your lovely nipples, and had you spread your legs nice and wide for me.'

He was watching her face now, and she realised suddenly that she was quite safe with him. It was her reactions that he wanted to see. She also guessed that he did not want her to brazenly swop lewd comments with him. It excited him to think that he was embarrassing a well-brought-up young woman. Very well, she thought, if those are the games you want to play, I'll oblige you.

He leant closer and she could see a sheen of sweat on his face. 'Tell me, my dear, do you shave?'

She lowered her head demurely. 'I have been taught to observe the local traditions,' she said.

'Werner taught you, eh?' He was obviously delighted. 'Did he shave you himself, or make you do it?'

'Really, sir,' she said. 'That is a very indecent question.'

'Haven't shocked you, have I?' He was clearly delighted at the idea.

'Surprised me,' she corrected.

He chuckled, pleased. 'I'll surprise you again before the night's over. Eat your cakes, my dear. Then come and see what I've arranged to entertain you.'

She managed to eat another cake, although they were really too sweet for her taste, and washed the sugary confection down with a mouthful of wine. When she finally convinced him that she could not manage another mouthful he stood up and held out his hand.

'Come with me, my dear. I'm going to let you see my private playroom.' He led her to a door which opened into a dark passage. 'Not afraid of the dark, are you?'

'No,' she said truthfully.

'It's part of the surprise,' he said. 'Take my arm. I'll guide you.'

She allowed him to lead her along the passage, fully expecting him to try and touch her, or maybe try to kiss her, in the darkness. She was prepared to repulse him, but was surprised and glad when he made no attempt at physical contact. Instead he hurried her along by pressure on her elbow. They went through another door and, although it was still pitch-black, she instinctively felt that she was in a large room. The grand duke guided her to a chair and sat down next to her. Then he clapped his hands loudly.

'Lights!' he ordered.

Katherine saw servants in dark clothing slipping round the walls, igniting the lamps. The effect was almost as if they had sputtered into flame on their own. Then a row of lights appeared on the floor in front of her and she realised that what she had taken for a wall was actually a curtain. It swished open and she was looking at the interior of a room, with paintings on the wall and a large chaise longue occupying a central position. It was only when she looked more closely that she realised the pictures were all of nude women sprawled about in sexually explicit positions. She guessed the kind of entertainment the grand duke was going to provide in his private theatre, and when it began her suspicions were confirmed.

A young woman came through a door and mimed exhaustion, sinking on to the chaise longue and loosening her clothes. A young man appeared almost immediately, and after a very short exchange of compliments, suggested

177

that if she was very hot she should remove her dress. She demurred with fake modesty, but was soon persuaded. He helped her. Before long she was naked. He tipped her backwards, legs outspread, and began to explore her with his mouth, tugging at her nipples while she moaned encouragements, and moving slowly down to her thighs. Katherine watched him, partly out of interest, and partly because she had a curious feeling that she knew him. A feeling that she realised was ridiculous. Unless, she thought, I've seen him at a party, and maybe been introduced to him, but forgotten him until now.

'Not shocking you too much?' The grand duke's voice startled her, close to her ear.

'Well, yes,' she lied. 'It's very explicit.'

'Never seen anything like it, eh?'

'Oh, never,' she agreed.

In fact, she thought the sexual coupling being enacted in front of her was remarkably restrained. The young man remained fully clothed, using only his mouth and hands to pleasure his companion. He spent a long time with his head between her legs, while she squealed and moaned, and finally thrashed about in a noisy orgasm. As she did so, another woman opened the door. She wore a rather masculine riding habit and carried a short whip. Apparently furious, she rushed forward and separated the rutting couple. The naked woman mimed contrition, kneeling on the floor, but it was quickly decided that she should be punished. She was unceremoniously hauled to her feet and bent over a small stool. Her hands were held by the young man, and the older woman whipped her with a great show of enthusiasm, while she kicked and struggled ineffectively. Katherine felt the grand duke's eyes were on her and not on the stage.

'Have you ever been whipped like that, my dear?' It was a hoarse stage whisper. 'By Werner, maybe?'

'Certainly not,' she said, rather more sharply than she intended.

'But you'd like to be?' the grand duke guessed. 'Most women like the man to take control, eh?'

'I'm not sure that I would like it,' Katherine said, untruthfully.

A commotion on the stage distracted the old man. The naked girl had been banished from the room, but the young man was now making up to the older woman. While she pretended to protest, he stripped her as neatly and expertly as a lady's maid. She was large-boned and buxom, and was soon on her back being tongued enthusiastically by her male companion. After reaching the inevitable noisy conclusion, she fell back on the chaise longue and appeared to fall into a contented sleep. The door opened and the original woman appeared again, still naked. Helped by the man, she upturned her original tormentor and spanked her soundly, her own laughter overriding the other woman's yells of protest.

The grand duke was clearly enjoying himself, alternating his attention from the performers to his companion, but Katherine was beginning to feel bored. It was all too obvious and too repetitious. And she was surprised – and just a little disappointed, she had to admit – that the young man was not given the opportunity to display his masculinity. What was the matter with him? Was he a eunuch? And where, she thought, irritated by the mystery, had she seen him before?

A commotion on the stage brought her back from her brief reverie. The two women seemed to have heard her unspoken thoughts. The larger one had grasped the young man and held him captive while the younger woman knelt in front of him and began to open his trousers. But instead of revealing an erect penis she mimed delight as she uncovered a huge dildo, unrealistically thick and with an obscenely painted red end. It was then that Katherine realised the truth, and felt

179

ashamed of herself for not guessing it sooner. The young 'man' was in fact a woman. She also realised, almost at the same time, why this 'man' looked familiar. It was Yvonne Tressilian!

The dildo was so clumsily ludicrous that, as Yvonne proceeded to couple with each of the women in turn, Katherine was briefly embarrassed for the first time that evening. She was genuinely glad when both women had been 'satisfied' and the curtains closed.

'Have I shocked you too much, my dear?' the grand duke asked hopefully, with such pathetic eagerness that she almost felt sorry for him.

'Yes, indeed you have,' she said. She smiled at him, and then demurely lowered her eyes. 'But you've excited me, too.' She looked up at him appealingly. 'I would so like to meet the performers. Can you arrange it?'

'Of course I can.' The old man sounded delighted. Then he hesitated. 'Would you like to play games with them, too? I can arrange that. Would you like to be an actress, eh?'

With you watching me, no doubt? Katherine thought crossly. Any feelings of pity she had for him evaporated.

'Oh no, that wouldn't interest me,' she said. 'I'd just like to speak with them.'

The three women were still in their heavy stage make-up when Katherine went behind the curtains. The two who had been cavorting naked were wrapped in shawls. They greeted the grand duke with a mixture of familiarity and servility. From her shocked expression Katherine knew that Yvonne had not recognised her behind the footlights, either. While the two other women were teasing the grand duke by pretending to be too modest to display themselves to him, she managed to edge closer to Yvonne.

'This isn't the kind of acting I expected you to be doing,' she whispered.

'This isn't the kind of performance I expected you to be attending,' Yvonne whispered back.

'We must meet,' Katherine said. 'Where are you staying?'

'At an inn on Glockenstrasse, but you can't visit me there. It's a very rough area.'

'Tomorrow night,' Katherine interrupted. 'Eight o'clock.'

As Yvonne was about to protest, the grand duke turned towards them. 'Now, my dear, stop making assignations with young men.' For a moment Katherine thought he had actually overheard her conversation with Yvonne. 'Well-endowed young men, too,' the old man added, wagging his finger. 'I think I'd better send you home. Can't have you making Werner jealous.'

Sending one last meaningful look towards Yvonne, Katherine followed the grand duke out of the room. In the carriage she felt suddenly elated. She genuinely wanted to meet Yvonne again, but she also felt certain Yvonne would know about Sergei von Lenz. Maybe she could answer some questions about his background – including the details that the count had refused to tell her.

Putting on her male clothes again gave Katherine a strange sense of freedom. As she had never ventured out on the street in these clothes before, she took a few extra precautions. Strips of cloth bound round her breasts flattened them, and ensured that her riding jacket no longer bulged in the front, disguising her female shape quite adequately. With her hair tucked up under her hat and the brim pulled down at a rakish angle, she felt that she made quite an acceptable young man. All that was needed now was to lengthen her stride and swagger a little.

She had planned a secret escape route from the house as an idle entertainment, never believing that she would have to use it. Now, as she clambered through a downstairs window in the dark, she felt a thrill of excitement. This was one jaunt she was certain the count – and Frau Grussell – would never know about.

She felt surprisingly safe walking through the streets in her male clothes. It was a strange experience to be jostled by passers by, and to have other men push in front of her as they hurried past. It was even stranger to be looked up and down invitingly by two women in fashionable clothes who had just stepped out of a carriage.

The inn on Glockenstrasse was not difficult to find. Once inside, Katherine soon spotted Yvonne sitting in the far corner. Yvonne looked up when Katherine entered, but obviously did not recognise her. Amused, Katherine made her way over to Yvonne's table. Yvonne hardly glanced at her.

'You look lonely, madam,' she said, dropping her voice to a lower octave. 'May I sit with you?'

'No, you may not,' Yvonne said sharply. 'I'm waiting for a friend.' Suddenly she added, 'Oh, my God!'

'Changed your mind?' Katherine asked softly, sitting down.

'What are you doing in those clothes?' Yvonne demanded.

'Meeting you,' Katherine said. 'And you're a fine one to look shocked. At least I'm not wearing a dildo.'

'Are you crazy?' Yvonne was laughing now. 'Suppose someone recognises you?'

'You're the first one who has,' Katherine said. 'Did you expect me to come out here in Count von Krohnenstein's carriage?'

'I didn't really expect you to come at all,' Yvonne admitted. 'Even with my limited German, I've picked up the gossip. The Count von Krohnenstein's mistress? You're famous!'

'I do hate being called a mistress,' Katherine said.

'You mean you're not fucking him?' Yvonne asked, bluntly. 'Why ever not? I've seen him. From a distance, it's true, but he looks like everything a woman could want in a man.'

'We have a close relationship,' Katherine said. 'It's just that I don't consider myself his mistress.'

'Well, everyone else does,' Yvonne said. 'And if you want to give him up, there'll be no shortage of offers to take your place. As you'll find out,' she added slyly, 'when you marry his son.'

'If I marry his son,' Katherine corrected. Before Yvonne could say anything more, she added, 'But I want to hear about you.'

'Well, you saw what's happened to me.' Yvonne shrugged. 'The troupe I joined disbanded after a couple of weeks because they never could decide who was going to play the leading roles. The trouble was, I wasn't paid. So I was on my way back to England with what was left of my savings, when I met these two women. I told them my sad story, and they told me they were actresses too, and performed dildo plays. Maybe you won't believe me, but I didn't really understand what they meant at first. When they asked me to join them it sounded like a good way to fill my purse. We take it in turns to play different roles and, to be honest, being tongued by a woman who enjoys doing it is a lot better than having it done by a man.' She looked at Katherine speculatively. 'Well, most men, anyway. Perhaps your dashing count is an exception?'

Katherine deliberately ignored the question. 'But how did you come to be performing for the grand duke?' she asked.

Yvonne shrugged. 'Because we were paid. I don't make the arrangements. Lise – she's the younger one – does all that. I just turn up and wear my dildo, or get spanked or tongued, or both, and take my money. When

I've saved enough I'm going back to England to start my own troupe.'

'So you don't know how long you'll be in Heldenburg?'

'Well, a little while yet,' Yvonne said. 'We're very popular, and not only with the men. Women pay us, too, and they often want to join in our scenes. You wouldn't believe it, would you? These people look so straight-laced, but they're worse than the French! And the grand duke loves us. We've done three performances for him already, and he always brings different young women, although I never thought one of them would be you.'

'Neither did I,' Katherine admitted.

'But surely you've been invited to some of the less conventional parties?' Yvonne hinted. 'I understand that this country isn't as dull as it appears, once you know the right people.'

Katherine shrugged. 'I really don't know much about that.' She added casually, 'I imagine you're the kind of person such people would invite though, aren't you?'

'Oh, I wouldn't say that,' Yvonne said, equally casual. 'I'm usually too tired for such pleasures, or too busy.' There was another pause, then Yvonne laughed. 'Come on, now, you're angling to ask me something naughty, and I do believe you're too embarrassed to come out with it.' She leant forward. 'What is it? Do you want to employ our troupe to spice up your evenings with the count?'

'Certainly not,' Katherine said. 'It's just that I met someone. And I wondered if you knew him. Or anything about him.'

'Like whether it's safe to fuck him?' Yvonne nodded. 'Well, if it's someone you think is better than your count, I'd like to meet him myself. Who is it?'

'A man named Sergei von Lenz,' Katherine said.

Yvonne's smile disappeared. 'You've met him?'

'Briefly,' Katherine hedged.

'He's gorgeous,' Yvonne said. 'But don't even think about having any kind of affair with him.'

'Why ever not?' Katherine asked. 'I know he's a gambler, and probably a dishonest one, but . . .'

'Gambler?' Yvonne laughed disbelievingly. 'Well, that's what he'd like everyone to think. But Lise told me his real profession is theft. He's been at some of the performances we've given, the very private ones, in rich patrons' houses, and she pointed him out to me. She saw him in Florence, and later on she heard there'd been a big robbery there. Mainly jewellery. Sergei von Lenz, or whatever he calls himself, charms his way into people's houses, and into women's beds, and before they realise it he's disappeared with their diamonds.'

'But there's no proof,' Katherine objected.

'Where does he get his money from?' Yvonne said. 'He claims to be Russian, and he's always hinting at rich family connections, but I think that's all lies. He lives well, and spends generously on his women, so where does he get it all from? Certainly not from gambling. That's just a disguise. He's a thief, believe me.' She leant forward and grasped Katherine's hand. 'He's not the kind of man you want to become involved with. You've got too much to lose. And you don't need him. The von Krohnensteins are rich. You have a future with them. If Sergei von Lenz stays in Heldenburg, and tries anything here, he'll end up in Schloss Ohlm. The big prison, you know? Or if your count gets hold of him, he may even end up dead.'

Before Katherine could answer a man lurched past their table, tripped and flailed wildly to keep his balance. His arm struck Yvonne's glass, and tipped the remains of her wine into her lap.

'Clumsy oaf!' Yvonne said furiously, in German. She stood up and shook her skirts. 'Look at that. You've ruined my dress.'

The man rocked on his feet, and squinted in an effort

to focus. Yvonne's cloak had slipped from her shoulders and as she brushed at her skirts the man was treated to a good view of her ample breasts. He leered at them, admiringly.

'Well now, little darling.' His voice was slurred. 'Why not take the dress off?' Yvonne gave him a furious look, which he ignored. 'Come on now, let's see all of those lovely tits.' Reaching forward he grabbed at Yvonne. She slapped his hand away. 'Not shy, are you?' He laughed harshly. 'You don't look the shy sort.'

'Bugger off, you drunken pig,' Yvonne said viciously, in English.

The man might not have understood the language, but he certainly understood the sentiment. His expression turned ugly. 'Who'd you think you're talking to, you foreign bitch?' He reached forward and clamped a huge hand round Yvonne's wrist. 'I bet lots of men have paid to stick their pricks up you. And I'll bet you enjoyed every minute of it, too.'

Yvonne tried to disengage herself, without success. As he reached out with his free hand to grab at the front of her dress, Katherine stood up.

'You're annoying my lady friend,' she said, as gruffly as she could.

The man turned to her in surprise. 'And who are you?' he jeered. 'Her baby brother?'

He let Yvonne go and turned to tower over Katherine. She guessed he was more than double her weight, but he was also drunk and obviously unsteady on his feet. And she had another advantage over him. He would not be expecting her to give him any trouble.

'My lady friend doesn't want your company,' she said, 'and neither do I.' She saw Yvonne gazing at her in horror, and was also aware that the other customers in the inn were now watching with interest. She knew she had done the one thing she should have avoided, drawn attention to herself, but she did not care. A strange surge of excitement was making her feel reckless. 'And if your prick is the same size as your brain,' she added, 'you won't be much good to her anyway.'

Yvonne moved forward, pushed past the man, and grabbed Katherine's arm. 'Are you mad?' she muttered. 'Let's go.'

Katherine turned towards her, but out of the corner of her eye she saw the man lurch forward again.

'Not so fast, you. I want an apology.'

His forward movement was just what Katherine had been waiting for. She grabbed him, and pulled him forward, off balance, as he came for her – just as Jack Telfer had taught her, kicking at his ankles at the same time. It was the last thing he was expecting, and it worked perfectly. He pitched forward and crashed over a table, demolishing it as he slithered to the floor.

Yvonne and Katherine made good their escape during the resulting commotion, but it was only when they were several streets away that they finally stopped for breath.

'I can hardly believe what I've just seen,' Yvonne said. 'I've tackled some rowdy men at times, but I'd never try to throw one like that. I usually kick them in the balls.'

'I didn't throw him,' Katherine said. She was delighted to find that the tricks Jack Telfer had taught her actually worked. 'His own weight did that.'

'Well, you helped it,' Yvonne said. She looked at Katherine admiringly. 'You are full of surprises, aren't you? God help your husband if he deceives you.'

The incident had made Katherine feel light-headed. She almost felt like going out and picking a quarrel with another man, just to see if the same trick would work twice. But common sense prevailed, and instead she made arrangements to keep in touch with Yvonne for as long as she was in Heldenburg, and then made her way back to her house.

As she took off her male clothes and hid them away again, she thought about Yvonne's comments on Sergei.

Was he really a jewel thief? She had to admit that it sounded quite plausible. She remembered their very first meeting, when Sergei thought she was a local boy. He had offered her money for information about the area. Why else would he need such details?

Strangely, the idea of Sergei as a thief did nothing to diminish her feelings for him. If anything, she felt even more attracted to him. She imagined him slipping through the darkness like a cat, his lean body wearing tight black clothes to enable him to move swiftly and safely. It was an arousing and attractive image. She knew that she was romanticising an illegal activity, and if someone had robbed her she would have been angry and upset, but she could not help visualising Sergei's lithe figure appearing at a darkened window, climbing silently in, rummaging in jewellery boxes and finding diamonds, pearls, drop earrings, bracelets. Stuffing them in his pockets and then realising, suddenly, that he was being watched by a woman on the bed. What would happen? In real life, she thought, the woman would probably scream and Sergei would escape, maybe leaving the jewellery behind. But supposing she was the woman on the bed, and he came towards her, the jewellery still in his hands, and asked her what price she would pay to get her baubles back?

She lay down and closed her eyes, and let her thoughts wander. He would suggest that she dress in the diamonds, and dance for him. She imagined herself clothed in nothing but gems. Strings of pearls wound in her hair, bracelets round her feet and ankles. A belt of sparkling diamonds round her waist, with a little loincloth of woven pearls in front, covering her shaven lips. And a collar round her neck, she thought, with a leash made of strung pearls. He would hold one end and pull her to him, inch by inch, a glittering prize.

She imagined swaying, her body tantalising him, and each time she moved he would tug her closer, until at last he could reach out and touch her shoulders, forcing her down to her knees. He would stand in front of her, a dark contrast to her own pale ornamented flesh. He would unbutton his tight breeches for her, and she would nuzzle her mouth close to his erect cock and hold it between her lips, exciting it with her tongue. Maybe he would permit her to place her hands on his taut buttocks and hold him as his body shook with mounting delight. Maybe he would refuse to pleasure her, and simply insist that she pleasured him.

What was it she found so irresistible about him? she wondered. Did she envy him the way he lived his life without conforming to the kind of conventions she knew would soon rule hers? Or was it simply that he was so physically attractive she could not think of him without also thinking about undressing him, and making love? She ran her hands over her body. Her nipples were already hard from her fantasy. Did he feel this way about her? Did he dream of her? She rather doubted it. Her common sense told her that he might well forget her as soon as she was out of his sight. Did she mean anything to him at all? she wondered. Or was she just a passing amusement, perhaps just a little bit special because she also belonged to Count von Krohnenstein?

And that's who I should be thinking of, she told herself. The man I hope to persuade to marry me. And it would be easy to think about him if I hadn't met Sergei. That Russian gipsy jewel thief, with his wonderful smile, has pushed his way into my mind, and I can't forget him. I don't want to forget him.

She wriggled uncomfortably as her body reacted to her thoughts. Her hand crept down between her legs. She felt her clitoris peeping out between her parted shaven lips, and stroked herself urgently. This could be Sergei, she thought. Or it could be the count. Either of them would please me. I could watch them as they performed, and know that they were enjoying it as much as I was.

Her orgasm came suddenly, but left her frustrated rather than satisfied. Why can't I have them both? she fretted. Men marry and have mistresses. Why can't I marry Werner von Krohnenstein, and keep Sergei von Lenz as my ... what? There isn't even a word for the male equivalent of a mistress. What an unfair world this is.

She remembered her thoughts as she lay next to the count after making love. He had been remarkably tender, almost romantic, undressing her very slowly, kissing her in unexpected places. The crook of her elbow, the soft skin behind her knees, the hollow of her neck. He turned her over and ran the tip of his tongue lightly down her spine, to linger at its base, making her squirm with pleasure as he circled the little spot between the cleft of her buttocks. When he turned her again she needed no pressure on her inner thighs to encourage her to part her legs for him and let his mouth reach its intended goal. She was already wet and swollen, and the rapid movement of his tongue sliding over her clitoris incensed her still more. She writhed on the bed, thrusting her hips towards him with such wanton movements that he stopped what he was doing and laughed softly.

'Whoever said that English women were cold? They had certainly never met you.'

'Did anyone tell you,' she groaned, 'that men should not talk when they should be performing?'

He propped himself on one elbow, and she felt the heat of his naked body warming her. 'So you want me, do you?' His fingers touched her lightly, offering relief, and then straying up to her navel, and circling there, frustrating her. 'So ask me. Beg me, Lady Katherine. Let me hear you talk like a whore.'

190

'Fuck me, please,' she moaned. 'Now. I want you now.'

He straddled her then, and entered her swiftly, thrusting deeply, and her orgasm came almost at once, surprising her with its intensity. She heard him laugh. He took longer over his own release, using her body almost roughly, as if he were extracting payment for his previous unselfish foreplay. Afterwards, when his own orgasm had subsided, he lay next to her. 'Did you enjoy that, Katherine?'

'I always enjoy it with you,' she said truthfully.

'Did you find the grand duke's little entertainment equally arousing?'

Startled, she turned to him. 'No. Why do you ask?'

'I've often wondered how women react to watching members of their own sex tongue each other. Did it shock you?'

'The performance didn't,' she said. 'But I was surprised to see the grand duke drooling over a group of woman playing around with a dildo. I thought he was a nice old gentleman.'

'What a funny set of values you have, Katherine,' the count said, amused. 'Because a man is old, or even a gentleman, it doesn't mean he stops thinking about sex. At one time His Excellency would have been up there joining in the performance. What would you have thought about that? Nowadays he just has to be content to watch, while a pretty young lady sits next to him.' He glanced at her. 'I provide suitable young ladies, from time to time.'

'So you procure for him?' she observed, tartly.

She saw the count's face change. 'I serve the grand duke,' he said coldly. 'This little weakness of his doesn't affect his position as Head of State. As long as he holds that position, and the people love and respect him, Heldenburg will have political stability. Discrediting the grand duke would be the first step to deposing him, and deposing him would be the first step to union with Prussia. What I think of his private life is immaterial. If he enjoys himself with women that I approve of, women that I know will not tell tales, his little secrets will not become the subject of public gossip.' He glanced at her. 'Do you find that immoral?'

'As a matter of fact, I do,' Katherine said. 'I'm sure the people wouldn't respect him if they knew he was a lecher and a voyeur. He's getting their loyalty under false pretences.'

The count's face relaxed again, and he laughed. 'My dear Katherine, a man's performance in the bedroom doesn't affect his ability to govern, and the world contains very few saints.' He reached out and touched her cheek in a surprisingly affectionate gesture. 'You must learn to accept life as it is, not try and make it into something that it never can be. That way you won't ever be disappointed.'

Katherine had several opportunities to reflect on the count's words during the next few weeks. What she wanted most was to carry on her affair with Sergei von Lenz, without the count knowing. And what seemed to be happening was that she was being frustrated at every turn.

The only point of contact that she had with Sergei was Marie Holzmann, but although Marie had sent her several invitations, the count always wanted her company on the days in question. She received another invitation from Countess Montrossi. Although she was no longer excited by it, she accepted. This time one of the small groups that seemed to drift away to pursue entertainments of their own suggested that she joined them. But when she realised that their intention was to indulge in multiple sexual couplings, she refused to participate. The countess expressed surprise, and Katherine guessed that she would not be invited to attend any more of the famous Montrossi parties.

She knew she should be happy with the knowledge that the count seemed more relaxed with her now. Maybe, she thought, because he knew that he was preventing her from seeing Sergei? And he had not mentioned her marriage to Ruprecht for some time. But the need to see Sergei filled her with frustrated desire. She began to try to think of ways to get to him. She dared not use Marie Holzmann, partly because the count seemed to know everything Marie did, and partly because she did not really trust Marie not to gossip. But she did trust Yvonne Tressilian. If only she could get a message to Yvonne she was sure the Englishwoman would be able to find out exactly which house Sergei had rented on Hochmeisterstrasse. Then, dressed in her male clothes, she would pay Sergei a visit.

She decided that the direct approach was best. She would leave a letter for Yvonne at the inn, suggesting a meeting place in a few days' time. That should give Yvonne enough time to find Sergei's full address, if she did not know it already. She was ready to go out when a carriage clattered to a halt outside. The front door slammed and there was the sound of raised voices. 'No, no,' she heard Frau Grussell say, 'Lady Katherine has not been out. She stayed in yesterday evening. She has been in all day.'

The door opened and Frau Grussell burst into the room. Before she could speak, Katherine demanded, 'What has happened? Who is asking questions about me?'

'The count is here.' Frau Grussell glanced round nervously, as if expecting eavesdroppers. 'Something bad has happened. Very bad.' She gave Katherine a guarded look. 'And it concerns someone you know.'

'Someone has been hurt?' Katherine felt her stomach churn in apprehension. Had Sergei been shot during a robbery? She imagined him lying in a pool of blood on the floor. 'What has happened?' she demanded, suppressing a desire to shake the information out of Frau Grussell. 'Tell me at once!'

'The count will tell you himself,' Frau Grussell said. 'But it's bad,' she added dolefully. 'Very bad indeed.'

Chapter Seven

'*A* robbery?' Katherine did not know whether to be relieved or angry. 'Is that all? From the way Frau Grussell was carrying on I thought there must have been a murder, at least.'

'A murder would have been better,' the count said grimly. He flung himself in a chair. 'Get me wine, Katherine. I need it.'

'I have schnapps,' she offered. 'It works faster than wine.' He accepted a glass and downed it in one gulp.

'Surely you don't need to be involved in a robbery investigation?' she asked.

'In this one, I do,' he said. He stared at her, his face unreadable. 'It involves jewellery, and some papers that could be worth much more than the jewels, if they were offered to the right people.'

'Blackmail?' she guessed. He nodded. 'And you think Sergei is involved?' she said.

'Of course von Lenz is involved,' the count snapped. 'He's obviously been·planning this for some time. Planning and waiting. But I have no proof yet.'

'Do you need any?' She smiled sweetly. 'Why not just

drag him off to a dungeon? I thought you did that kind of thing here.'

The count gave her a look of exasperation. 'We don't do that kind of thing here, as you are well aware. This is a civilised country. Herr von Lenz has provided me with the names of people he claims will give him an irrefutable alibi. At the moment all I can do is suggest that he doesn't consider leaving Grazheim. If he ignores my suggestions, then I can detain him.' The count stood up and began to pace about. A caged panther, she thought. Waiting to pounce. 'The names he's given me are unusual,' he said. 'They're respectable people. Not the kind I would have thought would lie for a man like von Lenz.'

'Have you considered that you're condemning him without proof simply because you don't like him?' she suggested.

'No, I haven't,' he said, irritably. 'He's guilty. And I intend to prove it.'

'And then?' she asked.

'He goes to Schloss Ohlm,' the count said. 'For a very long stay. A long stay with no sunshine, and no women.' He gave her a sharp, cruel look. 'And no visits from friends.'

'You hate him a lot, don't you?' she said.

The count shrugged. 'He's a criminal. He doesn't know the meaning of the words patriotism, loyalty or honour. I despise men like that.'

'Sergei might think that your dedication to that old lecher, the grand duke, was equally reprehensible,' she said.

'My dedication is to Heldenburg,' the count said. 'And the people of Heldenburg. The grand duke is just a symbol. My loyalty to the grand duke is the same as my loyalty to the flag.'

'I think Sergei would find that ridiculous, too,' she said.

He took a couple of steps towards her and put his hands on her shoulders. 'Tell me the truth. When did you last see Sergei von Lenz?'

'At Marie Holzmann's party,' she answered.

'I believe you,' he said.

'Mainly because you've made it impossible for me to arrange to meet him again,' she added.

'Perhaps I've done you a favour,' he said. 'At least you won't be involved in any investigations.' He paused. 'And you won't be tempted to try and give him an alibi.'

'You think I'd lie for him?' She hoped she sounded suitably shocked.

He put one hand under her chin and tipped her face up. 'You'd lie for him,' he said, softly. 'And the trouble is, you're not the only woman in Heldenburg who'd do so.' He glanced at the schnapps. 'One last drink, and then I must go.'

'To carry on with your investigation?'

He looked at her with a touch of humour in his eyes. 'To visit a brothel,' he said. He downed the schnapps in one gulp. 'The best brothel in Heldenburg, as it happens. Have you heard of Madame Jardinne?' When she shook her head, he smiled. 'I'm not surprised. I doubt if you could afford her fees.'

'It's a brothel for women?'

'It's a brothel for anyone,' he said. 'Anyone rich, who needs absolute discretion.' He looked at her for a long moment. 'You may as well hear the correct story from me,' he said. 'The rumours will be spreading soon enough. Madame Jardinne was robbed of jewellery, and also of some papers. Letters from clients, asking for certain services. Letters from people who have now risen to high positions. The scheming bitch has been in business a long time, and she kept everything. Over the years there have even been communications from the grand duke.' He paused. 'Those are the ones that worry me. The other idiots can take their chances.'

'Surely it was foolish of the grand duke to write to a madam?' Katherine said.

'Times change,' the count said. 'In the past, His Excellency could more or less do as he wished. He was secure. No one in Heldenburg would even think of deposing him. Now, in the wrong hands, those letters would be fuel for the opposition. They could be the sparks that ignited a fire we would not be able to put out.'

'And you think Sergei would sell them to the grand duke's enemies?'

'Of course he would,' the count said. 'Thieves have no honour. The papers are probably worth as much as the jewellery, and they'll be much easier to get rid of.' He put his glass down. 'The only thing I don't understand is how von Lenz knew about them. And how he knew where to find them. He's a foreigner, and Madame Jardinne is not as quick to open her mouth as she has been in the past to open her legs.' He looked at Katherine suddenly. 'Have you ever been to a brothel, Katherine?'

'Certainly not,' she said, surprised at his sudden question.

'Don't sound so virginal.' He held out his hand. 'You're dressed to go out. Come with me. You might find it interesting.'

Madame Jardinne's house was surrounded by wooded ground and a high wall. The count's carriage drew up outside the massive front door. The count banged unceremoniously on the door with his fist, and a demure girl in a plain dress answered immediately.

'Tell your mistress I'm here,' the count said abruptly.

The girl glanced briefly at Katherine and then bobbed a curtsey and scurried off. Katherine looked round. The hall was the epitome of good taste. Beautifully carpeted, with elegant furniture and a magnificent chandelier. It would not have disgraced a duchess. And when Madame Jardinne appeared, Katherine reflected that she looked quite at home in these surroundings. A tall, middle-aged lady in a dress that was a perfect example of unobtrusive good taste. Her temper, however, was less restrained.

'Well?' she demanded imperiously. 'Have you arrested him yet?'

'No,' the count said. 'He has an alibi.'

'Of course he has an alibi.' Madame Jardinne's accent was refined, but it had the slightly forced sound of someone who had learnt such speech patterns, rather than someone who had grown up with them. 'Throw him in the Schloss, and check his alibi later.'

'I can't do that, Helga,' the count said, rather wearily. 'We have laws in this country.'

'Laws that protect thieves?' Madame Jardinne snapped. 'I want my jewels back. That Russian bastard has hidden them somewhere. I want to see some evidence that you're going to find them. And don't call me Helga. It's Monique.'

'Everyone seems very keen to condemn Sergei without proof,' Katherine said.

Madame Jardinne laughed harshly. 'Ha! You're another of those fools who've fallen for his charming smile, are you? He's guilty as Judas! Twice he's been in a town where there's been a big robbery, and each time he's lived like a lord afterwards.'

'He's a gambler,' Katherine said. 'He makes money by gambling.'

'He makes money by stealing,' Madame Jardinne said. 'But until now he's been too clever to get caught.' She looked meaningfully at the count. 'Only maybe this time he's met his match, eh?'

'Maybe,' the count said. 'You say the thief appeared to know exactly where to go, both for your jewellery and for the papers?'

Madame Jardinne nodded. 'My jewels are either in my safe or on my body. Some of my older girls know where the safe is. But the papers were in a strong box, and very few people knew where I kept that.'

'But von Lenz knew?' the count said.

'Obviously someone told him. And it has to be someone who knew me. Knew me for a long time. Someone I trusted.' Madame Jardinne put her hand on her heart, a theatrical gesture. 'That's what hurts me the most. A friend betrayed me to that pig of a Russian.'

'Or a disgruntled client,' the count said.

'Werner,' Madame Jardinne said imperiously. 'I don't have any disgruntled clients.'

'Helga,' he said, 'how would you know? They wouldn't tell you to your face. They'd simply go away and plot revenge.' She glared at him, and he smiled. 'If you can think of anyone who might have a grudge against you, let me know as soon as possible. In the mean time – ' he reached out and put his hand on Katherine's arm ' – we want to look round. Do you have any clients on the second floor?'

'Not at the moment,' Madame Jardinne said. 'But in two hours' time, I am expecting company.'

'We'll be gone by then,' the count said.

'Do you want a woman?'

'Of course not.' The count touched Katherine's face briefly and possessively. 'I've got one.'

Katherine contained her anger until they were alone in the corridor. Then she turned to face him. 'I don't like being spoken of as if I'm a possession.'

'Why not?' he asked mildly, guiding her up a flight of thickly carpeted stairs. 'That's exactly what you are.'

'Paying for a house doesn't mean you've bought me,' she said.

'Are you trying to tell me that in England a man sets a woman up, pays for her house, her servants, her clothes and her food, and expects nothing back?'

'I am waiting to be married to your son,' she said. 'The least you can do is provide accommodation.'

'You should have been married weeks ago.' He pushed open a door. 'And if it wasn't for that damned Russian, you would have been.' He crowded her into the dimly lit room, but before she had a chance to look round he grasped her by the shoulders and turned her round to face him. 'He's the one who told you about Ruprecht's tastes, isn't he? And you used that knowledge to manoeuvre me into giving you some free time. So that you could open your legs for von Lenz, and probably anyone else you fancied.'

'And you haven't made love to a single other woman since I came to Heldenburg?' she flung back at him.

'Well, not as many as usual,' he said.

'Am I supposed to applaud your self-control?'

'No.' He stepped back. 'What you have to do right now is take your clothes off.'

She had begun to look round the room, and for a moment his comment did not register in her mind. She saw wooden covered vaulting horses, frames and ropes, and several strangely fashioned pieces of equipment that she could not even guess the purpose of.

'What is this place?' she asked.

'A playground,' he said. 'And we're going to play.' He moved close to her. 'Are you going to do as you're told, and undress? Or shall I do it for you? I have to warn you that at the moment I'm not feeling inclined to be gentle.' He saw her glance towards the door. 'It's locked,' he said.

'And what if I'm not inclined to play?' she asked.

'I bought you, remember?' he said. 'It's about time you realised that I have first claim on you.' He began to take off his coat. 'I dislike sharing you with men like Sergei von Lenz.' He flung his coat down and began to unbutton his waistcoat. 'Or any other charming liar who happens to take your fancy.'

She removed her hat, but that was all, and stood back and watched him discard his cravat and shirt. He tossed his shirt on the ground, and stretched, flexing his muscles. His pale, close-fitting trousers were pulled down tightly by the stirrups under his boots, and the taut cloth did nothing to disguise his impressive erection.

'Come over here,' he said. He led her to a sturdy wooden frame that resembled a box without sides, and with a variety of poles and chains criss-crossing its interior. 'What do you think this is?'

She shook her head. 'I've no idea.'

'A pleasure box,' he said. 'Have you never wanted to take complete control over a lover, Katherine? Twist them, and turn them, and upend them, and put them in any position you fancied, without them being able to do a thing about it?'

She had to admit that it was one fantasy she had not considered, but now, looking at him standing in front of her, shirtless and very obviously aroused, she was beginning to see its attractions.

She touched the wooden frame. 'How does it work?'

He began to explain how the willing participant could be fastened by wrists, ankles, knees, waist or neck. How the various bars and shackles on the frame could be moved, leaving the victim spread-eagled between the four posts, bent over a central bar with arms out-stretched, or twisted into any number of other uncomfortable and delightfully humiliating positions that made all the secret places of their body available to their partner. She could hear the suppressed excitement in his voice as he described how a victim could be bent over and restrained.

'I still can't see exactly how it works,' she hinted.

'Take your clothes off,' he said, 'and I'll show you.'

'Oh, no,' she said. 'I want to see it demonstrated on you.'

She knew from his expression of pleasure that she had made the right decision. She realised that his pride prevented him from asking her outright for this gratification. He relied on her to read the hidden meaning in his suggestions. She also wondered if his previous comments had been a deliberate attempt to annoy her, to put her in a suitable state of anger for what he knew was coming next.

He stepped into the frame and told her how to fasten his wrists and ankles. The heavy central bar was brought forward against his waist. As she fastened him with another chain she brushed his erection with her hands, and felt his body shake with anticipation. Without asking his permission she unbuttoned the tight trousers and tugged them down to his knees. He groaned softly as her hands moved intimately over him.

'Open the cupboard,' he said. 'On the wall behind you.'

She knew what she would find and she was not disappointed. A selection of whips, ranging from a vicious-looking cat-o'-nine-tails with metal spikes on the end of its thongs to standard riding crops and canes, was hanging on hooks.

She chose a cane, and walked back to him, swishing it against her palm. She stood behind him so that he would not know exactly when the first blow would land and, when it did, drawing a red line across his tensed buttocks, she was rewarded with a grunt that indicated both relief and pleasure.

As she caned him she reflected once again how surprising it was that she found this activity so arousing. Until she had been introduced to it by the count it had never figured in any of her fantasies. And she would never have believed that she could still find a man desirable while she was treating him in such an undignified fashion. But seeing the red lines criss-cross the count's flesh, hearing him gasp as he struggled with increasing difficulty to withhold his orgasm, watching his attractive and beautifully muscled body jerk and twist as each stroke of the cane landed, she could only think how magnificent, and indeed how masculine, he looked.

'Harder,' he muttered. The cane whistled down and she put more force behind it. 'Again,' he said.

'Ask me nicely,' she taunted.

'Again, please,' he groaned. 'Don't stop now.'

She remembered him telling her that he had bought her, and also that she was never going to see Sergei von Lenz again, and she began to beat him with renewed enthusiasm. But as the cane landed, raising thin red weals on his flesh, she saw his body jerk uncontrollably and he gave a hoarse cry of mingled pleasure and satisfaction. She waited for the spasms to subside, and then began to unfasten his hands and feet. Even watching him climax made her feel good. She felt deliciously swollen and tense with reciprocal need.

'Katherine,' he said, unsteadily. 'I sometimes think you are as strong as a man.'

'Oh, hardly,' she said, demurely. 'But perhaps I'm stronger that you expected, especially when I'm angry.' She watched him wince as he carefully buttoned his trousers. 'You'll remember this for a while, I imagine,' she said. 'Especially when you sit down.'

'It'll be a good memory for me,' he said. He turned to her, a sheen of sweat making his tanned face glow. 'And what about you?' He stepped towards her. 'Was it good for you, too?'

She stood with her back to the wooden frame. His closeness made her shiver with expectation. 'Yes,' she said, 'it was.'

'Prove it,' he said. 'Lift your arms and grasp the rail above your head.' Curiously, she did as she was told. He bunched her skirts up and tucked them round her waist. 'Spread your legs,' he ordered. 'And lean back. Rest your bottom on the beam behind you.' She did as he instructed, and remained half sitting, with her legs apart and stretched out in front of her. Her state of arousal was now self-evident. He inspected her with obvious delight. 'Yes,' he murmured, 'you enjoyed it too, didn't you?' He put his hand on her inner thigh, and moved it slowly up until his fingers touched her clitoris. She gave a shudder of delight. He moved closer, standing between her legs. His fingers played with her, and his mouth was close to her ear. 'And you enjoy this, don't you?' She felt his warm breath on her skin, like a light caress. 'Do you do this to yourself, Katherine, in the privacy of your room?'

'Yes,' she whispered.

'Just like this? Or harder? Or faster?' He altered his rhythm to suit his words. 'Tell me, Katherine. I want to make it good for you.'

'It's good,' she muttered. She was so aroused that any touch would have made her body shiver with delight. She wanted to pull him even closer but she knew that, stretched out as she was, she would fall on the floor if she let go of the beam above her head. So she hung there and allowed him to work on her expertly, until she was so tense with sexual need that she felt she would scream with frustration if he did not make an effort to encourage her to a climax. And then, suddenly, she felt her pleasure reach bursting point, and her body jolted and bucked with one of the best orgasms she had experienced in her life. He held her while the sensations subsided, and her breathing slowed to normal.

'I don't need to ask if that felt good,' he said.

'It's always good with you,' she said truthfully.

'I could say the same,' he said. He helped her to her feet, and encouraged her skirts to fall back into place. Then he turned to fetch his own clothes. 'And it's a pleasure to find a woman who enjoys the same games as I do. A woman I can trust.'

'You've never found one before?'

'Once or twice I thought I had,' he said. 'When I was younger. And even then I was sometimes foolish in my choices. One girl actually suggested that if I didn't buy

205

her an expensive piece of jewellery she would spread some interesting stories about me.'

'And did she get her present?' Katherine asked.

He laughed. 'Of course not. I wasn't that foolish.'

'So what did she do?' Katherine asked, intrigued that women had tried to best him.

He grinned. 'She disappeared out of my life,' he said.

Katherine stared at him. 'You had her killed?'

This time he laughed in genuine amusement. 'What a terrible opinion you have of me, Katherine. I simply made it clear that threatening me was not a good idea.' He began to button his shirt. 'I wonder what happened to her? She was a pretty girl, with a nice strong arm, and I think she enjoyed using it. Pity she was so greedy.'

'Would you have carried out your threats, whatever they were?'

'Of course.' He picked up his cravat. 'Never make threats you don't intend to keep, Katherine. It destroys your credibility.' He knotted his cravat loosely, shrugged on his waistcoat and began to button it. 'Since then I've been cautious about relaxing completely.' He smiled at her. 'Not that rumours about my particular pleasures would destroy me, but they might weaken my dignified reputation a little.'

'Well, you certainly have a reputation,' she agreed. 'Although fear would seem to play more of a part in it than dignity.'

'Good,' he said. 'I've worked hard to achieve that. In my position, being feared is an asset. You've no idea how many rumours I've spread about myself. But it does mean I have to choose my friends carefully.' He smiled at her. 'That's why it's so pleasing to know that I can trust you, Katherine.' He reached for his coat, and added almost casually, 'What a pity you have to marry Ruprecht.'

'But I don't,' she said, wondering if she had correctly interpreted his allusion. 'Do I?'

'Of course you do,' he said. 'If you want me to settle your father's debts.'

'I could marry into your family,' she hinted. 'But not Ruprecht.'

He gave her a long, quizzical look. 'The idea is appealing,' he said at last. 'But unfortunately it isn't practical.'

'Why not?' she demanded.

'Because in law Ruprecht is my first-born, and he takes precedence over any children I might have from any subsequent marriages,' the count said. 'But if he has a son, I do have the right to make him my successor, when he comes of age.' He smiled. 'So there's a good chance that I will live to see a suitable grandson taking over from me. That would give me a great deal of satisfaction.' He gave her another calculating look. 'But Ruprecht has to be the father. There must be no doubt about that.'

'Must you do everything according to the rules?' she demanded, angrily.

'Without rules, society falls apart,' he said. 'If those of us in positions of authority are lax about observing the rules, it's too easy for any smooth-tongued insurrectionist to persuade the people that they need not obey them either. That's why I guard the grand duke's reputation. That's why I feel I must also set an example. I may be feared, but I believed I'm known to be fair.' His voice was suddenly hard, and she sensed the steel behind it. 'I knew you came with a price, Katherine, and I'm willing to pay it. I would not be happy if you tried to renege on your part of the bargain now. There is far too much at stake. I would not be happy at all!'

So he doesn't intend to marry me, Katherine thought. She paced about her room in frustration. At least, not as long as Ruprecht is around! I would make him a splendid wife, in every sense, but he clearly cares more about his position as self-appointed protector of Heldenburg's future than me. I'm to marry Ruprecht, am I? She spun on her heel and kicked at the nearest chair. I think *not*!

Her male clothes were laid out on the bed and she dressed swiftly. She had decided to contact Yvonne as quickly as possible. If she could not see a future with the von Krohnensteins, she wanted to discover whether or not she had one with Sergei von Lenz. She did not believe he was a jewel thief. If he had money, he had made it from gambling. She knew that was possible, as long as you kept in control of your fortunes. It was the compulsives like her father, the ones who could not resist just one more throw, or one more bet, in order to double what they already had, who ended up penniless. Sergei von Lenz, she felt certain, had far more self-discipline than that.

Having passed successfully as a man already, she now walked the streets with far more confidence, and even returned the smiles of several ladies. Yvonne was in her room when she arrived at the inn, and the grinning inn-keeper was happy to give Katherine the room number.

'You'll be getting me a reputation,' Yvonne teased when she walked in. She stood back and smiled. 'But you do make a handsome young man.' She took a pile of clothes off the only chair in the room, and Katherine sat down. Yvonne hunted for a bottle of wine and some glasses. 'I know why you're here,' she said. 'You've heard about Sergei's latest escapade.'

'I've heard the *rumours* about Sergei,' Katherine admitted.

'Rumours?' Yvonne snorted with amusement. 'You'll be telling me next that you think he's innocent.'

'Well, I'm rather annoyed that everyone assumes he's guilty,' Katherine said. 'Apparently he has a splendid alibi.'

'From what I've heard, he always does,' Yvonne said. She poured Katherine a glass of wine. 'When did you last see your wild and charming lover?'

'I've only seen him once since I arrived in Grazheim,' Katherine said. 'And I need to see him again.'

'Is that wise?' Yvonne sat down on the bed. 'I mean, you're virtually a member of the von Krohnenstein family now, and I don't think Sergei von Lenz is the kind of person they'd welcome as a wedding guest.'

'I don't think there's going to be a wedding,' Katherine said. 'That's why I have to see Sergei.'

Yvonne stared at her in alarm. 'You're not pregnant, are you?'

'No,' Katherine said.

'You haven't got any ridiculous ideas about getting romantically involved with that Russian heart-breaker?' Yvonne sounded anxious now. 'He's not the kind of man to want any kind of permanent relationship.'

'I'll be offering him a business partnership,' Katherine said.

Yvonne stared at her unhappily. 'I don't think he'd want that, either.'

'I need to hear him say so,' Katherine said. 'I know he has a rented house on Hochmeisterstrasse, and I want the number. If you don't know it, I'm sure you could find it for me.' She looked at Yvonne appealingly. 'I don't know who else to ask. I don't know who else I can trust.'

Yvonne still looked uncomfortable. 'Well, I do know the house number, but I'm not sure I should give it to you.'

'If you don't, I'll get it some other way,' Katherine said, recklessly. 'Help me, Yvonne. I'm trying to rearrange my life. My future happiness could depend on this.'

Yvonne looked serious for a moment longer, and then smiled. 'All right. That charming bastard seems to have bewitched you, but if I don't tell you how to get to him I suppose you'll go round asking questions, and making yourself so obvious that the whole of Grazheim'll know about it. It's number twenty-three, the house with three big trees in front of it. But for heaven's sake, be careful. Your count is just waiting to pounce on Sergei, and although no one's managed to catch him out before, this time von Krohnenstein just might.' She held up a hand to silence Katherine's objections. 'And don't try and tell me that he's innocent. The only one who believes that is you.'

Katherine had intended to go straight home after visiting Yvonne, but now that she knew Sergei's house number, and she was feeling increasingly comfortable in the freedom of her male clothes, she decided that at least she would check the address for herself. Her intention had been to simply stroll past like a casual passer-by, but when she realised that the house was set back from the road and surrounded by a thickly wooded garden, she could not resist slipping through a gap in the iron railings and making her way towards the building itself.

The trees thinned and a lighted ground-floor window faced her. The shutters were open. She crept closer, and peered in. She was rewarded by the sight of Sergei von Lenz picking up two large cushions and tucking them under his arm. He was casually dressed in pale trousers and a dark beautifully cut jacket. His white shirt was undone and open to his waist. She tapped on the window and he looked round, startled. She tapped again, and this time he not only saw her, she knew that he had recognised her. He dumped the cushions and was over by the window in three long strides. He opened it and leant out. 'Katherine? What the devil are you doing out there?'

'Looking for you,' she said. 'Can I come in?'

'Of course not,' he said. 'Haven't you heard that I'm the prime suspect for a robbery and your lover, von Krohnenstein, is doing his damnedest to get me into Schloss Ohlm?'

'I've heard all that,' she said. 'I still want to come in.'

'It's too dangerous for you,' he said.

210

'Be damned to the danger,' she snapped back, grasping the window sill. 'I have to talk to you.'

'All right,' he said. He smiled down at her, the dazzling smile that she remembered so well. 'We'll talk. But not now. Not tonight. I'm expecting an important visitor, and although he'd probably love to see you, I don't think a meeting would be wise.'

Captivated by the smile, by his dark, wild face framed by the jet-black hair, she was about to obey him and back away from the window. Then the door opened and a girl came into the room. Katherine registered first that she was young and pretty, with tousled brown curls. And secondly that she was half-naked; her pert round breasts with nipples so pink they looked as if they had been rouged were jostling each other over the top of her unlaced corset. Sergei half-turned to the girl, and then back to Katherine.

'English Rose,' he said. 'I can explain.'

'Good,' Katherine said. She swung one leg over the window sill. 'I shall be delighted to hear you try.'

Sergei tried to prevent her from climbing into the room. 'But not now,' he added. 'Later.'

'Right now,' Katherine said. She pushed him, far harder than he expected, and sent him staggering back. Before he could recover she had jumped into the room.

The girl stared at her curiously. '*Liebchen*, who's this pretty young man? Have you arranged a *ménage à trois*?' She smiled at Katherine. 'Can I have him first? Can he make love to me as if he's a woman?'

'No,' Katherine snapped, 'he can't.'

'Oh.' The girl looked startled for a moment. 'You *are* a woman.' She turned to Sergei. 'Just what have you planned for this evening? I thought you wanted me all to yourself.' She smiled sunnily at Katherine. 'But I don't mind sharing.'

'Minna,' Sergei said, 'go back into the bedroom. My friend and I have to talk.'

'All right. *Liebchen*,' Minna seemed unperturbed. She blew Sergei a kiss and then, smiling mischievously, blew one to Katherine too. Katherine stared stonily back, and then surprised herself by thinking that Minna really was rather pretty. When the girl had gone Sergei turned to Katherine. She was slightly mollified to see that he was at least a little shamefaced.

'So?' she said. 'Important visitors, eh?'

'I have had a terrible time,' he said. 'I've been accused of committing a robbery. I needed a little relaxation.' He managed another delightful smile. 'And you seemed to have disappeared from my life, English Rose. I thought you'd abandoned me.'

'You were quick to find a replacement,' she observed acidly. 'A schoolgirl, from the looks of it.'

He laughed. 'She's older than she looks, English Rose. But I'd much rather have you. Minna's very expensive.'

Katherine slapped him, and felt much better for it. And even as his head jerked back, and his hand went to his stinging face, she felt a stab of desire at the sight of him. She suddenly remembered the wooden frame at Madame Jardinne's. I'd like Sergei on that frame right now, she thought. Stripped naked. Or maybe with his shirt on, the tails tied round his waist, so that the white cotton stretched over his back made a nice contrast to his tanned legs and his neat bottom. And then I'd change the colour of that delicious behind of his!

'Would you still much rather have me?' she asked, sweetly.

'Yes,' he said. He took a step nearer to her, and rubbed his face again. 'By God, Katherine, you can be a bitch, can't you?' Suddenly he threw back his head and laughed. 'If any other woman did that, I'd pitch them out of the window. Why do I take it from you, English Rose?'

'Because I'm so inexpensive?' she suggested, demurely.

212

'Maybe.' He smiled again, and caught her arm. 'Come and meet Minna, English Rose. She's a professional lady, and very discreet. Independent too. A bit like you.'

She went with him, knowing that he had captivated her again, but not really caring. Minna was sitting on the bed. There was a bucket of ice with an unopened bottle of wine in it on the table next to her.

'Pour Katherine a glass of wine,' Sergei said. 'You know who Katherine is, don't you?'

Minna stared, and for a brief moment Katherine saw a worldly-wise woman, rather than a bubbly girl. Then Minna shrugged. 'No,' she said. And smiled. 'But then I have a perfectly terrible memory for names and faces.'

Sergei laughed. He took Katherine's hand. 'Take off that hat and coat and sit down,' he said. Minna struggled to uncork the wine, succeeded, and poured a glass. Sergei helped Katherine out of her coat and guided her to the bed.

'Drink,' he ordered. 'This is a celebration. You've come back to me.'

He sat down next to her and Minna poured more wine. To be so near to Sergei again made Katherine feel aroused and light-headed. After several glasses of wine, and some slightly risqué conversation, she was feeling even more light-headed and pleasantly relaxed. Sergei was unbuttoning her man's waistcoat, but she did not care. Once it was unbuttoned, Minna helped her remove it, and suddenly she found herself lying back on the bed, between the two of them, with Minna delicately fumbling with the buttons of her shirt.

'No,' she protested half-heartedly. Mina's face was close to hers, her full red lips smiling.

'Let her do it,' Sergei's voice caressed her ear. 'Let her undress you, Katherine.'

Because she was sleepy from the wine, and the closeness of his body aroused her, and because, much to her surprise, she did not find Minna unattractive, she let the girl finish unbuttoning her shirt. Sergei helped her to shrug it off.

'Whatever's this?' Minna looked at the wide strips of cloth wound round her body. 'A new kind of corset?' She unwound the strips and suddenly Katherine's breasts were bare. 'Oh, I understand,' she laughed. 'You wouldn't be so convincing as a young man with these under your jacket.'

Her hands touched Katherine, lightly and intimately, and for a moment Katherine felt like recoiling. But Sergei was behind her, his mouth close to her ear. 'Let her do it, English Rose,' he whispered. 'I want to watch her pleasing you.'

She leant back against his chest, feeling the strength and warmth of his body supporting her. His hands moved under her breasts, lifting them towards Minna's mouth. Minna's lips made a round shape and closed over Katherine's nipple. She sucked gently, and used the tip of her tongue to increase the pleasurable sensations. Katherine gave a little gasp of surprise. Instead of feeling repulsed she was actually excited. And all the more so when she heard Sergei's breathing quicken as he watched.

When Minna's hands slipped down and expertly unbuttoned her tight riding breeches, Katherine made a movement of protest. Mina hesitated, obviously not wishing to do anything that Katherine did not approve.

'Have you never been tongued by a woman, English Rose?' Sergei murmured.

'No,' Katherine said. She felt his hands supporting her breasts, his fingers taking over where Minna's tongue had been moments before.

'You'll like it,' Sergei promised. 'And so will I.'

With his breath soft on her ear and his hands massaging her, Katherine felt her body responding to the sensuous atmosphere in the room. 'Take her boots off,' Sergei ordered.

As Minna obliged, Katherine protested passively, 'No.'

Sergei laughed softly. 'And her breeches,' he said. 'Make her comfortable.'

It was sensuously relaxing to be undressed so gently. Sergei's voice in her ear encouraged Katherine's thoughts to form erotic images as he described how expertly Minna was going to arouse her. When Minna's mouth first touched her knee, and began to work its way up, Katherine could not help making a little movement of resistance.

'Keep still,' Sergei ordered. His hands suddenly moved down her body and he grasped her wrists, pulling her arms behind her back. Katherine sat upright, with a cry of surprise. Minna crouched between her outstretched legs, waiting.

'Do it!' Sergei ordered.

'Only if she agrees,' Minna said.

'She agreed when she let you strip her,' Sergei said. 'And if she's changed her mind, it's too late now. Tell her that you want it, Katherine.'

The sensation of being held captive, and the hard bulge of Sergei's erection against her back, aroused Katherine to such a state of sexual need that all she could do was moan softly. Minna read this as a sign of compliance, and bent her head forward, between Katherine's legs. Her warm tongue, flicking lightly and expertly, concentrating on her partner's swollen, throbbing clitoris. It aroused Katherine much faster than she expected. She made a little mewing nose of pleasure and found herself stretching back against Sergei, and thrusting her hips forward to Minna. Her climax came almost too soon, and she bucked and twisted in Sergei's grasp, with Minna holding her thighs and pleasuring her to the very last. When Sergei let her go she fell back on the bed, delightfully exhausted, her chest heaving.

'I told you I'd educate you,' Sergei said. He touched her damp face, affectionately. 'Lesson number one. Being

215

tongued by a woman is almost as good as being tongued by a man.'

'Conceited pig!' Minna laughed. 'It's better.'

'And this – ' he sat back on his heels on the bed, unbuttoned his tight trousers and displayed his impressively erect cock and heavy balls ' – is best of all.'

'Oooh, sir,' Minna teased. 'Is that for me?'

'Well, one of you had better take control of it,' Sergei said. 'Otherwise I'll have to waste it on my hands.'

His pose was so excitingly masculine that Katherine felt a surge of desire tingle her body again. And then another thought captivated her: the idea of watching him making love to Minna. She knew Minna was no rival for his affections. When she had been paid she would go off quite happily and service another man with the same display of believable enthusiasm that she was exhibiting now. There was no reason to be jealous of Minna.

'Educate me again,' she said to Sergei. 'Let me see you satisfy Minna.'

He grinned. 'You're a voyeuse, madam? Well, I'll give you something to enjoy.'

Minna jumped of the bed and Sergei caught her and pulled her to him. He lowered his head to her breasts and took her nipple in his mouth. She arched her back and half-closed her eyes. If she had been a cat, Katherine thought, she would probably have purred. She watched with sensuous approval as he sucked and licked. It excited her to see his sinewy body contrasted with Minna's soft roundness, and his glossy dark hair against Minna's white skin. His long fingers played with Minna as expertly as they riffled a pack of cards.

But he only indulged in a minimum of foreplay, before his need for relief overtook him. She noted how his muscles began to tremble as his sexual excitement mounted, then he grasped Minna, and thrust into her with urgent savagery. Katherine watched his body moving in the violent rhythm of desire. His buttocks tensed as his orgasm overtook him. She had never understood the pleasure of voyeurism before, but as she watched Sergei's spasms of uncontrolled lust, heard his gasps, and saw the expression on his face when he came, she felt as exhilarated as if she had been under him herself.

His needs satisfied, Sergei rolled off Minna and lay back on the bed with a contented smile. Minna sat up and thrust her fingers through her tangled hair, shaking her head as she did so. Katherine realised that she hadn't really been watching Minna's reactions. Had she come? Did she care whether she was satisfied or not? Did she even like men? It was difficult to tell. Minna was looking for her clothes now, while Sergei still lay stretched out on the bed, idly buttoning his trousers and looking rather smug.

Minna obviously considered that her obligations had been fulfilled, and did not stay long after she had dressed. When she had gone, Katherine shared another glass of wine with Sergei.

'When will I see you again?' she asked.

'Whenever it's safe for you,' he said. 'Your tyrant lover has suggested that I stay in Grazheim until he gives me permission to leave.' He smiled. 'So I might as well entertain you while I'm here.'

'The count believes you robbed Madame Jardinne,' she said. 'And so does everyone else I've spoken to.'

'What do you think?' he asked. 'Am I guilty?'

'I don't know,' she said, honestly. 'Are you?'

'Would you disown me if I was?'

'No,' she said. 'But I'd be afraid for you. The count is determined to find enough evidence to convict you.'

'Don't be afraid,' he said. 'I can take care of myself. And now that we're back together again, I'll take care of you, too.'

* * *

217

The week that followed was one of sheer delight for Katherine. The count was busy with his investigations, and visited her only briefly. When she told him that she was amazed he was taking so much trouble over a brothel-keeper's jewellery, he laughed wearily.

'If it was only the jewels, I wouldn't even be involved. It's the grand duke's letters that I'm really worried about. I need to get them back.' He smiled. 'And you're unlikely to see much of me until I do.'

Given the freedom to go out whenever she wanted, Katherine made a habit of leaving the house at different times, and never saying how long she would be. The carriage took her to the centre of Grazheim, and she would send it home with instructions to return for her later. She would claim to be shopping, or visiting friends, or riding in the Grazheim parks. Sometimes she did ride, hiring a horse from an excellent livery stables that she discovered, although she disliked the side-saddle she was obliged to use. But after the ride she always went to Sergei. She slipped through the trees, grateful that the house itself was situated in an area where there were few people walking, and only the occasional carriage rattled past.

Sergei entertained her with food and salacious stories about his life in Russia, where he claimed his father encouraged voyeurism as a weekend entertainment for guests, encouraging lusty estate workers to visit selected participants, who may or may not have been told that their antics were being enjoyed by an audience behind cunningly positioned peep-holes.

'Women would agree to assignations,' Sergei said. 'And you'd be surprised how the most refined ladies, those with cultured airs and graces, just loved to be serviced by the most muscular and roughest workers. It really educated the gentlemen when they watched their wives perform, so I was told. My father claimed to have saved several marriages by showing lax husbands just what they had to do to their wives to keep them satisfied in bed.'

According to Sergei, his early life in Russia had been one round of sexual adventure and discovery. Katherine certainly did not believe all the stories, but they were diverting to listen to, and usually ended with them both making love, either acting out some of the scenes Sergei had been describing, or simply giving way to the delightful feelings of sexual need that his monologues had encouraged in them both.

But when it came to discussing their possible future together, Sergei was infuriatingly vague. He agreed that they would make a fine couple at the gaming tables, each supporting the other, but laughingly deflected any suggestions that they turn talk into reality. And despite her prompting, he also refused to be drawn into any discussion of the robbery, leaving her with a frustrated feeling that he did not trust her.

But then, why should he trust me? she asked herself, as she tried to sleep at night, with the memories of her lovemaking still fresh in her mind. I'm still living in the count's house. As far as Sergei is concerned I'm unofficially the count's mistress. And I'm still expected to marry Ruprecht. Why should he make any commitment to me? I haven't shown any sign of making a commitment to him.

She knew she had to make a decision herself, but she wanted to be certain about him. If she left Heldenburg it would have to be done secretly. The count, she was sure, would not let her go. She had made a promise, and he intended her to keep it. She knew that he would make an implacable and dangerous enemy. But what if I were to run away, she thought, and then Sergei refused to help me? I should be penniless and alone, and my father would lose everything.

She tossed and turned in her bed, wondering what course to take. Her mind showed her pictures of a marriage ceremony, with a petulant Ruprecht by her side, and the count, grimly attractive in his ceremonial uniform, watching the wedding ring being slipped over her finger. If only he would agree to marry me himself, she thought. I'd forget Sergei, eventually. I'd make myself forget.

But Sergei still inhabited her dreams and most of her fantasies. She longed to see him again. It frustrated her that her time with him was so short, and when she had to leave him all she could think of was their next meeting. I have to ask him outright, she thought. Am I going to be part of his life or not? I have to force him to answer me directly. And if he says no? Her mind wrestled with the possibility. A possibility that her common sense told her was very likely to become a reality. If he says no, she thought, I'll accept it. I'll marry Ruprecht, and stay in Heldenburg, and try to forget Sergei von Lenz ever existed.

'It has to end now,' the count said. 'I've been very patient, but now things have to change.'

He had ordered her to stay in for him, and she had spent the afternoon waiting. An afternoon when she was supposed to be seeing Sergei who, she thought, was probably wondering where she was, and why she had not contacted him.

'What has to end?' she asked.

'Your freedom,' the count said. 'You came here to be married, and now it's time for you to fulfil your obligation.' He smiled, and stretched out his legs, watching her. 'As a married woman you'll still have a certain amount of personal liberty, of course.' He paused. 'But all visits to Sergei von Lenz must obviously stop.'

She drew breath sharply, and felt her cheeks flush. Clearly he had been spying on her. For a moment she hated him.

'Congratulations for not trying to deny it,' he added dryly. 'Has he said anything to you about the robbery?'

'We didn't discuss the robbery,' she said coolly. 'We had other things on our minds.'

He laughed. 'That's what I like about you, Katherine. You don't make excuses. It does seem a waste to marry you to Ruprecht, but that's what I have to do.' He looked at her silently for a moment. 'If it's any consolation to you, I don't believe Sergei will stay in Grazheim much longer.'

She arched her eyebrows. 'Why do you say that?'

'Because I can't legally hold him,' the count said. 'I've checked his alibi. It's unshakable. Two titled gentlemen, and two very worthy elderly citizens, all claim he was with them, playing cards. They are not the kind of people I would have believed would support von Lenz. How can I call them liars?'

'So Sergei is innocent?' she said.

'I didn't say that,' the count corrected. 'I said I couldn't shake his alibi. So I'll have to lift the restrictions on his movements.'

'And you think he'll leave Grazheim?'

'Of course.' The count smiled. 'But don't let that raise your hopes, Katherine. He certainly won't take you with him.' His smile was cruel now. 'You didn't really think that he would, did you? I told you once, men like von Lenz are not knights in shining armour. They're hyenas. Scavengers on the edge of decent society. Men without honour.'

'But for all my association with hyenas,' she said, 'I'm still considered to be a suitable wife for your son?'

He stood up, still smiling. 'I'm sure you'd like me to say no, and cancel the wedding. But I have no intention of doing that. We made a bargain. As soon as you marry, your father's debts will be paid in full. Just remember that.'

221

'And have I any say in the marriage arrangements?' she asked.

'No,' he said. 'It will be traditional and impressive. One must put on a show. It's expected of me. The official date will be announced at a grand masked ball. I will take you there, and hand you formally to Ruprecht. I'm afraid you'll have to dance with him a few times. If it's any consolation to you, he'll probably hate it even more than you do.' He walked to the door, then turned towards her. For a moment she thought he was going to suggest making love. The way she felt at that moment she would have slapped him for such a suggestion. Instead he said mildly, 'Perhaps you'd like to arrange a shopping trip to choose your gown and mask? And this time, Katherine, you really will go to the shops. Hecht will accompany you, just in case you lose your way, and end up at Hochmeisterstrasse by mistake.'

At least the servants think all this is wonderful, Katherine thought. The house was buzzing with activity. Arrangements for the marriage, and arrangements for the ball, which was to be held at the grand duke's palace, proceeded in tandem.

Katherine felt like a spectator. She was to be the centre of the celebrations, but no one asked her opinion on anything. She was told who the guests would be, told that the colour theme for the masks would be blue and silver, told that the Bishop of Grazheim would perform the wedding ceremony, and told that her dress would be embroidered with thousands of tiny seed pearls.

'The flowers at the ball will be blue and silver,' Frau Grussell informed her, excitedly. 'They'll put white flowers in water stained with dye, and the petals will soak up the colour. Can you imagine? The foliage will be painted. No one has done such a thing before.' When Katherine looked less than enchanted at the idea, she added, 'You're not worried about anything, are you, gracious lady? We'll make sure everything is carried out correctly.'

'No, I'm not worried,' Katherine said.

But it was a lie. I'm worried because I can feel life slipping out of my control, she thought. I'm worried because I'll never see Sergei again. I'm worried because I know I have to go through with this thing, and I don't want to any more. Nothing has turned out how I expected. Including me!

'I think everything has gone very well,' the count said. 'And you look beautiful,' he added. Katherine's elaborately decorated white satin dress had a draped bodice and an embroidered skirt. Her mask, which would be held by silk ribbons, was made from blue velvet ornamented with sweeping white feathers that arched back over her head. In contrast, the count's clothing was quite plain. His single-breasted cutaway jacket was dark blue, and his trousers pale grey, tucked into short leather boots. His white ruffled shirt was topped by a dark blue cravat. He lifted a plain blue mask to his face. His eyes glittered at her through the slits.

'Would you recognise me? ' he asked.

'Of course I would,' she said abruptly.

He stood in front of her with his legs braced apart, his tight trousers doing nothing to disguise the bulge of his sexual equipment. 'Well,' he said, 'I suppose you know me so well by now you'd recognise me even if I had my back to you.'

'Particularly when you have your back to me,' she said.

He laughed. 'We must play those games again sometime, Katherine.'

'I don't think so,' she said. She smiled sweetly. 'I shall soon be a respectable married woman.'

'But I do think so,' he said. His hand slid down to his

crotch. 'By God, Katherine,' he muttered. 'It's making me hard just thinking about it.'

'Well, stop thinking about it,' she said coolly. 'Or you're going to be very uncomfortable all evening.'

'I'm not,' he said. In two strides he was in front of her. When she tried to take a step back he grasped her wrists and held her. 'Kneel down,' he said.

'I will not!' She was furious with herself because she knew she wanted to obey him. He pushed her down to her knees, her skirts ballooning out around her. 'Unbutton me,' he said. 'And get your mouth working.' His grip tightened. Now he was genuinely crushing her wrists. 'Or I'll hold you here until you do.'

She hated herself for actually enjoying the sensation of being forced to obey. She fumbled with the buttons on his trouser flap and then he helped her by opening his legs wider as she freed his heavy balls and now stiffened cock.

'Your mouth,' he ordered, less steadily now. 'Do it!'

She closed her lips round him, enjoying the intimate taste of him and the musky scent of his masculinity. He did not help her by moving but made her work hard, sliding her mouth up and down his shaft, nibbling, licking and sucking. When his release came he was deep in her mouth, and he pushed his hips forward then, intent on keeping her there. Unable to help herself, she grasped his buttocks, feeling the muscles hard and tense under her fingers, feeling his body shake as his climax overtook him. As she pulled him close she heard him made a sound between a groan and a cry of delight. He buttoned himself up and she was back on her feet when Frau Grussell knocked on the door and announced that the carriage had arrived.

'I need time to tidy myself,' Katherine muttered, as the count urged her forward.

'You don't,' he said. He turned her towards him for a moment. 'You look like a woman who wants to make

224

love. It's very becoming. What a pity you'll have a mask over your face for most of the evening. Or perhaps it's not such a bad thing. We don't want the male guests queuing up to offer you relief, do we?'

'What a disgusting suggestion,' she said primly.

'What a strange combination you are, Katherine,' he said, as they climbed into the coach. 'A mixture of wanton and innocent. A strict mistress and a compliant slave.' He smiled at her. 'When I agreed on this marriage I never expected to get such a complex daughter-in-law.'

'I'm not your daughter-in-law yet,' she said, crisply.

She felt like telling him he was an equally strange amalgam. A totally masculine man who enjoyed being whipped by a woman.

'You can back out of the arrangement any time you wish, Katherine,' he said, pleasantly. 'And ruin your father. Is that what you want?'

She refused to answer him. When they arrived at the grand duke's palace she placed her hand on his arm and allowed him to escort her inside. Ruprecht was waiting for her in the entrance hall, dressed in a surprisingly conservative evening suit. After being formally handed to her future husband by the count, Katherine accompanied Ruprecht into the ballroom, allowing him to lead her from guest to guest. She smiled, and accepted congratulations and compliments from people that she knew were well aware that her marriage would be a sham.

'That's our duty done,' Ruprecht said as he took her aside and the orchestra began to play.

'Maybe you should make an effort and dance with me,' she suggested, sarcastically. 'At least once.'

He sighed irritably. 'I suppose I should.' As he moved stiffly round the floor with her, she wondered if he was finding their close contact as unpleasant as she was. She hoped so. After the dance he gave her a small, quick bow and managed to disappear into the crowd of masked guests.

Someone touched Katherine's arm. She turned to see a woman in a mask that fully covered her head and a bright blue dress, lavishly trimmed with lace.

'Congratulations, dear Katherine,' the woman said.

'Thank you,' Katherine said flatly.

'Well, don't sound so enthusiastic,' the woman giggled. 'But then, Ruprecht is hardly Sergei, is he? Wouldn't you love to be marrying your wild Russian gambler?'

'Marie?' Katherine recognised the voice now.

'Of course,' Marie Holzmann said. 'I can't promise you a wedding ring, but do you see that gentleman over there?' She flipped her fan over Katherine's shoulder, and Katherine saw a tall slim man standing on his own, a glass in his hand. He looked elegant and relaxed in a beautifully cut dark coat and tight white trousers tucked into black calf-length boots. Although his face was almost totally obscured by his wrap-around silk mask, and his jet-black hair was beautifully combed, he was heart-stoppingly familiar.

'Yes,' Marie whispered, when she heard Katherine's sharp intake of breath. 'It's exactly who you think it is.'

'But in God's name, what's he doing here?' Katherine demanded breathlessly.

'God knows.' Marie shrugged. 'Or maybe you know? He obtained an invitation from somewhere, and I'm certain he didn't come to pay his respects to Count von Krohnenstein.'

The man sauntered over to them, and no mask in the world could disguise his flashing smile. 'Congratulations on your impending marriage, Lady Katherine,' he said, with a brief bow. 'May I have the pleasure of a dance?' Without waiting for her reply he led her onto the floor. 'Try and relax,' he advised, as she held herself stiffly against him. 'You look terribly uncomfortable. Is my dancing that bad?'

'Are you mad?' she said, hoping her smile did not look

too fixed and nervous. 'If the count knows you're here, if anyone knows you're here, you'll probably be arrested. Or at least thrown out.'

He laughed. 'The count's been trying to arrest me all week, without any success. I have a genuine invitation. Obtained by bribery, it's true, but I'm hardly going to be sent to Schloss Ohlm for dancing with several bored wives.' He sighed. 'The things I do for you, English Rose.'

'But why have you come here?' she asked.

'What a question!' He spun her round. 'The count has obviously been preventing you from meeting me. You're obviously going through with this absurd marriage of convenience. And this was obviously the only way I could get to see you again.'

'Was that so important to you?' The closeness of his body was beginning to affect her.

'Of course,' he said. She felt his hand press against the small of her back. 'I rather thought we had an understanding, English Rose.'

She felt suddenly giddy. 'What kind of understanding?' she asked faintly.

'Well, not marriage,' he admitted bluntly. 'But an adventure, maybe?' He smiled again. 'I have plenty of money, and when I run out I can always persuade some willing gambler to give me more.' His dark eyes were amused, behind the black mask. 'And so can you, I imagine, Lady Katherine. With my help you can sort out your father's debts yourself. You don't need von Krohnenstein's help.' Being so close to him was intoxicating her. Anything seemed possible. 'I told you once we were two of a kind, remember?' he said. 'We should form a partnership. Doesn't that sound more interesting than marrying Ruprecht von Krohnenstein?'

The music, and his words, both spun dizzily round in her head. 'Why didn't you ask me before?' she asked.

'Because I never really believed you would go through

227

with this ridiculous charade,' he said. 'And I was worried that the count would try and manufacture some evidence against me, and throw me in that damned Schloss for twenty years.'

'But it's too late to do anything,' she said. 'I'm committed.'

'That doesn't sound like the English Rose I remember,' he said softly. 'That doesn't sound like the woman who defied Count von Krohnenstein and went out for a walk in the forest wearing boy's clothes.' The music stopped. 'Come to me tomorrow night,' he said. 'At nine o'clock. I'll have a carriage waiting that will take us over the border to Prussia. The count isn't very popular with the Prussians, and they won't help him find us. From there we'll go to France, or maybe Italy.' He held her hand for a fraction longer than politeness demanded, and gave her one last dazzling smile. 'Remember,' he said. 'Nine o'clock.'

'But I'm being watched all the time,' she said.

'If you really want it, English Rose,' he said softly, backing away from her into the crowd of dancers, 'you'll manage it.'

She spent the rest of the evening in a half-dazed state. She saw Sergei many more times, on the dance floor and off, but he did not approach her again. She saw the count, although she did not dance with him, and she saw Ruprecht, usually surrounded by a crowd of friends. He did not dance with her again, either.

People chatted to her, but she hardly heard them. Her mind was on Sergei, and on a future spent at his side. On travelling through Europe together, laughing, gambling, making love. She imagined herself returning to her father with the news that not only could she pay off his debts, she had not been obliged to enter into a marriage she did not really want. Instead she had found a man she felt certain she could spend the rest of her life with. If he did not want to marry her, she was willing to flout convention and set herself outside polite society, by travelling with him anyway.

The sense of euphoria lasted until she got home. When she finally took off her mask and her dress, and relaxed on her bed with Frau Grussell's obligatory glass of spiced wine, her common sense began to take over. Why had Sergei really suddenly decided he wanted her to go with him? What guarantee did she have that he would stay with her? Or let her use any money they made to pay her father's debts?

She wanted to believe that Sergei was genuine, and he cared about her, but now she began to wonder if she was letting her sexual need for him blind her to his real character. She had had no chance to question him properly at the ball. If she made the decision to go with him, was burning her boats with a vengeance. She would be cutting herself off from the society she knew. If he did not support her she would be penniless. And she knew very well that there would be only one way to support herself if that happened. It was not a way that she wanted to think about.

And another thing bothered her, as she lay there in the semi-darkness. She had recognised Sergei fairly easily. Surely the count would have recognised him too? Why did he not only let the two of them meet and talk, but allow Sergei to stay at the ball until it ended?

There were too many unanswered questions. And she wanted answers. This is my life, she thought. If I make the wrong decision now, I could be ruined forever. I don't want to marry Ruprecht, but I certainly don't want to be left destitute somewhere in Europe if Sergei von Lenz ever gets tired of me. He may not be a jewel thief, but I believe the count was probably right when he warned me that Herr von Lenz is no knight in shining armour.

She knew she had to see Sergei again. She had to ask him questions, and she had to believe in his answers. If necessary, she thought, he should be willing to show good faith by lending me enough money to pay my father's debts. Then I could work to repay him. Would he do that? She did not want to ask herself that question, because she was unsure of the answer.

And she did not want to wait until the following evening before she settled this, she decided. She wanted her answers now. She got up off the bed and went over to her leather-bound box. Before long she had transformed herself into a young man again. She looked at her pistol. After a moment's hesitation, she picked it up and pushed it in the top of her tight riding breeches. Would Hecht still be up and watching out for her, she wondered? She rather thought not. No one would be expecting her to go out at this hour.

It was strange walking through the streets at night and, she realised, probably dangerous. But she did not care. Once again she felt the odd surge of excitement that these adventures always gave her. It was as if she had been asleep and was now awake. All her senses seemed heightened, and the pistol felt comforting, snug under her coat. If someone accosted her she would defend herself. But she reached Hochmeisterstrasse without incident, and slipped through the trees to the house. It was in darkness. Well, she thought, that's not surprising. Sergei is probably in bed. A little voice prodded her with the question: *who with?* She ignored it.

She had an intimate knowledge of the house from her previous visits. Getting in through the window gave her no problems. She moved easily across the room to the door and into the passageway. She knew where Sergei's bedroom was. Reaching that was easy, too. She pushed open the door and stepped inside. The room was dark, and she sensed immediately that it was empty. She went over to the bed. It had not been used. Either he had not been home at all, or he was in a different part of the house. But in that case, she thought, why weren't there any lamps alight?

'Stay right where you are! If you give me any trouble, I'll shoot.'

The voice spun her round. 'Sergei?'

'He's not here.'

Her moment of surprise over, Katherine remembered to deepen her voice. 'Then where the devil is he?' she demanded. She could see a man's bulk in the doorway. Although she could not see his pistol, she did not doubt that he had one.

'Von Lenz has gone,' the man said. 'Servants paid, rent paid, contract of tenancy ended. I'm caretaking for Herr Köchler, the owner.'

For a moment Katherine could hardly believe what she was hearing. But in her heart she knew that she should not be surprised. This was far more believable than Sergei offering to include her permanently in his life.

'Where's he gone?' she asked truculently.

'What's that to you?' the man responded, equally aggressive.

'He owes me money,' Katherine improvised. 'A lot of money.' She put a note of desperation into her voice. 'I have to find him.'

The man moved slowly into the room. 'Owes you, does he? What for, I wonder?' She sensed that he was smiling now, and heard his voice change. 'You're one of those pretty boys, aren't you? Like men, do you? What does this Sergei owe you for, eh? Did you sweeten up some of his gambling friends with that little mouth of yours?'

'Never you mind,' Katherine blustered. 'He owes me money. Where's he gone?'

'Well, now.' The man was very close now, 'I could tell you where he was heading, because I don't owe him anything, and they reckon he stole a load of jewellery, so he deserves what he gets.' He stopped in front of Katherine. 'But why should I tell you for nothing?' She saw his hand move down the front of his body. 'I'm not one of those man lovers, but one mouth is as good as another in the dark.' She hear the rustle of his clothing as he unbuttoned his trouser flap. 'What do you say, pretty boy?'

'One cock's as good as another, in the dark,' Katherine said. 'But I want my information first.'

The man was very close now, big and burly. She saw him tuck the pistol into his belt. She could smell his body, sweaty and none too clean. 'He was heading for the castle at Rotwald. God knows why. I'd have thought he'd go straight to the border.'

She saw him struggling to hoist himself out, ready for her. 'When did he leave?'

'You ask a lot, don't you?' the man grumbled. 'About half an hour ago. Gave me the house keys, and rode off.' He grabbed at Katherine's head and pulled her towards him. 'Come on, get sucking! You'd better be worth it.'

Katherine moved towards him, but not in the way he hoped. Her head slammed forward and hit him exactly where he was expecting to feel her mouth. He gave a bellow of pain and staggered back, doubling up and clutching himself. By the time he had recovered sufficiently to drag the pistol out of his belt, Katherine had run downstairs, and vaulted out of the window. She continued to run until she reached the street.

Now her mind was working clearly, and fast. She knew she should forget Sergei, go back to her house, and prepare to marry Ruprecht von Krohnenstein. But she also knew that if she did that, if she meekly let Sergei walk out of her life, she would never forgive herself. She wanted to confront him, if only to let him know that she was not like all the other women he had probably used and discarded in the past.

She tucked the pistol more securely in at her waist and set off to the livery stables she had used for her rides in the park.

Chapter Eight

*A*s she headed out of Grazheim on horseback, Katherine marvelled at how easy it was to become a thief. The horses at the stable yard had snickered softly when they recognised her voice. It had only taken her a very short time to saddle her favourite gelding, Samson, mount him, and walk him gently out to the street. Her only thought was that, when she returned the horse, she would suggest to the stables that they employed a night watchman.

Once she was out of Grazheim, she urged Samson into a canter, and then a gallop. It was exhilarating to be riding astride again. Exhilarating to be heading into the unknown. To have no idea what the next few hours would bring. She did not even know if she would catch up with Sergei, although the fact that he was heading for Schloss Rotwald was encouraging, if puzzling. Who was he going to meet there? If I find him with another woman, she thought, I'll kill him. And then the absurdity of her feelings struck her. Sergei von Lenz had deliberately walked out of her life. Why should she have any feelings at all for him, one way or another? After half an hour's hard riding on the road she saw the outline of a castle on the horizon. Instead of keeping to the road she cut across country. It was a difficult terrain, but once again she found it exciting to be pushing her horse, and herself, to the limits.

When she finally reached Schloss Rotwald she wondered if the caretaker at Hochmeisterstrasse had been lying to her. The place looked deserted. In fact, at closer inspection, it looked half-derelict. She dismounted and approached the gates. They stood open, and she saw two horses tethered in the courtyard. Once again she felt both jealousy and anger. Then she noticed that both horses had standard saddles. If Sergei had come here to meet a woman, she was also someone who rode astride.

She tied her own horse out of sight of the other two, and went up the steps to the castle doors. They were not locked. Clearly Sergei and whoever he was with felt certain they would not be interrupted. Once inside, she realised that the castle was not derelict, although it gave her the impression that it was not often used. The air smelt cold and musty. There were sabres and hunting trophies on the walls, and rugs scattered on the stone floor. A few lamps were alight, giving the whole place a shadowy, eerie look.

The ground floor seemed deserted. She climbed the wide stone steps to an upper balcony. Then she heard voices. Following the sounds she found herself outside a door. She could hear voices and realised that she recognised them both. She cocked her pistol, and opened the door.

Sergei von Lenz and Ruprecht von Krohnenstein were facing each other across a table. Sergei was seated. His coat was slung over the back of a chair, almost covering a small saddlebag. Ruprecht was standing on the other side of the table. As Katherine pushed open the door he spun round, and stared at her in open-mouthed amazement.

235

Sergei merely smiled. 'Obviously I underestimated you, English Rose. Do come in.'

The room was as sparsely furnished as the hall, and with more swords and animal heads decorating the walls. A huge fireplace stood soot-blackened and empty. One lamp left most of the room in shadow. Katherine closed the door behind her and stood with her back to it.

'You told her!' Ruprecht's face was ugly with anger. 'You betrayed me. I knew I shouldn't trust a thief.'

'What an idiot you are, Ruprecht,' Sergei drawled. 'I didn't tell anyone anything.' He smiled at Katherine, his bewitching smile. 'You didn't believe my request for a romantic rendezvous at nine, did you, English Rose? Perhaps it was foolish of me to think you would.'

'Very foolish,' she agreed. 'Why did you do it?'

'For selfish reasons,' he said. 'I knew the count would recognise me at the masked ball. In fact, I was counting on it. I hoped he would believe we were planning something together. And I hoped he would think that, as long as you were in Grazheim, I would be there as well. That would give me time to get away.' He shrugged. 'It nearly worked.'

'You underestimated the count, too,' she said. 'He never thought you'd take me with you.'

'Everyone seems to have a very poor opinion of me,' Sergei said.

'Did you really steal the jewellery?' she asked.

He nodded.

'And the letters?'

He nodded again. 'You didn't think Ruprecht burgled Madame Jardinne, did you? He hasn't got the skill, or the courage.'

'If I hadn't told you where to look, you wouldn't have got anything,' Ruprecht snarled.

'I'd have robbed someone else.' Sergei shrugged. 'It'd probably have been a lot less troublesome, in the long run.'

'And I almost believed you were innocent,' Katherine said.

'I know.' He smiled. 'It was charming of you. I'm sorry I've disappointed you.'

'I'm only disappointed because you're helping Ruprecht,' she said. 'And you both want to destroy Heldenburg.'

'You're talking like my father, dear,' Ruprecht said, cattily. 'What a bore you are.'

'Actually, I despise Ruprecht,' Sergei said. 'He and his friends wanted the letters. I wanted the jewels. So we came to an agreement. They supplied the information, and I took all the risks. They even gave me an alibi.' He grinned. 'I'm sure it puzzled the count when those worthy old men backed me up. But the count doesn't know everything, you see. Those fine upstanding citizens want to see Heldenburg unite with Prussia. They'd have given the Devil an alibi to achieve that aim.'

'You might despise me,' Ruprecht said, 'and the feeling is mutual, I can assure you, but I've made you rich. Now hand over the letters. I have a contact waiting for me at the border.'

Sergei laughed and pulled a flat packet out of his pocket.

'Don't,' Katherine said.

Sergei laughed. 'It's rather charming of you to care about what happens to little Heldenburg. In fact, I wouldn't be happy to see the Prussians swallow the country whole, which is probably what they're planning to do.' He pushed the packet of letters across the table to Ruprecht. 'But I made a promise. And I always keep my word.'

'You have a choice,' Katherine said to Ruprecht. 'You can attempt to pick up the letters, and get killed. Or you can leave now, without them, and stay alive.'

Ruprecht stared at her, his face twisted with frustration and fury. 'I don't believe you. You're bluffing.' He reached for the letters, slowly, testing her. She lifted her arm and took aim.

'At this range,' she said, her voice calm, 'I can't miss.'

'You wouldn't dare!' Ruprecht blustered. He turned to Sergei. 'Don't just sit there,' he snarled. 'Do something.'

Sergei shrugged. 'Why should I? I'm a thief, but you're a traitor. In my opinion that makes your hands far dirtier than mine. Let's see if you've got the courage of your convictions. Maybe the English Rose is bluffing. Pick up the letters, and find out.'

For a moment Ruprecht hesitated. He looked at Sergei, lounging elegantly in his chair, and then at Katherine, her arm steady, her aim unwavering. And he made his decision. He backed away from the table and stalked over to the door.

'I'll remember this, you whore!' His voice was thick with hatred. 'And you, you Russian bastard. I'll get even with you both.'

They heard his footsteps going down the stairs, and then heard the door slam.

Sergei stood up. 'Well, I wonder what story he'll tell his contact. Not the truth, I'm sure.' He smiled at her. 'Do put that pistol down now, English Rose. It might go off by accident.' When she did not move, he shrugged and slid the letters across the table. 'These are what you want, aren't they? A nice wedding present for Count von Krohnenstein.' He smiled, the brilliant smile that always made her heart suddenly ache. 'You will marry him now, won't you? Ruprecht won't come back to Heldenburg. He has a new lover in Prussia. That's really why he wanted the letters: a romantic gift for his boyfriend.' Sergei picked up the packet and held it out to her. She did not move. 'Now you can have them as a romantic gift for the count,' he said. When she still did not move, but kept the pistol pointing at him, he added a little uncertainly, 'What else do you want, English Rose? One last bout of lovemaking, maybe?' He took a step towards her. 'Well, I'm willing. Those male clothes always did make you look surprisingly desirable.'

'The jewellery,' she said.

For a moment he stared at her, blankly. Then he laughed.

'What use is that to you? You couldn't wear it.'

'Neither can you,' she said.

'Katherine –' his voice was harder now, and his smile had become dangerous '– don't tempt fate. I like you better than any other woman I've ever met, but regrettably I don't have a private fortune. I need that jewellery.'

'Well now,' she said pleasantly, 'isn't that a coincidence? I don't have a private fortune either, and I need it too.'

'But you're going to marry the count,' he said. 'Aren't you?'

'I don't know,' she replied. 'But it would still be nice to have my own money.' She glanced at the saddlebag slung over his chair. 'Hand it over, please. Or I'll come and get it.'

He was moving closer to her now. She backed a step, and immediately regretted it.

'You wouldn't shoot me, Katherine,' he said. 'You might have put a hole in Ruprecht, but not me.' He held out his hand. 'Come on now. Stop being silly. Give me the pistol, and let's part as friends.'

He was close to her. Too close. And then he moved. One hand aimed at her face, distracting her momentarily. The other knocked the pistol barrel aside. There was a sharp bang, and an acrid smell of gunpowder. The pistol clattered to the floor. She was both angry and relieved. She knew that she could never have shot him. For a moment they both stared at each other. Then he laughed good-humouredly.

'I would have been very disappointed if you'd killed me, English Rose. Although I wouldn't have minded if you'd shot Ruprecht.'

239

He turned away from her and walked back to the chair. She looked at the useless pistol, and then a pair of sabres hooked on the wall. While Sergei was picking up his coat, she ran to the wall and grasped one of the swords. He turned. The table was still between them. His eyes went from the sword, to her angry face, then back to the sword again.

'You never give up, do you?' he said. 'Are you going to wave that at me now?'

'I want the jewellery,' she said.

She began to walk round the table. The sabre felt heavy but comfortable in her hand. He backed away. His eyes flicked to the wall. Before she could stop him he had vaulted over the table. In another second he had a sabre in his hand too. He made a few experimental moves, and she knew at once he was quite capable of using the weapon.

'Rather evens things up, doesn't it?' He smiled. 'Ever been stripped at sword-point, English Rose? I think you'll enjoy it.'

They stalked round each other like two cats.

'Is that another trick you learnt on your father's estates in Russia?' she asked.

He laughed, but his eyes were wary. 'Actually, that was a slight exaggeration. My mother worked for a Russian aristo, but I haven't any idea who my father was. I have no family name to uphold. No stupid ideas about family honour.' He smiled at her, his charming, irresistible smile, and then moved so quickly that he almost caught her off guard. Their blades clashed, and she withdrew. 'And no foolish ideas about being chivalrous to women who threaten me with swords,' he added.

He attacked her then, with an obvious determination to end the duel as quickly as possible. She backed, defending herself. She knew his superior strength would weaken her if she let the fight go on too long. She deflected several slashing assaults, and backed some more. But strength, she noted, seemed to be his main asset. As a swordsman he was fast, but lacking in technique. She was used to the much lighter fencing foil, which utilised the wrist rather than the arm, but she deliberately fought as if she was both clumsy and inexperienced. She wanted to lull him into a false sense of security – and it worked. When her chance came, she hooked the sabre out of his hand with a self-assured proficiency that took him completely by surprise. Before he could recover, the point of her weapon was at his throat.

'Touché?' she said politely.

He recovered fast. 'I suppose it is,' he said. 'You ride like a man, you fight like a man, and you cheat at cards. What other tricks can you perform, English Rose?'

'I can steal from a thief,' she said. 'But first, a little fun.' She pressed the sabre gently against his throat. 'Strip,' she said. 'I think you'll enjoy it.'

He untied his cravat, and unbuttoned his waistcoat. Slowly. She moved warily round him, keeping her distance. They were like two animals, testing each other. She guessed that he would not grab at the sabre blade with its sharpened edge. She also knew that he was aware she would not hurt him. When he finally dropped his shirt on the floor and stretched his lean body, she felt her own body respond to the sight of the taut muscles moving under his tanned skin. 'Like what you see so far, English Rose?' He walked over to a chair, sat down and began to pull off his boots. Standing up, he started to unbutton his breeches. 'I hope you're going to take advantage of me,' he said. He took the breeches off, pulling them over his swelling cock with some difficulty. Then he faced her, legs slightly apart. He shielded himself briefly with his hands, then displayed his impressive erection. 'Otherwise this will be wasted.'

'Sit down,' she said. She prodded him and he moved back, slightly puzzled but obedient. Once he was in the chair she picked up his shirt from the floor, then went behind him. Leaning forward she put her mouth close to his ear, resisting the temptation to touch his glossy hair. 'I'm going to tie your wrists,' she said softly.

'Don't take too long,' he murmured. He stretched his legs forward, and she looked down at his waiting cock.

He clearly trusted her now, believing this to be part of the game she wanted to play. She put the sabre down and twisted the shirt into a rope. Then she secured his wrists to the chair, using knots that her father's gamekeeper had taught her. When Sergei felt the strength of his bonds, he began to struggle. But by then it was too late.

'You believe in realism, don't you?' he muttered.

'I believe in winning,' she said. She backed away from him. 'I imagine the jewellery is in that saddlebag?'

He struggled even harder then. 'I trusted you,' he said, almost plaintively.

'That was foolish of you,' she said. She checked the saddlebag. It contained a tightly wrapped packet. She knew it was the jewellery. She walked back to him, smiling. His position had not damped his sexual ardour. He looked, she thought, incredibly attractive tied helplessly to the chair, and with a massive erection.

'Poor Sergei,' she said, softly. She straddled his lap and leant forward. Taking one of his nipples between her teeth, she tugged at him gently. He groaned and writhed under her. She reached down and captured his engorged cock, sliding her hand up and down its length.

'Damn it, Katherine,' he muttered. 'Untie me. We'll share the jewellery, if that's what you want.'

She laughed, and knelt down in front of him. 'Unlike you,' she said, running the flat of her hands up his lean thighs, 'I'm not a trusting person at all.' She felt his body quiver as she reached his balls, and cupped them. 'If I untied you –' she massaged him gently '– you might try and turn the tables. And strip me. Or beat me.' She let go of him and sat back on her heels. 'And I might just enjoy being stripped by you, Sergei. And spanked. And forced to perform all sorts of interesting tricks.'

She could see his body responding to the images she was producing in his mind. His cock was so hard now she was surprised he had controlled himself for so long. 'You really are impressive when you're like that, Sergei,' she said. She reached forward and smoothed her hands up to his stomach, resting them there, feeling his muscles tense under her fingers. 'Almost the best I've ever seen. Maybe you are the best.'

'Stop talking,' he groaned, 'and use your mouth for something useful.'

'Useful?' She captured his erection, and felt it throb in her hands. 'Like this?' Leaning forward she ran her lips up and down the length of his shaft, licking him lightly. 'Or like this?' She transferred her attention to his balls, nipping them with her teeth, while her fingers found the sensitive rim at the head of his cock and teased it. When she felt his body begin to tremble uncontrollably, she took him in her mouth and held him until his body spasmed violently, rocking the chair.

Afterwards he relaxed with a deep sigh. 'That was almost worth losing a fight for,' he said. 'Although it was most embarrassing to be beaten by a woman. I hope you won't tell anyone.'

'I won't,' she promised, standing up.

He watched her. 'So are you going to untie me now?'

'No,' she said. 'I'll let whoever finds you do that.'

He looked horrified. 'Are you mad? No one comes out here. This castle belongs to the count, did you know that? Ruprecht had keys, but it's hardly ever used. I could be here forever.'

'You won't be,' she said. 'I'm sure you'll manage to free yourself after a bit of struggling. But I'll make sure someone comes out here, anyway.' She smiled sweetly. 'It's just that I don't want to be here when they arrive.'

'If I ever meet you again, English Rose,' he said. 'I'll repay you for all this – with interest.'

She was about to reply when she heard the muffled sound of hoofbeats approaching the castle. She ran to the window. From her vantage point she could see some way across the open countryside. And she could certainly see the group of riders approaching the castle at speed. In less than a minute she could make out men in the uniform of the Heldenburg Hussars. And leading them was a man she could recognise even at that distance.

'Oh, my God!' She drew back from the window. 'It's the count.'

'I won't ask you if you told him you were following me,' Sergei said, calmly. 'Because I'm sure you didn't. But I am asking you to release me. I really don't like the idea of a long stay in Schloss Ohlm.'

She had untied him before he had finished speaking. He tugged on his breeches.

'Hurry!' she said. She turned in a panic. 'You can't leave by the front gate, they'll see you. Take my horse. He's tethered round the corner.'

He was pulling on his boots when the sound of voices reached them.

'Go! Please go!' She pushed him towards the door. 'Is there a back way? A window?'

'Don't worry,' he said. 'I'm an expert at escaping.' Even then he paused. 'Katherine, the jewellery?'

'Don't be a fool,' she said desperately. The men had reached the courtyard and were dismounting. 'If you take the jewellery I won't be able to prevent them from following you.'

They could both hear the sounds of the Hussars searching the downstairs rooms and corridors. But even then Sergei paused at the door. 'You win, English Rose,' he said. 'This round, at least.'

And then he was gone, leaving her with the memory of his lean, half-naked body, his wild gipsy beauty and his dazzling smile. She just had time to take the saddle-bag and drop it from the window into the bushes below before the door opened.

Count von Krohnenstein, armed with a pistol and followed by two Hussars, came into the room. The Hussars could not disguise their surprise at the sight of Katherine, in her breeches, boots and man's jacket. They gaped at her for longer than the count, who glanced at her briefly and then looked round the room.

'He's gone,' Katherine said. 'He was gone when I arrived.'

The count walked towards her, his face grim. 'I don't believe you,' he said. He turned to the Hussars. 'Head for the border. I think you'll catch him. And remember, I want him alive.'

'No!' Katherine stepped forward. The Hussars were halfway down the stairs. 'Please stop them,' she said. 'I have the letters, but if you value your family honour, please let Sergei go.'

For a moment she thought the count was going to ignore her. Then he strode into the passage and counter-manded his previous order. 'Wait in the courtyard,' he added to the soldiers. Turning back to Katherine, he repeated, 'My family honour? Explain yourself.'

She went to the table and picked up the packet of letters. 'Sergei didn't want these,' she said. 'He came here to hand them over to his accomplice. An accomplice who wanted them for his lover in Prussia. An accomplice who told him how to get to Madame Jardinne's strong box and safe. An accomplice who had the keys to get into this castle.'

She saw the count's expression change. 'I don't believe what you are trying to tell me!' His voice was hoarse, and she could hear the pain in it.

'I'm sorry,' she said inadequately. 'But Ruprecht was here. He wanted the letters, but we forced him to leave without them. If you capture Sergei, he'll be obliged to divulge names. This way you can say that Ruprecht ran away because he didn't want to marry me. That, at least, is better than having him branded a traitor.'

'But he is a traitor, damn him,' the count muttered. 'And so are the men who helped him, the men who gave that Russian thief an alibi. To think I serve under one of them in the army. Unbelievable! And that damned Russian has got away with it. He's heading for the border right now, with the jewellery.'

'That's better than Ruprecht heading for his Prussian contact with the letters,' she said.

'True,' the count agreed. Suddenly he slumped down in the chair and rubbed his hand over his face. 'Damn it, Katherine, I feel as if my world's fallen apart. For all his faults, I didn't expect my own son to be a traitor. I should send the Hussars after him, and tell them to have an accident while bringing him back.'

'Tell them to kill your own son?' She was genuinely shocked. 'You wouldn't do that!'

His eyes were bleak, dark and cold. 'What else do you do with traitors?' Then he shrugged. 'But I'll let him go to his Prussian boyfriend. No one in Heldenburg will be surprised to hear that he's run away to some worthless lover. I wonder what sort of reception he'll get when he arrives without the letters. The Prussians don't take kindly to failure.' He stood up suddenly. 'Katherine, you've exhausted me. I've been following you ever since you left the masked ball.'

'I didn't know that,' she said.

'You weren't supposed to.' He smiled briefly. 'I hoped you'd lead me to Sergei. I hoped I'd be able to arrest him.' He strode over to the window. 'Why the devil did I let you persuade me to let him go? I could have offered him terms. He need not have mentioned Ruprecht.'

'This way is better,' she said.

'But you've done von Lenz a favour,' the count said. 'How much did it cost him?'

She looked surprised. 'I did it for you,' she said. 'To save you embarrassment.'

He gave her a frankly disbelieving look. 'You didn't accept any small payment from Sergei, then?' He paused. 'A small token of his thanks?' He paused. 'Like an item of jewellery, maybe?'

'What a ridiculous suggestion,' she said.

'It would be in keeping with his ridiculous sense of gratitude,' the count said.

'Well, he didn't give me anything.' She stared at him defiantly. 'Do you want to search me?'

'Yes,' he said. 'Later.' He sighed. 'You've bewitched me, Katherine. I shouldn't have listened to you. I shouldn't have let him go.'

'You've done the right thing,' she said. 'He'll never come back to Heldenburg.'

'He might,' the count said. 'If you're still here.' He stood up, suddenly, and turned to her. 'I don't feel like riding back to Grazheim tonight. Will you stay with me, Katherine? There's wine in the cellar, and we'll light a fire. Just the two of us, for old time's sake?'

'That sounds good,' she said. 'What about the Hussars?'

'They know their way back to town,' he said. 'I'll get them to send a carriage for us tomorrow. And some suitable clothes for you.'

'You think I'm indecently dressed?' she enquired.

'Very,' he said. 'Women should not wear men's trousers. But I plan to do something about that very shortly.'

'I thought you were exhausted?' she teased.

'Not that exhausted,' he said.

When they made love, later that evening, she felt for the first time that they were really like an established married couple. A couple who had grown to know each other intimately, and who undressed each other with

247

leisurely familiarity, lingering to tease and stroke as they removed each other's clothes.

The count kissed her with gentle passion, running his tongue over her lips and taking her own tongue into his mouth. He sucked her nipples gently, and she responded by performing the same caress on him, feeling his nipples harden under the flicking of her tongue. When she moved her head down, tracing a line of kisses over his stomach, and then took his rising erection in her mouth, she heard him sigh with pleasure.

Again by silent mutual consent, their bodies moved round each other until he was also able to reach between her legs and taste her, his tongue stroking her swelling clitoris. They remained entwined in this most intimate embrace until he rolled away from her and turned her on her stomach. Lifting her gently to her knees, he entered her. She was relaxed, moist and welcoming. He thrust unhurriedly, and she matched his rhythm. His hands cupped her breasts and his fingers caressed her. Her climax preceded his, making her body tremble, and filling her with a sensation of peaceful release. He continued thrusting until he reached his own climax. It shook his body gently, and subsided like a sigh.

Afterwards they lay close together, without talking. Just before she fell asleep she thought: this is how it should be. Maybe this is how it will be, in the future.

She remembered her thoughts a week later, when the count came to see her.

'I have arranged a financial settlement for you,' he said. 'I think you'll find it adequate and generous.'

'Settlement?' she repeated. 'I don't understand.'

'It will go some way towards alleviating your father's debts,' he said. 'It will buy you some time to find another husband.'

For a few moments she was disoriented. 'But I don't want another husband,' she said, unsteadily. 'I want to stay here, with you.' He said nothing, and she added, 'Surely we can spend some time together now? Openly, I mean?' When he did not respond, she persisted, 'You don't believe Ruprecht will come back, do you? And if he did, you would not still expect me to marry him?'

'This has nothing to do with Ruprecht,' he said. He turned away from her and walked towards the window. 'I am getting married.' He turned back to her then, and she saw something like pity in his face. 'I hope you will give me your blessing?'

For a moment she did not believe she had heard him correctly. Then she flung herself across the room. 'Married?' She dragged him round to face her. 'But you can't marry someone else! I thought . . . I believed . . .'

He gently disengaged her hands. 'I can't marry you, Katherine. Did I ever give you cause to believe that I would?'

'No,' she said. 'But what's wrong with me? I was good enough for your son.'

'That's partly what's wrong,' he said. 'You were engaged to Ruprecht. And also, I'm twenty years older than you.'

'I don't care about the age difference,' she said. 'Lots of men marry younger wives.'

'All right,' he said, with a trace of impatience now. 'There are other reasons. You have acquired a reputation. If you had married Ruprecht, it wouldn't really have mattered. But married to me, it would.' She stared at him, anger taking over from surprise. 'And you have no money,' he said. 'The Hungarian countess I intend to marry has vast estates, and . . .'

She slapped him, rocking his head back. For a moment she saw anger blaze in his eyes. Then he put one hand up to his stinging face.

'You have such a delightfully strong arm, Katherine,' he said, regretfully.

'I hate you!' she said.

'You don't.' He smiled. 'Katherine, if you wish to stay with me, I'll give you your house in Grazheim, and I'll make you a monthly allowance.'

'So?' she challenged. 'I'm good enough to be a mistress, but not a wife?'

'I don't make the rules of our society,' he said.

'The rules are made by men, for men,' she threw back at him. 'From now on, I'm going to make up my own.'

'I believe you will,' he said. 'And very successfully too.' He gave her a lingering look of admiration, touched with desire. 'I'll miss you, Katherine. Will you go back to England?'

'Probably.' She shrugged.

'I'll have my carriage take you to the border,' he said. He paused. 'And, Katherine, you wouldn't try to leave the country with anything that should rightly remain here, would you? The border guards have permission to search anyone they distrust. I wouldn't want them to embarrass you.'

Katherine left Heldenburg after a week. It was a busy week that included another secret trip on horseback in male clothes, back to Schloss Rotwald. She was certain that the count was not aware of this journey. She looked at the small saddlebag and smiled.

On the day that the carriage was to come for her she went out, telling Frau Grussell that she wanted one last walk in her favourite park. She would be about two hours. She did not return.

The theatre troupe crossed the border with the minimum of fuss. The two border guards looked at the buxom woman driving the ramshackle cart, and let their eyes stay on her swelling chest for much longer than necessary.

'Where are you ladies heading?' the larger man asked, grinning.

'Maybe France,' the woman said, letting her breasts jiggle enticingly. 'Or Holland. Or maybe even England. Who knows?'

'We've been told to search everyone, ladies.' He looked at the cart unenthusiastically. It was piled high with a jumble of boxes and wooden scenery. 'But I don't suppose I need to search you, do I?'

'Depends what you're hoping to find,' the woman said.

The guard tapped the side of his nose. 'Oh, maybe stolen gold and jewellery. Things like that.'

The woman laughed. 'We've got lots of jewellery. Crowns and tiaras. Do you want to see them?'

The guards laughed too. 'No thanks, ladies. On you go.'

'You're welcome to search us,' the buxom woman tempted. 'All four of us.'

The guards laughed louder. 'Next time, maybe. When you come back to our country.'

'And that,' Yvonne said, as the border post receded behind them, 'will probably be never.'

'Oh, I don't know,' one of the women said. 'That grand duke of theirs certainly paid well.'

Yvonne turned to her companion, a pretty girl with curly black hair and a gold bangle. 'Will you come back again, Katherine?'

'I doubt it,' Lady Katherine Gainsworth said. 'I'll stay with you until we reach the coast, and then I have to return to England. After that?' She smiled. 'Who knows?'

Maybe Holland, she thought, where I believe they have merchants who deal in diamonds and jewellery, and don't ask too many awkward questions. And then, maybe I'll come back to Europe, and travel as an independent woman of means. And maybe my reputation will precede me. And maybe Sergei von Lenz will hear about me, and seek me out. I believe he thinks I owe him something, and he did say he would like to repay it, with interest. She felt the familiar rush of excitement stirring her blood. It will be a good life, she thought. And it's only just beginning!

BLACK LACE NEW BOOKS

Published in February

MÉNAGE
Emma Holly
£5.99

When Kate finds her two male flatmates in bed with each other she is powerless to resist their offer to join them in kinky games. She's a woman who has everything: a great job, loads of friends, tons of ambition. As she embarks on a strange ménage à trois, she wants nothing more than to keep both her admirers happy but, inevitably, things become complicated. Can the three lovers live happily ever after ... together?

ISBN 0 352 33231 X

THE SUCCUBUS
Zoe le Verdier
£5.99

Adele is a talented ballet dancer thrown into the role of the Succubus – a legendary sex-crazed demon who is thought to haunt the house of her wealthy patron, Rafique. Adele feels insecure; her every move is shadowed by Jessica Sharpe, her rival and understudy who has her eyes on Adele's boyfriend, Jamie. As Adele learns to relish her new-found success, she finds a sudden, voracious appetite for new experiences. Can she discover the strength to conquer the other demons in her life?

ISBN 0 352 33230 1

Published in March

THE CAPTIVATION
Natasha Rostova
£5.99

It's 1917 and war-torn Russia is teetering on the brink of the Bolshevik revolution. The Princess Katya is forced to leave her estate when a mob threatens her life. After a daring escape, she ends up in the encampment of a rebel Cossack army. The men have not seen a woman for weeks and sexual tensions are running high. The captain is a man of dark desires and he and Katya become involved in an erotic power struggle.

ISBN 0 352 33234 4

A DANGEROUS LADY
Lucinda Carrington
£5.99

Lady Katherine Gainsworth is compromised into a marriage of convenience which takes her from her English home to the Prussian Duchy of Heldenburg. Once there, she is introduced to her future in-laws but finds they have some unconventional ideas of how to welcome her into the family. Her father-in-law, the Count, is no stranger to the underworld of bawdy clubs in the duchy and soon Katherine finds herself embroiled in political intrigue, jewel theft and sexual blackmail.

ISBN 0 352 33236 0

FEMININE WILES
Karina Moore
£7.99

Young American Kelly Aslett is due to fly back to the USA to claim her inheritance according to the terms of her father's will. As she prepares to fly home she falls passionately in love with French artist Luc Duras. Meanwhile, in California, Kelly's stepmother is determined to secure Kelly's inheritance for herself and enlists the help of her handsome lover and the dashing and ruthless Johnny Casigelli to assist her in her criminal deed. When Kelly finds herself held captive by Johnny, will she succumb to his masculine charms or can she use her feminine wiles to gain what's rightfully hers?

ISBN 0 352 33235 2

To be published in April

PLEASURE'S DAUGHTER
Sedalia Johnson
£5.99

1750, England. After the death of her father, headstrong young Amelia goes to live with her wealthy relatives. During the journey she meets the cruel Marquess of Beechwood, who both excites and frightens her. She escapes from him only to discover later that he is a good friend of her aunt and uncle. The Marquess pursues her ruthlessly, and persuades her uncle to give him her hand – but Amelia escapes and runs away to London. She takes up residence in an establishment dedicated to the pleasure of the feminine senses, where she becomes expert in every manner of debauch, and is happy with her new life until the Marquess catches up with her and demands that they renew their marriage vows.

ISBN 0 352 33237 9

AN ACT OF LOVE
Ella Broussard
£5.99

In order to be accepted at drama school, Gina has to be in a successful theatrical production. She joins the cast for a play which is being financed by kinky control freak, Charles Sarazan, who begins to pursue Gina. She is more attracted to Matt, one of the actors in the play, but finds it difficult to approach him, especially after she sees Persis, the provocative female lead, making explicit advances to him. Gina learns that Charles is planning to sabotage the production so that he can write it off as a tax loss. Can she manage to satisfy both her craving for success and her lust for the leading man?

ISBN 0 352 33240 9

If you would like a complete list of plot summaries of Black Lace titles, please fill out the questionnaire overleaf or send a stamped addressed envelope to:-

Black Lace, 332 Ladbroke Grove, London W10 5AH

BLACK LACE BOOKLIST

All books are priced £4.99 unless another price is given.

Black Lace books with a contemporary setting

ODALISQUE	Fleur Reynolds ISBN 0 352 32887 8	☐
VIRTUOSO	Katrina Vincenzi ISBN 0 352 32907 6	☐
THE SILKEN CAGE	Sophie Danson ISBN 0 352 32928 9	☐
RIVER OF SECRETS	Saskia Hope & Georgia Angelis ISBN 0 352 32925 4	☐
SUMMER OF ENLIGHTENMENT	Cheryl Mildenhall ISBN 0 352 32937 8	☐
MOON OF DESIRE	Sophie Danson ISBN 0 352 32911 4	☐
A BOUQUET OF BLACK ORCHIDS	Roxanne Carr ISBN 0 352 32939 4	☐
THE TUTOR	Portia Da Costa ISBN 0 352 32946 7	☐
THE HOUSE IN NEW ORLEANS	Fleur Reynolds ISBN 0 352 32951 3	☐
WICKED WORK	Pamela Kyle ISBN 0 352 32958 0	☐
DREAM LOVER	Katrina Vincenzi ISBN 0 352 32956 4	☐
UNFINISHED BUSINESS	Sarah Hope-Walker ISBN 0 352 329 83 1	☐
THE DEVIL INSIDE	Portia Da Costa ISBN 0 352 32993 9	☐
HEALING PASSION	Sylvie Ouellette ISBN 0 352 32998 X	☐
THE STALLION	Georgina Brown ISBN 0 352 33005 8	☐

Black Lace books with an historical setting

----------✂----------------------

Please send me the books I have ticked above.

Name   ....

Address ....

       ....

       ....

    .... Post Code   ....

Send to: **Cash Sales, Black Lace Books, 332 Ladbroke Grove, London W10 5AH, UK.**

US customers: for prices and details of how to order books for delivery by mail, call 1-800-805-1083.

Please enclose a cheque or postal order, made payable to **Virgin Publishing Ltd**, to the value of the books you have ordered plus postage and packing costs as follows:

UK and BFPO – £1.00 for the first book, 50p for each subsequent book.

Overseas (including Republic of Ireland) – £2.00 for the first book, £1.00 each subsequent book.

If you would prefer to pay by VISA or ACCESS/MASTERCARD, please write your card number and expiry date here:

....

Please allow up to 28 days for delivery.

Signature   ....

----------✂----------------------

WE NEED YOUR HELP . . .
to plan the future of women's erotic fiction –

– and no stamp required!

Yours are the only opinions that matter.

Black Lace is the first series of books devoted to erotic fiction by women for women.

We intend to keep providing the best-written, sexiest books you can buy. And we'd appreciate your help and valued opinion of the books so far. Tell us what you want to read.

THE BLACK LACE QUESTIONNAIRE

SECTION ONE: ABOUT YOU

1.1 Sex *(we presume you are female, but so as not to discriminate)*
   Are you?
Male	☐
Female	☐

1.2 Age
under 21	☐	21–30	☐
31–40	☐	41–50	☐
51–60	☐	over 60	☐

1.3 At what age did you leave full-time education?
still in education	☐	16 or younger	☐
17–19	☐	20 or older	☐

1.4 Occupation _____

1.5 Annual household income _____

1.6 We are perfectly happy for you to remain anonymous; but if you would like to receive information on other publications available, please insert your name and address

_____

_____

_____

_____

SECTION TWO: ABOUT BUYING BLACK LACE BOOKS

2.1 Where did you get this copy of *A Dangerous Lady*?
Bought at chain book shop ☐
Bought at independent book shop ☐
Bought at supermarket ☐
Bought at book exchange or used book shop ☐
I borrowed it/found it ☐
My partner bought it ☐

2.2 How did you find out about Black Lace books?
I saw them in a shop ☐
I saw them advertised in a magazine ☐
I read about them in _____
Other _____

2.3 Please tick the following statements you agree with:
I would be less embarrassed about buying Black Lace books if the cover pictures were less explicit ☐
I think that in general the pictures on Black Lace books are about right ☐
I think Black Lace cover pictures should be as explicit as possible ☐

2.4 Would you read a Black Lace book in a public place – on a train for instance?
Yes ☐ No ☐

SECTION THREE: ABOUT THIS BLACK LACE BOOK

3.1 Do you think the sex content in this book is:
    Too much   ☐   About right   ☐
    Not enough   ☐

3.2 Do you think the writing style in this book is:
    Too unreal/escapist ☐   About right   ☐
    Too down to earth   ☐

3.3 Do you think the story in this book is:
    Too complicated ☐   About right   ☐
    Too boring/simple ☐

3.4 Do you think the cover of this book is:
    Too explicit   ☐   About right   ☐
    Not explicit enough ☐

Here's a space for any other comments:

SECTION FOUR: ABOUT OTHER BLACK LACE BOOKS

4.1 How many Black Lace books have you read?   ☐

4.2 If more than one, which one did you prefer?

4.3 Why?

SECTION FIVE: ABOUT YOUR IDEAL EROTIC NOVEL

We want to publish the books you want to read – so this is your chance to tell us exactly what your ideal erotic novel would be like.

5.1 Using a scale of 1 to 5 (1 = no interest at all, 5 = your ideal), please rate the following possible settings for an erotic novel:

Medieval/barbarian/sword 'n' sorcery ☐
Renaissance/Elizabethan/Restoration ☐
Victorian/Edwardian ☐
1920s & 1930s – the Jazz Age ☐
Present day ☐
Future/Science Fiction ☐

5.2 Using the same scale of 1 to 5, please rate the following themes you may find in an erotic novel:

Submissive male/dominant female ☐
Submissive female/dominant male ☐
Lesbianism ☐
Bondage/fetishism ☐
Romantic love ☐
Experimental sex e.g. anal/watersports/sex toys ☐
Gay male sex ☐
Group sex ☐

5.3 Using the same scale of 1 to 5, please rate the following styles in which an erotic novel could be written:

Realistic, down to earth, set in real life ☐
Escapist fantasy, but just about believable ☐
Completely unreal, impressionistic, dreamlike ☐

5.4 Would you prefer your ideal erotic novel to be written from the viewpoint of the main male characters or the main female characters?

Male ☐   Female ☐
Both ☐

5.5 What would your ideal Black Lace heroine be like? Tick
as many as you like:

Dominant	☐	Glamorous	☐
Extroverted	☐	Contemporary	☐
Independent	☐	Bisexual	☐
Adventurous	☐	Naïve	☐
Intellectual	☐	Introverted	☐
Professional	☐	Kinky	☐
Submissive	☐	Anything else?	☐
Ordinary	☐	_____	

5.6 What would your ideal male lead character be like?
Again, tick as many as you like:

Rugged	☐		
Athletic	☐	Caring	☐
Sophisticated	☐	Cruel	☐
Retiring	☐	Debonair	☐
Outdoor-type	☐	Naïve	☐
Executive-type	☐	Intellectual	☐
Ordinary	☐	Professional	☐
Kinky	☐	Romantic	☐
Hunky	☐		
Sexually dominant	☐	Anything else?	☐
Sexually submissive	☐	_____	

5.7 Is there one particular setting or subject matter that your
ideal erotic novel would contain?

_____

SECTION SIX: LAST WORDS

6.1 What do you like best about Black Lace books?

_____

6.2 What do you most dislike about Black Lace books?

_____

6.3 In what way, if any, would you like to change Black Lace
covers?

_____

6.4   Here's a space for any other comments:

_____

_____

_____

_____

Thank you for completing this questionnaire. Now tear it out of the book – carefully! – put it in an envelope and send it to:

> **Black Lace**
> **FREEPOST**
> **London**
> **W10 5BR**

No stamp is required if you are resident in the U.K.